THE IRISH REDEMPTION

AVA GRAY

Copyright © 2025 by Ava Gray

All rights reserved.

No part of this book may be reproduced in any form or by any electronic or mechanical means, including information storage and retrieval systems, without written permission from the author, except for the use of brief quotations in a book review.

❦ Created with Vellum

ALSO BY AVA GRAY

CONTEMPORARY ROMANCE
Mafia Kingpins Series

His to Own

His to Protect

His to Win

His to Possess

The Valkov Bratva Series

Stolen by the Bratva

Kept by the Bratva

Captured by the Bratva

Captivated by the Bratva

Festive Flames Series

Silver Hills' Christmas Miracle

Holly, Jolly, and Oh So Naughty

The Christmas Eve Delivery

Valentine's with the Silver Fox

Harem Hearts Series

3 SEAL Daddies for Christmas

Small Town Sparks

Her Protector Daddies

Her Alpha Bosses

The Mafia's Surprise Gift

The Billionaire Mafia Series

Knocked Up by the Mafia

Stolen by the Mafia

Claimed by the Mafia

Arranged by the Mafia

Charmed by the Mafia

Alpha Billionaire Series

Secret Baby with Brother's Best Friend

Just Pretending

Loving The One I Should Hate

Billionaire and the Barista

Coming Home

Doctor Daddy

Baby Surprise

A Fake Fiancée for Christmas

Hot Mess

Love to Hate You - The Beckett Billionaires

Just Another Chance - The Beckett Billionaires

Valentine's Day Proposal

The Wrong Choice - Difficult Choices

The Right Choice - Difficult Choices

SEALed by a Kiss

The Boss's Unexpected Surprise

Twins for the Playboy

When We Meet Again

The Rules We Break

Secret Baby with my Boss's Brother

Frosty Beginnings

Silver Fox Billionaire

Taken by the Major

Daddy's Unexpected Gift

Off Limits

Boss's Baby Surprise

CEO's Baby Scandal

Playing with Trouble Series:

Chasing What's Mine

Claiming What's Mine

Protecting What's Mine

Saving What's Mine

The Beckett Billionaires Series:

Love to Hate You

Just Another Chance

Standalone's:

Ruthless Love

The Best Friend Affair

PARANORMAL ROMANCE

Maple Lake Shifters Series:

Omega Vanished

Omega Exiled

Omega Coveted

Omega Bonded

Everton Falls Mated Love Series:

The Alpha's Mate

The Wolf's Wild Mate

Saving His Mate

Fighting For His Mate

Dragons of Las Vegas Series:

Thin Ice

Silver Lining

A Spark in the Dark

Fire & Ice

Dragons of Las Vegas Boxed Set (The Complete Series)

Standalone's:

Fiery Kiss

Wild Fate

BLURB

God, I never asked for this life.

Just needed to pay rent, clean rooms, keep my head down.

Then I found him—lifeless in that cheap motel bathtub.

And his brother found me.

Cormac's hands aren't gentle when he takes me in the night.

His eyes burn with something darker than just grief.

"Tell me what you saw," he demands, but keeps me after I confess.

Strange how captivity feels like salvation when he shields me from my past.

The Russians think I'm a spy, the Italians want me silenced.

Between powerful men and their bloody vendettas, I'm just trying to survive.

His family's ranch should feel like prison, but it doesn't.

When did his anger soften into something that makes my heart race?

I hate how his touch sets my skin on fire.

I hate even more that I crave it when he's gone.

The same hands that kill without mercy now trace my curves with reverence.

I never meant to need the devil, but here we are.

They're hunting us now. My blood has already stained these streets.

And the killer who murdered his brother won't stop until I join the body count.

This isn't some fairytale—it's a death wish wrapped in forbidden desire.

But the Irish devil has marked me as his, and I've already sold my soul.

The question isn't whether I'll survive loving Cormac Gifford.

It's whether any of us will survive what he'll do when they try to take me away.

Author's Note: This mafia romance features a possessive alpha male, kidnapping, stalking, obsession, power play, steamy scenes, and a dangerous criminal empire. Not for the faint of heart.

1

EVELYN

It's three thirty in the afternoon and Lana Del Rey's *Summertime* is the only thing dragging me through a workday that never ends. On paper, being the cleaner for the Sunrise Motel is fairly simple. Keep the rooms clean and tidy, don't disturb the guests, and make sure each room sweep takes no longer than fifteen minutes.

Reality is much different. There's a constant under-the-counter policy here that has empty rooms becoming occupied at the drop of a hat, guests who think the cleaner is also the one in charge of the booze and snacks, and the occasional argument over the cleaning cart when someone high on God knows what decides that my bleach is going to give them a better fix.

Paint peels from the walls, creating an array of crisscross cracks between each rust-covered drainpipe. When the sun is high enough, baking the Sunrise Motel like an overturned cake, a distinct scent of stale piss, old vomit, and something painfully acidic fills the parking lot. The Sunrise Motel shouldn't be anyone's choice to live or work. If I had any other choice, I definitely wouldn't be here.

As unattractive as this place is, it's rarely empty. My boss has a revolving door policy, and I try to keep my nose out of it. If I don't know what's going on in those rooms, I won't be liable if anyone ever gets caught doing something shady. I think that's why Gerald hired me.

"Pretty to look at and silent to boot!" he'd snorted when signing my employment papers. I keep my distance as much as I can.

Squeezing the last drop of moisture from my mop with the revolving bucket, I brush back a few loose strands of my dark hair and puff out my cheeks. Fourteen rooms done, eight to go. Then I can go home and hope my next paycheck is enough to tide me over for the rest of the month.

Humming softly, I push the cart in front of me toward the elevator. My next rooms are on the top floor and they should all be empty, provided that my manager hasn't invited any sudden guests.

"Think I'll miss you forever," I sing softly, lost in a world of nostalgic musical notes drifting from my earphones. "Like the stars miss the sun—"

"Surprise!" With a stomp of his boots and a loud clap of his hands, Dillon Stewart leaps out of the side corridor and lands in front of my cart.

I scream in fright, narrowly avoiding ramming into his shins with the cart, and immediately leap back. My heart pounds painfully while a rush of static heat floods up my arms and legs.

"Dillon!" I yell, tearing my earphones out by the cable. "What the hell do you think you're doing?"

Dillon places both hands on the end of my cart and leans forward, using his body weight to prevent it from rolling any further.

"Surprising you, obviously." He rolls his eyes and grins, displaying all his teeth like some kind of feral animal.

"You scared me half to death!" My voice trembles faintly from how hard my heart beats in my chest, so hard, in fact, that I swear my tongue pulses in time to the rhythm.

"You've been ignoring my calls," Dillon remarks, scrunching his nose upward. "What else was I supposed to do?"

Shit.

A few weeks ago, I weakened under Dillon's unrelenting pressure and agreed to one date. A date that was a few drinks at a local bar where he got so incredibly drunk that he started a fight with the barman. He ended up being thrown out by security, which was much deserved, but rather than stumbling home, he decided to start a fight with security until I was kicked out too. It was humiliating and painful since they wouldn't let me leave until I paid Dillon's tab. As if I wasn't in enough debt. As dates go, it was terrible and he was not deserving of a second.

"I don't know how much clearer I can be." Suddenly, I'm glad the cleaning cart is between us. "I didn't have fun and I don't want to see you again. I can't believe you're even here. You don't even work here."

"Wasn't hard to track you down." Dillon snorts, and the amused look on his face quickly fades. "Let me take you out again."

"No."

"A proper date this time. Last time only felt bad because you didn't drink enough, and if that bastard at the bar had listened to me then, we wouldn't have had a problem."

My brow raises at the memory of Dillon demanding shots of absinthe after four Vodka limes. The barman refused due to the high proofing of absinthe and Dillon decided he knew better. Trying to climb over the bar to prove his point was the spark that started it all.

"No," I repeat with slightly less confidence. I'm suddenly acutely aware of how it's only the two of us in this corridor. The six rooms along this walkway are all empty—and very clean, if I do say so myself. It was one thing to dodge Dillon at the laundromat, the gas station, and my grocery store, but now he's here at my work.

Not ideal.

"Come on," Dillon whines, and he moves around the cart, swaying toward me like a palm tree caught in a light wind. "This playing hard-to-get schtick is getting old, Evelyn."

"Dillon, we're not compatible, okay?"

"I heard you singing, you miss me…"

"No, I—"

"The fuck is going on here?" With a bundle of papers in hand and a chewed toothpick hanging from his fat lips, my boss rounds the corner with a dark scowl on his face.

Never have I been gladder to see my horrible boss than at this moment.

"Nothing," I say quickly, stepping around Dillon. "I was just—"

"Who the fuck are you?" Gerald tilts his head back, creating the illusion that his fat neck is only swollen due to his hunched form. "You're not a guest."

"No." Dillon sighs and shoves his hands deep into the pockets of his jacket. "A friend."

"I don't give a fuck. Either buy a room or get the fuck out," Gerald barks.

I can feel Dillon staring at me, perhaps hoping I will speak up and save him from my boss's wrath, but I won't help. I'm more than happy for Gerald to send him packing.

"Well?" Gerald barks when Dillon doesn't reply. "You forget how to speak, boy? Buy a room or get the fuck off my property."

"Alright, Gramps," Dillon grumbles. "Don't have a heart attack." He slouches away, leaving Gerald to grumble darkly about insolent young men and how if he were twenty years younger, he would teach that fucker a lesson. His face reddens with each passing second, and then he fixes his beady eyes on me, and my heart sinks.

Looks like it's me who will get that lesson.

"I don't pay you to stand around flirting on my time," Gerald barks. "I pay you to clean. It's not fucking hard, Evelyn. In fact, the only thing easier than this would be if I paid you to fuck each guest. Should I be doing that instead? Would I make more money off you then? I wouldn't have to put up with complaints about your shoddy work or how you disturb guests who want to be left alone, would I? The dirtiest thing about that job would be your cunt, but no one would complain, would they? Should I add self-service to your duties, Evelyn?"

My stomach churns hotly and disgust worms its way up my throat as we stare at one another. As he talks, little flecks of spittle fly past his fat lips, raining through the air toward me. It takes all my restraint not to flinch, and I'm amazed that his toothpick hasn't dislodged from his lip. Maybe it's been there so long that it's become part of him.

I've never seen him without it.

"No, sir," I say when Gerald finally pauses for breath. "I didn't know he was here so I—"

"I don't care," Gerald yells, making me jump. "There are a thousand girls who would kill for this job, understand? You're more trouble than you're worth."

"No!" The word bursts out of me before I can stop it. "Please, sir. You know how much I need this job. Please, I promise this won't happen again!"

A shitty job in a seedy motel that's more like a reputable drug den is the only thing I have. I made some bad decisions when I was a teenager, seeking love and comfort in material things I could only afford with credit cards. A lot of credit cards. With my financial history in ruins, getting a job to pay off the debt had been almost impossible until I found this place. I can't afford to lose it.

Gerald steps forward, and while the anger lingers in his eyes, there's something else there too. A glint of something dark, like he knows exactly how to wear me down and get what he really wants from me. The skimpy maid outfit was hint enough that it's not just my stellar cleaning skills he wants from me.

"No more boyfriends in my motel, you hear me?" Gerald snaps.

"He's not my boyfriend, trust me," I say, fighting to keep the shake out of my voice when Gerald's meaty hand lands on my upper arm. For a man so rotund, his grip is alarmingly powerful. It feels like he could snap my arm in two with just a flex of his fingers.

"Good," Gerald replies breathily, and when he breathes in through his mouth, there's a gurgling sound at the back of his throat. "You can apologize to me later. Back to work, there's a good girl."

My skin crawls fiercely with disgust as I force a smile, grab my cleaning cart, and run toward the elevator. His gaze remains on me, heavy and unrelenting as I wait for the doors to slide open and whisk me away to the next floor.

I need this job, I tell myself as I force myself to wave at him when I step into the elevator. I need this job, I need this job, I need this job.

The mantra continues until the doors close, sealing me away from the disgusting, hungry look in my boss's eyes. I sag back against the wall with a groan and close my eyes. What I would give for the elevator to just keep going up, carrying me away to a life better than this one.

My debt is my own fault, although deep down, I blame my mother's neglect for pushing me toward seeking validation in material items. I just need to keep my head down, away from any kind of drama and just work until my credit is back to a place where I can get a better job.

And a better apartment. My shitty home is the only apartment in the whole of New York City that makes this motel look like a five-star. Burned credit gets you a waterlogged shoebox.

I take several deep breaths of acidic, smoke-tainted air to calm myself and slide my earphones back in place. Eight more rooms, then I can go home.

Eight more.

'relate to desperation. My give-a-fucks are on vacation.' Espresso filters into my mind, chasing away the lingering negativity from my boss and Dillon.

Focusing on the lyrics, I find my rhythm once more and hum softly while changing my gloves. Cleaning has always been therapeutic for me in a way I don't fully understand. It might be because my own life is such a mess, so there's something satisfying about wiping stains away, cleaning up a mess, and tidying up a place like it's my own mind. Leaving a freshly cleaned room is like the first burst of crisp, cold air in your lungs when you open a window on a wintry morning.

I love it.

My next two rooms are swift cleans. Nothing more than ashtrays to empty, bins to unload, and a restock of the bathrooms. By the time I reach the third, I'm calm once more and fully engrossed in the music pouring through my brain. There's nothing but me, my summer playlist, and the sharp scents of bleach, drain cleaner, and the peach scent bombs I leave as I exit each room. It's hardly a deserving scent for a place like this, but I've seen the people who stay here. Many look like they're in need of an escape, so I like to think they are the ones who appreciate the fruity or floral scents I leave behind.

The third room shows evidence of a party, and it takes me longer to clean up the empty beer cans and chip bags. I make the bed, timing myself and cheering softly when I beat my record of three minutes and eighteen seconds.

"Tastes like strawberries on a summer evening," I sing to myself, nudging open the bathroom door with my hip. "And it sounds just—"

My singing halts abruptly and my breath catches in my throat as my chest seizes up tightly. The cleaning basket in my hand clatters to the floor, landing in a large pool of blood and sending a spray of crimson droplets up the walls already covered in the thick, dark gore.

My heart freezes, turning my blood to ice as the carnage of the bathroom registers in my mind.

I scream.

Loud and sharp.

Splayed out like a twisted piece of art is the blood-soaked body of a man with his throat slit so wide I can see the white bone of his neck.

There's a corpse in the tub.

Holy shit.

2

EVELYN

I've never seen a dead body before.

In the movies, they make them look peaceful. Like death was something they expected and was as painful as ripping off a Band-Aid, and like the blood is nothing more than the strawberry syrup you pump into your morning coffee.

Reality is painfully different.

I can't get that man's face out of my mind. His eyes were open, staring at me but not seeing. His mouth hung open, twisted in a silent cry that still oddly rings in my ears, and his fingers were rigid and claw-like as if he were still gripping onto his attacker for dear life.

But what haunts me the most is the wound at his throat. It was so wide and open, stretching the width of his neck as if his entire skeleton was trying to claw its way out of his flesh. There was so much blood soaked into his suit, sprayed up the walls, and pooled out across the floor.

And the smell.

A terrible wet, coppery smell that clings to my nose and floods my lungs even now as I sit in my manager's office clutching a paper cup filled with cold, terrible coffee.

That man. That poor man.

How can he be dead?

How can someone be murdered here and no one heard a thing?

"You know what to say, right?" Gerald paces in front of me, wearing a hole into the floor with how frantically he walks back and forth. "You tell them nothing, you hear me? Not a fucking thing."

I don't speak. I can't. I'm frozen, staring at the dirty carpet as if the body is still there staring back at me.

"Do you hear me, Evelyn?" Gerald snaps. "You don't say a thing."

Slowly, I lift my head and stare at the blurry version of him that dances through my unshed tears.

"Are you even fucking listening? Those cops upstairs don't care about you, alright? They don't give a shit about anything, so you don't say a word about how we run things here, understand?"

We.

As if I have a stake or responsibility in running this place. As if the dead body in the bathtub is my fault as much as it is his.

"Are you fucking listening?" Gerald surges forward and painfully grasps my shoulders in his meaty hands. He brings his face so close that I should be able to smell the stale stink of his breath, but all I smell is blood.

"The under-the-table payments, the whores who use this place, the drugs. Not a fucking peep, you hear me?" Gerald snarls. "You know nothing. You're just the fucking cleaner."

Gerald darts back when there's a knock at the door, and a second later, the white door swings open and in steps a woman. Her blonde hair sweeps up to the top of her head, and square spectacles balance on the bridge of her nose. Her grey pantsuit hugs her body and as our eyes meet, I can't help but wonder if the fabric is as soft as it looks.

Should I be thinking about that right now? I have no idea.

"Good afternoon. I am Detective Sarah Gogs." She introduces herself with a flat smile. "You are the business owner, correct?" Her sharp gaze lands on Gerald and he nods quickly, offering her a hand to shake.

"Gerald, yes."

She doesn't take it. Her eyes snap back to me, and I'm rooted to the spot. "And you, you're the one who found the body?"

I nod slowly, unable to take my eyes off her.

"Gerald, my colleague outside wants a word with you. Do you mind?" Sarah steps aside and tilts her head, indicating that Gerald should leave. He hesitates but leaves after a moment, but not before he shoots a warning glare in my direction. Once the door closes, Sarah perches on the edge of Gerald's messy desk and sucks in air through her teeth.

"What's your name?"

Finally, I find my voice. "Evelyn," I croak. "Evelyn Morris."

"How are you doing, Evelyn?"

"Is he really dead?" I ask softly, despite the answer being clear in my mind.

"Yes."

I close my eyes and the tears fall. "I can't stop thinking about it. I can't get the image of him out of my head."

Sarah's tone softens and there's a note of sympathy. "You never forget seeing a dead body, I'm afraid," she replies. "Evelyn, I'm sorry to have to do this, but I need to hear it while it's still fresh in your mind. Can you tell me what happened?"

Nodding, I open my eyes and stare up at her. Despite the hard lines creasing her forehead and the tight purse of her lips, her eyes hold an unexpected warmth. I cling to it as I speak.

"I was cleaning as usual and just listening to music. I didn't hear anything or see anything. I just… I did the room and then I went into the bathroom to clean, and that's when I saw the… the…" My throat closes and heat rushes up my neck, settling behind my eyes. The tears come thick and fast, forcing me to dip my head away in embarrassment. Abandoning my pathetic coffee, I fight to wipe the tears away.

"Did you recognize the victim? Did you see him at all?"

I shake my head, struggling to picture his face. All I can see is the gaping wound on his throat and in my mind, it spreads across his body until it consumes him.

Sarah makes a soft noise, then her hand lands gently on my shoulder. "I understand this will be difficult for you, Evelyn. I'm going to have one of my officers take you down to the station so we can talk properly, okay?"

My head snaps up as my heart jumps like a punch. "What? You think… You think I did this?" I weep.

"It's protocol," Sarah replies, smoothly dodging the question. "It will be more comfortable for you to talk away from the crime scene."

The crime scene.

Of course.

That man is dead and someone killed him. Could it be someone else who is staying here?

Or something much worse?

* * *

The bright lights and antiseptic smell of the police station are starkly different from the motel. It's like I've been whisked away into an entirely different world. Sarah seats me in a comfortable office and brings me a cup of real coffee, one with a taste and scent strong enough to cut through the copper smell that's following me like a ghost.

She sits on the couch across from me, notepad in hand, and taps her pen lightly against it while watching me drink. The heat from the coffee trickles slowly through me, and I can trace it in my mind's eye as tight muscles slowly ease from the heat.

"How long have you worked at the Sunrise Motel?" Sarah asks.

"Two years," I reply hoarsely.

"And in those two years, have you ever seen that man before?"

I can't think. His face is lost to me, swallowed by that wound and his claw hands. Trying to picture him each time fails, so all I can do is shake my head. "No."

"According to the books, there was no guest staying in that room, yet you were there today to clean it," Sarah says. "Is that common?"

I nod and lift my attention to her. "Gerald wants every room cleaned every day."

"Why?"

I can't tell her the truth. Gerald has too many people staying there who want to remain invisible or are up to something illegal. I don't know what to do. If I cover for him, am I covering for the murderer?

"Sometimes we get people that sneak in through the back fence," I say, reciting the lie Gerald told me when I first started working there. It's the only thing I can think of right now. "They break into the rooms, so Gerald has me clean every room every day to check that we don't have anyone here who shouldn't be."

Sarah scribbles on her notepad. "Talk me through that room today. What did you do?"

I sip the coffee and briefly close my eyes. My tears have long dried on the drive over here, but the sting of them clings to my eyelids and the back of my throat.

"I unlocked the door with my key and went inside. The place was a bit of a mess. I figured a guest had checked out recently, so I just cleaned."

"What did you clean? Tell me exactly, Evelyn."

"I don't know," I say while shrugging. My thoughts are muddled like fog has slipped in between my ears and is hiding the details from me. "What does it matter? I cleaned and then I found a body."

"Because you cleaned the crime scene, Evelyn." Sarah leans forward and rests one elbow on the top of her thigh. "Either you're the murderer trying a very clever tactic to cover your tracks, or you're just caught up in this by accident."

"Murderer?" My stomach lurches with the force of a wave. "I didn't do it! I swear I didn't kill him, I could never kill him! I could never hurt anyone!" A wave of nausea forces me into silence, and I screw up my eyes, fighting the stomach cramps that follow.

"Which," says Sarah softly, "is exactly why I need to know every detail of what you did."

I take her through it all to the best of my ability. I detail everything I remember doing when I entered the room, everything I touched and cleaned including what products I used, and then my discovery of the body. I had dropped my basket of bathroom cleaning products in shock and then picked it back up, only to drop it again when I realized I was disturbing the pool of blood. Sarah writes it all down and gets me to repeat it several times, then she has me tell the same story to two other detectives who ask their own variations of the same questions.

I repeat it until my throat is dry and my shift feels more like a story than actual reality, but in a strange way, it does help me disconnect from the trauma of discovering a dead man. Constantly repeating the story makes me bored of saying the same thing over and over again, but I can't tell if that's a normal reaction to have, and I'm too scared to ask in case it makes me look guilty.

By the time we finish, it's pitch black outside.

"I can have an officer run you home," Sarah says as she walks me to the exit.

"No." I shake my head. "It's okay, really. I'd much rather walk. Gives me some time to process."

"Are you sure?" Sarah's prickly demeanor has softened these past few hours, and her sympathetic smile holds a clearer warmth.

"Yeah. I kind of want to breathe fresh air and just walk, y'know?"

"I understand," Sarah replies, though I can't tell whether she does or not.

As a detective, I'm sure she's seen her fair share of dead bodies. Maybe this is just a regular Thursday for her.

"Take my card," Sarah continues, sliding a small card into my hand. "If you need anything, please call me. And I'll be in touch, so make sure you don't go anywhere."

"Is that a don't leave the state kind of warning?" I try to joke, but even as Sarah smiles, the warmth doesn't reach her eyes.

"That's exactly what that is."

"Oh." I flip her card over in my hands, then nod quickly. "Okay. Thank you."

"Take care, Evelyn." She waves me off at the door, turns on her heel, and strides back into the police station.

I remain stationary on top of the steps, staring out at the busy streets still heaving with life despite the late hour. It's surreal to see people going on with their lives as if there hasn't been a murder.

And yet, I understand it. I can't count how often I've seen a death on the news and brushed it off as nothing. Only this time, it's tangled up in my life and I saw something I will never forget.

I start walking, loosely planning my route home as my thoughts turn back to the body despite my best efforts. His face is still a blur to me, and that wound is as clear as ever. It's seared into my mind as if my thoughts fell victim to the same blade that cut his throat.

Digging in my pockets, I retrieve my phone and Google the motel. The murder has hit the news already. I scan articles as I walk, but there's no mention of me, thank God. Is that a good sign? Maybe the cops don't see me as the culprit if it's not in the news.

I hope so.

Next, I search how to deal with seeing a dead body, searching to see if my growing numbness and lack of memory of his face are common reactions, but I don't get my answer.

Two steps down the next street and suddenly, someone slams into me so hard that all air is forced from my lungs in a rapid grasp. The impact sends my phone flying from my fingers and I stumble sharply, rolling over my ankle while I fight to regain balance.

I don't stand a chance. Before I can suck in a breath, arms lock around my body and lift me upward as a black car screeches to a stop at the roadside. The door swings open.

Terror grips me like a vise and I can't scream. I have no air in my lungs, and the tight grip across my body prevents me from gaining the space to breathe. I kick my legs and another set of hands grabs them.

"No!" tears from me in a hoarse, weak gargle as I'm dragged into the darkness of the car and the door slams heavily behind me.

3

CORMAC

"Please! No, no, please!"

The woman gasps haggardly, choking on her own air as she fights against the man holding her down in the seat. Her eyes are so wide in terror, reminding me of a dog fighting on its last legs. She throws out her arms, desperately trying to reach the door handle, but she is missing by an inch. Still she begs, still she screams and gasps like a yapping puppy unable to understand the will of its master.

"Shut her up," I order quietly.

Hank, the burly man holding the woman down, obeys in an instant. One well-aimed hit to the back of the head, and she slumps forward like a rag doll, unconscious and silent.

I breathe slowly and focus on the gold lighter between my fingers. Flipping it back and forth is the only thing that grants me momentary peace. The car sways back and forth as we weave through traffic. Hank, my bodyguard, eases the woman back against the chair and sets about wrapping a seatbelt around her body.

"So this is her."

"Aye." Hank nods once.

Her olive skin flares briefly under each passing streetlight. Dark lashes rest against tear-stained cheeks where her makeup streaks near her chin just under her full red lips, likely from crying. Black hair frames her sleeping face, and Hank smooths out a few strands after untangling them from the seatbelt.

I rotate the lighter and slide my thumb over the seam between body and lid. I didn't know what to expect when I heard that there was a witness, someone the cops were overly interested in. She looks nothing like I expected, and yet I'm not sure what I did expect.

"Search her pockets. I want to know who she is."

As Hank obeys, vibrations against my thigh pull my attention. I pull out my phone, and my heart immediately sinks to the dark depths of my gut when I see who is calling. It's a call I have to take but one I absolutely do not want to.

The lighter rotates faster in my fingers as I answer. "Ma."

"Is it true?" My mother's agonized tone floods my ear. "Tell me it isn't true, Cormac. Please, for the love of God, tell me it isn't true."

My throat is dry, my tongue is fat and useless in my mouth, and I search the passing world through the tinted windows for any kind of distraction. I'd take a pocket of no cell service, a cop car stopping us, or even a car crash. Anything to stop me from saying what I have to say.

My ribs become barbed wire, painfully closing around my pounding heart as my lips part and I speak the dreaded words.

"It's true, Ma. Brenden is dead."

The agonizing wail of pain that comes from my mother is enough to bring burning tears to my eyes, and I swallow thickly to keep the terrible grief at bay.

"No!" she wails. "Not Brenden. Not my baby! No!"

I blink furiously, and my world blurs with unshed tears, forcing myself to listen to every single one of my mother's heart-wrenching sobs.

Brenden Gifford, my older brother and Irish Captain of the Gifford Mob, is dead, murdered in cold blood in some disgusting motel that he never should have been anywhere near.

His death not only brings agony to my family, but it jolts me from the position of Underboss to Captain.

I am in charge now.

"I'm sorry, Ma," I choke out roughly. "I'm so sorry."

Our world is far from safe and not even close to perfect, but out of all the cunts and traitors who flood the Mafia ranks each day, my brother was one of the good ones. He had a strong head on his shoulders and sought peace over war whenever the situation arose. Through his careful negotiations and level-headed perspective, he became the first Irishman to negotiate a business treaty with the Italians, who were famous for trusting no one but their own blood.

In five years, both Irish and Italian Families flourished under the weapons trade deal, which boosted our standing with every Irish family who trusted us to keep them safe.

All of that happened because of my brother.

And now he's dead in the morgue.

"Ma." I try to reach her as her sobs finally die down.

"Cormac." Despite the thickness of grief clogging her voice, her sharp words cut through me with aching familiarity. "You find them, you understand me? You find the fucker that did this to our

Brenden and you make him pay. You hearing me, Son? You make him pay!"

"I will, Ma," I swear tightly. "I will. Saoirse is coming to see you—"

"No." She cuts me off while sniffling. "You need her with you. You need the family with you. I'll be fine."

"Ma—"

"I'll be fine, Cormac. You find the bastard that killed my baby." She hangs up, and a smothering silence falls. The air grows so thick that I have to unbutton my waistcoat and the top two buttons of my shirt, then lower the window just so I can take an easy breath.

No one speaks.

Brenden is dead. I am Captain now. And his murderer walks these streets thinking they are safe. But I will not stop, I will not breathe until I have that fucker beneath my boot, and they will know nothing but agony for the rest of their days.

And this woman is key to finding them. At least, the cops think so.

After a few deep breaths of night air, I glance at Hank who watches me with unspoken sympathy. He's been my bodyguard for over ten years and in this family, he's as much a brother as Brenden was. Which means he shares in my pain, to an extent.

"How is she?" Hank asks quietly.

"Heartbroken," I reply tightly. "She wants the killer found immediately."

"As do we all." Hank's head tilts to the left, and he tosses me the purse he had taken from the woman. "Her name is Evelyn Morris. Twenty-four years old. Lives about six blocks away under the off-ramp. Her phone is a bit fucked, though. She dropped it when Dale grabbed her."

As he talks, I rummage through her purse. She has twenty bucks, a couple of loose coins, and an old library card that's so faded I can't even make out the name of the library. The last item is a card with a detective's name scrawled across it in gold ink. Anger pulses through me like a flickering flame, and I flip the card around, showing it to Hank.

"I want to know who the fuck this is and if we pay them. I need to know what they know, or whatever the fuck they think they know."

Was it random? Was Brenden caught unawares by some fucker who didn't know who they were dealing with? Or was it gang-related?

The answer will determine whether dawn breaks on war.

* * *

I watch the unconscious woman slowly come too. She jolts her shoulders first and then registers that her hands are bound and inaccessible. Then comes the panic. Her head snaps up, sending her black hair back in a wave, and she begins to hyperventilate. Like a caged cat, she pulls at her bindings, rocking back and forth while wildly scanning the dark room.

I wait until tears flood her brown eyes, and then I turn on the small lamp on the desk beside me.

"Evelyn."

She screams immediately, throwing her head back, and her eyes grow so wide it's a wonder they don't pop right out of their sockets.

"Please! I haven't done anything, I haven't, I swear. I don't know anything. Please let me go. Please, please, I'm sorry!"

When her eyes drop to the handgun resting against my thigh, she screams louder and then trails off into a sob. Whoever she is, the police think she's important, which means I have to find out if that's true. If she has worth, she will live. If she doesn't, then I will kill her and move on to the next stone. And the next, and the next, until my brother's killer is in front me begging for their life as desperately as she is.

"Your name is Evelyn Morris," I say. "Twenty-four. Lives alone in a dogshit apartment not fit for a squirrel. Your mother, Amy, has lived alone since the death of your father eight years ago. You've spent the past two years cleaning up grime for the Sunset Motel. You're single, no pets, and you eat at the same Vietnamese restaurant every Friday."

I recite what we've learned in the time she's been unconscious, and with each word, Evelyn grows quieter. A different kind of fear overtakes her, and I see it in her eyes. The moment she switches from blind fear to cold terror is like a switch flicking in her mind, and her wails fall silent.

"How do you know all that?" Evelyn gasps, wetting her lips with her tongue as tears pour down her cheeks. "What are you, cops? Is this a s–scare tactic or something?"

"I'm not a cop." I stand slowly, and Evelyn's eyes snap to the gun in my hand. "I'm letting you know that I know everything about you so that you will think very carefully about how you answer my next question."

Swiftly approaching her, I wind one hand into her dark hair and jerk her head back. With the other, the gun rests lightly against her collar bone, and Evelyn whimpers in terror while more tears spill past her dark lashes.

"I d–don't know anything," she whimpers, trembling like a fragile leaf in my hands. "Please, I know nothing. I'm a nobody, I'm no one! I'm not important!"

"Nine hours ago, you found a body in that shitty motel you work at. I need to know what you saw."

"What? Th—The body?" Her trembling makes her words jerky, and her mouth struggles to obey her desire to talk.

I tighten my grip, drawing more of her hair into my first and forcing her head back further until a whimper of pain claws its way out her throat.

"I won't ask again. Tell me about the body."

"The body? The body… I don't know, okay! It was a body. He was just dead in the bathtub and—and there was blood everywhere and his throat was slit open, and that's it, okay? That's it, I swear, there's nothing else. It wasn't me. I just found him!"

His throat was slit.

I release her and turn away, barely hearing her terrified sobs as her description snakes through my mind like poison. He was murdered and dumped in the tub like he was trash. The coils of wire around my heart tighten, and for a split second, nothing exists inside me but pain. I want to scream and roar. I want to pound my fists into something until all of my anger has faded and there's nothing left but a hollow emptiness.

I can't.

But fuck, I want to.

"His throat was slit?"

"Yes!" Evelyn wails. "Wide open, and it was horrible, and that's all I saw, okay? I ran out and called the cops right after!"

"What was he doing there?"

"Huh?"

I grab her neck, forcing her to look me in the eye, and she sobs openly. The anger blinds me so I don't care how tightly I grip her or how I've pulled her up so that both she and the chair teeter on one leg.

"I said, what the fuck was he doing there?"

"I don't know," she sobs. "I n–never saw him, I never spoke to him. M–My boss leases rooms all the time with no names, no nothing. I don't know him and I don't know why he was there, okay? I don't know anything, please! Please don't kill me, please, I don't want to die!"

When I release her, she collapses back into the chair, and it rocks back once but doesn't tip over. She really appears to know nothing, nothing helpful, at least. Since she discovered the body, it explains why the cops were so interested in her. She's just a witness, not a suspect.

She's no use to me.

I pull back the safety on the gun, and Evelyn wails, but just as I lift it, the door opens and warm light pours in from the hallway.

"Cormac." My sister, Saoirse, stands there with her phone in hand, leaning against the door handle.

"Please," Evelyn begs weakly as I step away. "I have money. You can have all my money. You can have my car, my apartment, everything, please! Just take it. I don't want to die, please."

Ignoring her, I approach my sister who regards Evelyn with a curl of distaste. Once I'm close enough, her dark brows pinch over her green eyes. "Detective Gogs isn't one of ours."

"What?"

"She's new, from out of state. Transferred three months ago."

"Whose is she, Italian?"

"No one's." Saoirse sighs. "She's not on any payroll. She's a hundred percent legit."

A beat of anger pulses through my chest and I grit my teeth. Anyone else would be happy to have a non-corrupt cop on the case of their brother's death, but not me. I don't need the cops to do their jobs. I need them to help me and then stay the fuck out of my way. Their law isn't going to bring justice.

My law will.

"Can we get her?" I snap. "Pay her or use her, I don't care."

"We've got nothing, at least not yet," Saoirse replies sharply. "She's cleaner than a fucking virgin, and she's not open for business."

"Fuck!" Tension snaps up my arm and I lash out, slamming my fist into the door. Wood cracks under the force, and Evelyn whimpers behind me.

Saoirse doesn't flinch.

"What about someone on her team?"

She shakes her head. "She's pulling in green officers, even someone from out of state. She's going all out. Other than getting our hands on her, I don't see a way into this case."

Sarah Gogs pulling for outside help tells me one thing. She knows exactly whose body is in the morgue and what it will mean for this city. She knows war is coming and is arrogant enough to think she can get ahead of it.

Without someone on the force giving me the info I need, this suddenly became a hundred times more difficult.

Evelyn's sobs grate through me like chalk on a board, and then suddenly, they're the most beautiful thing I have ever heard.

The detective isn't on our payroll and won't talk to us, but there is one person she will talk to.

One person she won't ever suspect.

Evelyn.

"Well," I say, turning toward the cowering woman, "you suddenly have worth."

4

EVELYN

I'm in hell.

Maybe the sight of the body killed me and this is the eternal punishment I've landed in for being up to my eyeballs in debt.

Each breath tears through my raw throat like a razor blade. My heart pounds so fiercely that I can barely discern the individual beats, and my stomach has knotted so tightly from stress that I'm not even sure I can straighten up.

All I wanted was to go home. In a blink, I ended up dragged into a car, and then I woke up to an interrogation by a man as thickly muscular as a brick house. Like the cops, all he cares about is the body and none of my answers seemed to satisfy him. I was so certain he was going to kill me until that woman appeared.

I couldn't hear what they were saying, but something made him angry enough to punch and damage the door. Then something changed.

I beg for darkness to take me as the huge bulldozer of a man walks back toward me with his gun gripped tightly in his right hand.

"You want to live?" he asks in a voice tinged with an accent I can't currently place.

My mind races with a plethora of offers he might make, and I think I would say yes to anything if it would get me out of here. I nod rapidly, unable to stop my lower jaw from trembling enough to answer.

"You will do something for me," he states. "Once you complete it, you will be free to go. Do you agree to these terms?" He adjusts his grip on the gun, and my heart leaps painfully up into my throat.

I should ask him what he needs first rather than agreeing blindly, but that thought is drowned out by the sheer panicked need to survive and walk out of here.

Wherever here is.

So I nod again.

"Say it," the man barks, making me jump.

I sniffle, blinking rapidly through the ever-flowing tears. "Y–Yes," I manage to force out. "I–I'll do anything."

"If you want to live, you will return to the police station and bug the detective in charge of this murder case. You're familiar with her already, I imagine?" With the flick of a wrist, he pulls a card from his pocket and tosses it down onto my lap. "And if you value your life, you won't get caught. Are we clear?"

All I see is freedom, so I nod as fast I can. "Yes, I understand."

What the fuck?

Bugging Sarah? Is that because these people are responsible for the murder or because they want to know more? I can't tell. All I know for sure is that this man is dangerous and the dead body is important to him in some regard. But the details don't matter. I can play along until I get a window and then I can run. I can just run away and not stop until I reach a place where no one knows me.

"Cormac," calls the woman from the door, putting a name to the face of the muscular, armed man in front of me. "Cian will be here in the morning."

"Understood," Cormac replies. With a nod, the woman leaves and Cormac closes the distance between us. I flinch, fearing he's going to strike me or his fist is heading back into my hair, but neither of those things happen. He reaches around me and unravels the rope around my wrist in a matter of seconds.

"It's late," he says, his gruff voice thick. "Follow me."

He strides away, and I try to follow, but fear has my muscles locked up and I'm unable to stand from the chair. Hurriedly wiping away my tears, I massage my thighs and clutch the detective's card, begging my body to listen to me. By the time Cormac reaches the door and opens it, I'm finally on my feet.

Each step is jerky and I'm unable to control the tremor that's settled deep in my skeleton. Every part of me shakes as I stare at Cormac's back and follow him through a warmly lit hallway to a door near the end. He opens it and jerks his head inside.

"You can rest there until morning."

He doesn't even look at me as I pass him, and as soon as I'm inside, the door thumps shut.

I hold my breath, waiting for something to jump out at me in the darkness, but there's nothing—just a faint scent of cotton and vanilla and air that's cool against my skin. As my eyes adjust to the dark, I make out the shapes of a chair, a few cabinets, and a bed.

The bed is my destination, and the tears pour the second I throw myself onto the softness. Grabbing the nearest pillow, I curl around it and sob my aching heart out.

What the fuck is going on?

I find a dead body in my shitty job, become scarred for life at the sight of it, face intense interrogation by the cops, and then get kidnapped and have my life threatened by a terrifyingly large man.

All in the past twenty-four hours.

I'm scared, more scared than I've ever been in my entire life. This isn't what my life is supposed to be. I make bad financial choices, I fight with my mother over her neglect, and I work a shitty job to pay off debt. That's supposed to be the extent of my stress.

But that man knew everything, even my favorite restaurant. Whoever these people are, it's clear I don't belong here. I don't want to belong here.

I want to go home.

I cry into the pillow until the sheer exhaustion of the day steals over me, and I fall into a troubled sleep filled with gaping wounds, pools of blood, and gigantic shadows that smother me to silence.

One shadow in particular keeps its hand over my mouth and suffocates me to the point that my body is about to burst from the lack of air.

My eyes snap open and I jerk back from whatever is in front of my face, panting harshly. Fumbling with the bedside table, I scramble at the light and eventually turn it on, revealing that the only thing smothering me was the pillow I had chosen before I fell asleep. I must have rolled into it during my nightmare and become stuck.

As for the pain in my abdomen, that's not from the lack of air.

I really, really need to pee.

But I don't want to leave.

It becomes a debate between whether it would be scarier to run into Cormac in the hallway while looking for the bathroom or to face him after I have an accident in this bedroom. A bedroom that, at a glance, holds more expensive-looking furniture than I've ever seen in my life.

Soiling this room definitely wins out as the scarier option, so with my heart in my throat, I move on my tiptoes and sneak out of the room.

The place is quiet. As I hold my breath in the dark hallway, not a single sound reaches me. No voices, no clinking of dishes or signs of life. Everything is dark and quiet. They wouldn't leave me here alone, would they?

Maybe this entire thing is just one long, bad dream.

It takes me a few long minutes to find the bathroom by peeking into doorways, but eventually, I locate the facilities and relieve myself with a groan of relief. Washing my hands, I try not to look at myself in the mirror. What makeup does remain on my face is smudged and messy, barely covering my blotchy skin and red-rimmed eyes. Caring about what I look like hardly feels important right now, but having to go through all of this in the terrible maid's outfit from the motel just makes the entire past day feel like some horrid joke.

I splash water on my face, then cup some in my palm and drink a few sips. I have no appetite, but the growing ache in my skull is definitely from dehydration. Or Cormac's hand in my hair or the earlier blow to the head.

I can't decide.

Heading back to bed seems like the best choice. I'd rather sleep until someone comes to get me, but on the way back to where I think the bedroom was, I spot a light coming out from underneath one of the closed doors.

I should leave it alone. Every part of my body screams at me to leave it alone and go back to bed, but since I haven't seen a soul since I woke up, curiosity wins out.

The door opens silently, and I peer around to see what's inside.

It's a lounge filled with plush leather sofas and chairs, a wooden wall cabinet filled with alcohol bottles, and floor-to-ceiling windows opposite the door, through which streams of early morning light pour. Seeing a pink morning sky is beautiful, and I watch it for a few long seconds. Just as I'm about to leave, a soft thump catches my attention as a glass half full of amber falls into view on the other side of one of the chairs.

The glass teeters on its edge, and my heart jumps, watching it fall over. I dart inside the room without a second thought and snatch up the glass before too much of the alcohol spills onto the rug, but even a few droplets are enough to ruin the pure cream pattern on the rug. I should clean it. I want to clean it because it will bring me peace of mind, but I can't move.

Cormac is asleep in the chair. The glass must have fallen from his relaxed fingertips, and for the first time, I can look at him—really look at him.

He sleeps soundly with his auburn brows pulled low in a scowl, even in slumber. Thick copper-red hair sits quaffed on his head, and a dark five o'clock shadow hugs his wide, chiseled jaw. He's topless, exposing a broad muscular chest covered in a dusting of red hair and more thick scars than I care to count. There's a cluster of triangles tattooed onto his thick neck, and his left arm is wrapped in a colorful tattoo sleeve filled with flowers and birds.

He's incredibly handsome when he's not brandishing a gun and threatening my life.

Each slow breath makes his impressive muscles shift and rise, creating a ripple across his torso which draws my eyes down to his tight abs and the soft start of a snail trail that disappears into the waistband of his belted slacks.

Did he lose his shirt in another spilled alcohol incident?

The longer I stare, the harder it is to move, but eventually, I kick myself into gear and set the glass aside on a coaster resting on the glass coffee table. With limited access to any cleaning supplies, the best I can do is a small bottle of white vinegar that I find on the bottom shelf of the drinks cabinet. It will help only a little, but it will have to do.

I hurry back to the stain, but as I crouch down next to Cormac's sleeping form, my hair falls forward and brushes over his empty fingers. Every nerve in my body pulses in fright as his hand twitches, but he doesn't wake. I breathe out a slow sigh of relief and uncap the vinegar.

Cormac is on his feet in an instant with his hand around my throat, hauling me upward with a growl. The vinegar bottle slips away from my grasp as my hands shoot to clutch at his thick arm, and for a searingly terrifying second, I'm held aloft, staring into stormy blue eyes. In the same second, Cormac appears to realize what he is doing and he immediately releases me.

"Shit," he croaks gruffly. "Sorry."

I cough sharply, clutching at my throat as he steps away. My heart hammers and fear pours through me like acid in my veins, but then Cormac places his warm hand on my shoulder and the burn suddenly fades.

"I'm sorry," he says again. "Didn't expect you to be there."

"Do you always go for the throat?" I ask, my voice tight.

Cormac snorts as if he finds humor in my words. "Maybe. What are you doing?"

I suddenly remember the vinegar and dart down to grab the bottle, but it's too late. The vinegar has poured out and soaked into the rug, filling the air with its sharp scent.

"I was looking for the bathroom and then I came in here and saw the glass fall. I was just trying to stop it from staining. I'm so sorry, it was an accident!" Will he kill me for ruining the rug? For spilling the vinegar? This man scares me, and I tense up, ready for anger or the gun or anything.

Instead, there's nothing. When I glance up, Cormac waves one hand at me and turns away toward the drinking cabinet.

"It's fine. It's just a rug. Doesn't fucking matter." As he grabs a glass, he throws a glance over his shoulder. "Your life is on the line and you cared about my rug?"

I clutch the vinegar bottle to my chest. "I like to clean. It soothes me. When everything inside is a mess, it helps to clean the outside, y'know?"

Cormac grunts. "You're in the perfect line of work, then."

"Sort of." It's all I can think of to say. My stomach writhes like a nest of snakes as the awkward conversation falls into a lull, but my feet don't obey my desire to leave. I watch Cormac pour a full glass and then drain it in two gulps. He couldn't have been asleep long if I saw the other glass fall. I watch him pour another, then he glances at me again.

"Do you drink?"

"A little. Though maybe not right now."

"I shouldn't drink either," he replies, lifting the glass. "Shouldn't do a lot of things."

As he drinks, it suddenly hits me why there's something oddly familiar about this. My mother, as cold and distant as she was, had a period of drowning herself in wine after the death of my father. It made my teen years terribly painful, but the way Cormac bunches himself up as if trying to make himself small and drinks like the burn in medicine... It's familiar.

He's grieving.

"That man," I say softly, taking a cautious step forward. "He was important to you, wasn't he?" Previously, I worried that Cormac was the killer, or someone around him was. His earlier desire to kill me would make sense if he wanted to hide what I knew. But I see it now.

He wears grief on his wrist like the ink on his arm. It's just smothered in anger.

"He was my brother," Cormac replies finally, his words ejecting from him in sharp bursts. "Family." That word cracks out of him, and Cormac lifts his glass, but it doesn't meet his lips. A subtle shudder moves through his entire form.

I've seen a lot at that motel over the years, and I know the signs of someone in pain. Closing the gap once more, I lightly touch his arm, and he jumps ever so slightly, but he doesn't pull away. The glass lowers and he sends me a side-long glance.

"I'm sorry for your loss," I say softly. For a moment, staring into those blue eyes, I choose to forget the kidnapping and the threats just to let him know that I am sorry. My description of what I saw in the bathroom takes on a colder truth when I realize I was describing this man's brother.

Cormac holds my gaze, then his eyes narrow ever so faintly. "You should be telling me to go fuck myself."

"Maybe," I reply softly. "But I am still sorry about your brother."

There's a second where the world stops spinning, my heart stops beating, and a pulse of warmth rises between us. I can't decipher its meaning. Maybe it's just adrenaline from everything that's been happening or a mixture of fear and something else.

Something like attraction.

Whatever it is, it passes in a split second before the door opens and the man who dragged me in from the car walks in. His brow lifts like he's surprised to see me, and Cormac draws away from me as he turns.

"What is it, Hank?"

"Your mother," Hank says, and he holds out a phone.

Cormac accepts it, then glances at the silver watch on his wrist. "Hank, get Evelyn a change of clothes." He glances back at me, and the hardened coldness has returned to his eyes. "Time for you to plant a little bug."

5

CORMAC

"Do you have anything?"

My mother's sharp tones pull my thoughts away from Evelyn as I stare after her, watching her meekly follow after Hank. What was that sensation that passed between us? Her touch was so gentle, so alien compared to what I deserve. Especially after what I'm putting her through.

Confusion swirls like fog in my gut, so I push it down and stride toward the windows overlooking a city on the cusp of waking up.

"I have the witness who found Brenden."

"And?" Mom demands. "Do they have anything useful?"

"No," I sigh. "But I can use them to get us to someone who will have something useful."

"Good." She pauses heavily, and her voice is softer when she next speaks. "I called your father. I wanted to let him know about Brenden but he… well, you can imagine. He didn't know who I was, never mind his own son."

An older shard of pain embedded in my heart sinks in a little deeper at the thought of my father. In my youth, he was a vibrant and loyal man, but sickness stole him away from us and that pain knows no end. Early-onset dementia quickly spiraled into Alzheimer's. One morning, I woke up and the man I called my father was just an empty shell, unrecognizable even to my mother who had spent nearly her entire life with him. We made the decision to send him back to Ireland, hoping that being around his childhood scenery would help soothe his soul.

To an extent, we were right. He's alive and happy. He just doesn't remember he has a huge family that loves him.

"Perhaps it's a blessing," Mom says as my silence drags on. "It would break his heart to know about Brenden." Her voice cracks, and my heart follows with a sharp pain that lances right through my ribcage. I'm heartbroken, and the shards scatter around my insides with every angry beat of whatever is left.

"Brenden would understand," I reply tightly. "He knew better than anyone how much of Dad was just a ghost."

"I want their head, Cormac," Mom says, and the cracks keep forming in her words. "I want their head on a platter, you understand me? I need—" She cuts herself off and distant sniffling carries through the phone.

I tighten my grip on the device until the plastic begins to crack and the ridges cut painfully into my palm. I share the same fury. It sits like a knot in my chest, tightening with each passing minute that my brother's killer walks free. I want to soothe my mom, to comfort my siblings, and break the skull of the bastard who is causing such pain to everyone I love.

But I have no idea who it is, so that anger has nowhere to go. I'm going to drown at this rate.

"I need to go and deal with a detective, Ma. But if you need anything, you call me, alright?"

"Be safe," she says, her voice thick. "I love you."

"Love you too, Ma."

After ending the call, I throw on a shirt and take the stairs down to the lobby of my apartment building in an attempt to burn off some of the rage locking up my muscles. It helps for a few minutes as I arrive breathlessly and find my younger brother and sister, twins Saoirse and Cian, waiting for me.

"Did you sprint down here?" Cian asks with a snort, crossing his thick arms over his broad chest and straining his shirt to the point that the buttons are holding on for dear life.

"Gotta keep in shape, little brother," I reply, bouncing up to him and ruffling the tight collection of dark curls on top of his head. "Can't have you beating me."

"Fuck off." Cian slaps my hand away. "I'd beat you any day of the week."

"Time and place," I challenge.

"Right here." Cian starts to roll his sleeves up but stops when Saoirse elbows him sharply in the ribs.

"Put your fucking dick away," she snaps, then she moves closer to me and pulls me into a tight hug. "How's Ma?"

"About as bad as you can imagine," I reply, hugging her back with one arm and dragging Cian in under my other. He fights me for half a second and then melts into the hug with a grunt. "She tried to call Dad."

"And?" Saoirse looks up at me with old hope in her sparkling eyes. It fades the second I shake my head. "Figures," she mutters.

"What you got for me?" With the intimate moment over, we step back from one another and the sibling bonds melt away, replaced with the bonds of loyalty. Brenden's death catapulted me into the position of Captain, which had ripple effects on the entire hierarchy. Saoirse is now my underboss and Cian steps into her shoes as a General. In the space of a day, our lives and the entire layout of the Irish Mob changed.

Keeping a lid on her pain, Saoirse purses her lips and places a hand on her hip. "The Italians reached out. Matteo Barati, to be exact."

"He didn't send his son?" Cian snorts.

"Rocky's probably too balls deep in some poor hooker to give a shit about what's going on here," Saoirse retorts. "But Matteo offers his sympathies and resources. He claims it's in his best interests to get this matter resolved as quickly as possible."

"You think he's speaking out of guilt?" I ask. Saoirse's analyses have proven invaluable over the years, so when she shakes her head, I trust her implicitly.

"He didn't sound guilty. If he was, he would have sent one of his generals to offer sympathies rather than calling himself. I'm not ruling him out, but he's not at the top of my list."

"What would he even have to gain?" Cian remarks. "If he's behind this, the peace treaty he signed with Brenden would go up in smoke. No guns for them, no drugs for us. And only one of those wins a war."

Cian's right, but it doesn't soothe the growing itch under my skin to have a name and face I can pulverize. "One glance at our history and you can see how often someone fucks over something good for some small slight."

Cian grumbles under his breath. "Fair." Then he straightens up. "The Russians offered their own condolences in their own weird way. Flowers." He wrinkles his nose. "I'm not even fully convinced they came from Anastasia."

"Doubt it," Saoirse replies. "Anastasia took over what, four months ago? The entire Remizova clan has been in uproar ever since her father died, and it's no secret they hate having a woman in charge. Someone's probably trying to undermine her by sending flowers because that's what a woman would do." Saoirse dramatically rolls her eyes. "As if Anastasia isn't as fierce as they come."

"Undermine her enough to kill?" I ask.

Saoirse meets my gaze. "Maybe."

"Keep an eye on them."

"Understood."

"We do have a more immediate problem," Cian remarks. "We can't get into the crime scene. This new detective has the place sealed off and patrolled like crazy. None of them are ours, or Italian, so unless you know of a ghost that can get us in there, I have no idea how we can get in and find out what the fuck Brenden was even doing there."

That is a pressing problem. There are too many unknowns around Brenden's death like why the fuck he was even in that shitty motel in the first place. A look at the crime scene would give us a chance to check for anything he might have hidden before he died. I step away from my siblings, forcing myself to pace as my fingers seek comfort in the lighter buried in my pocket.

"The girl," I say eventually. "She works there. I bet she can get in."

"Really?" Cian snorts. "You want to entrust another thing to a fucking stranger?"

"What else do you want me to do, Cian?" I spin around, anger crawling up my spine like a rabid snake. "We don't have the cops, we don't have the crime scene. All we have is a fucking cleaner and a dead brother, so tell me, Cian, what brilliant plan do you have to get us in there, huh? Do you want to shoot your way in? Because more cop eyes on us right now would be fucking brilliant."

"I don't fucking know," Cian snaps back, his voice rising. "I'm not the fucking Captain. It's your job to guide us, but doing it on the back of some stranger?"

"Hey!" Saoirse steps between us, her eyes narrowed to dangerous slits. "One more word out of you and I'll rip your balls off, you understand?" She glares at her twin, pointing one sharp, manicured finger at him. "And you." Her angry eyes whip around to me. "I know you're itching for a reason to explode, but Cian is right. You're the Captain now, so rein it the fuck in, will you? I'm not some fucking mediator."

Cian and I glare at one another for a few heated minutes until sense and Saoirse's words finally sink in. She's right, annoyingly so. The urge to lash out is so strong that I'm latching onto the slightest hint of discourse, hoping it will let me pound some flesh. But my brother doesn't deserve it. He's in as much pain as I am.

A silent apology passes between the two of us and Cian steps away, rubbing at the back of his neck.

"If Ma were here, she'd slap the both of you," Saoirse mutters.

I clasp her shoulder and squeeze. "I'm sorry."

"Fucking emotional men," she grumbles, then she flashes me a sad smile. "It's fine."

Before I can say more, the elevator doors hiss softly and Hank strides out with Evelyn by his side. She's changed into a pair of blue jeans and a light green shirt that strains slightly over her chest and is open enough to give a tantalizing flash of skin just below her neck.

My eyes linger for a second, but Evelyn is too nervous to notice my wandering eye. Her own gaze darts back and forth between the three of us while she twists her hands together and chews on her lower lip.

"Boss." Hank greets me with a nod. "Satisfied?"

I follow the tilt of his head to Evelyn and nod. Having her turn up at the police station in the same clothes would have raised too many questions. She looks a little rough with messy hair and dark circles under her eyes, but she looks the part and that's all that matters.

"Hungry?" I ask as Evelyn stops nearest me, likely because I'm the only one out of the three of us whom she's spoken to.

Evelyn shakes her head.

"Right," Cian snaps, and he abruptly approaches Evelyn. "It's so fucking simple that a monkey could do it. You see this?" He pulls a tiny black square from his pocket and holds it in the palm of his hand. "You need to get this onto her desk near her computer. Stick it in a drawer or in a pen or something, as long as it's near her computer, alright?"

With wide eyes, Evelyn nods so quickly that her hair bounces about her face.

"And this one." He pulls out an even smaller one. "You need to get this on her person."

"I—" Evelyn squeaks. "Her person?"

"Yes," Cian sighs, visibly irritated. "On her person. How else the fuck do you want me to say it?"

The moment he roughly grasps her wrist, my spine jumps and I wrestle down the urge to shove his hand away from her. I've no idea where such a territorial urge came from, but it takes all my strength to remain still as Cian shoves the bugs into her hand.

"On her person. In her pocket, in her bag, hell, fucking kiss her and shove it down her throat for all I care." Cian snaps his hand away and grumbles something under his breath about uselessness. "Don't fuck it up."

Following that, he strides away with Saoirse and slams his way out of the building. His anger is justified and I don't hold it against him, but it irritates me the way he spoke to Evelyn when she's clearly shaken to the core.

However, why I even care remains a mystery to me. She's just a maid. The last person to see my brother. Other than that, she doesn't matter.

"Wow." Evelyn puffs out her cheeks. "No pressure." Her words are soft, as if she's talking to herself, so I don't respond as I lead her out of the building to the car parked outside. As Hank opens the door for her, I catch her firmly by the forearm and stop her from climbing in.

"It feels like a lot," I say as she turns those wide, doe-like eyes on me. "But you do this and one more thing for me, and then you are free to go."

"You won't kill me?" she asks, tilting her head slightly in a way that reminds me of a curious puppy.

"No," I reply honestly. "As long as you don't fuck this up."

6

EVELYN

As I climb the steps toward the police station, I contemplate running.

Would Cormac catch me? Or that other angry man who shoved the bugs into my hand? Would they catch me and kill me or would they let me vanish among the crowds?

I know the answer as I reach the door and feel the weight of their eyes on me from wherever they parked the car. I might be away from them, but I'm certainly not free.

As I head inside, my mind whirs.

I should tell the detective what's happening, get her to help me and save me from them so I can go back home and return to my boring, regular life. That's what the cops are for, right? To help people in any kind of situation.

I decide I'll ask her for help as I'm speaking to the desk sergeant about Detective Gogs. He takes me to her office and sits me down, telling me that she's busy in interrogation right now but will be with me shortly. When he leaves, he closes the door, and a soft silence falls around me like a warm blanket.

The past two days have been insane and for the first time since I walked into that bathroom, I feel like I can breathe properly. I'm alone. The soft hum of conversation and ringing phones from outside Sarah's office drift through the air, warming me with a distant presence that's far enough away to keep me at peace. I focus on my breathing and pick at a loose thread on my jeans, feeling the tightness in my chest relax and expand.

I'm exhausted. And confused. For whatever reason, the strange spark that passed between me and Cormac in his lounge lingers in my mind like some kind of alert.

He's a dangerous man who kidnapped me and tied me to a chair, then threatened me with a gun in my face. So why can't I stop thinking about him? About the way his hand wrapped around my throat and lifted me like I weighed nothing, about the way his eyes melted from angry to apologetic in just a flash, and how warm his arm was under my fingertips.

It has to be some kind of adrenaline-based reaction, right? There's no way I should be lingering on a man who threatened me and is forcing me to plant bugs inside a police station.

Footsteps draw closer outside and I open my eyes, but whoever it was merely passes by and I'm left alone with my turbulent thoughts.

And the bugs.

Despite their size, the ridges go through my pocket and burn into my thigh, threatening to set me ablaze if I don't do something about them soon. My heart begins to race when I slip my hand into my pocket and remove the largest bug. That man, Cian I think his name was, demanded I place this as near Sarah's computer as possible. Scanning her desk, there's not much for me to work with. It's incredibly neat,

THE IRISH REDEMPTION

with folders and papers lined up with the edge of the desk, a mug centered on a coaster, and dust covers over her keyboard and monitor.

My only option is the small succulent tucked just behind her monitor, to the left of her desk phone. Sarah's desk is so tidy that she'll surely notice if I touch anything, but I have no choice and my window for success is rapidly closing.

Rising from my chair, I lean over her desk and place the small square bug into the succulent's soil. My fingers tremble, so I grit my teeth, frowning as I use all my focus to press the little piece of plastic as deep into the soil as I can without disturbing it. Luckily, the bug blends in well, and I'm able to cover the small hole with a few brushes of dirt.

My ass is barely back in the hard plastic chair when the door swings open and Sarah strides in with a cup of coffee in hand, sending my heart racing wildly and my gut to punch down to my core.

Holy shit.

A second longer and I would have been discovered.

"Evelyn!" Sarah's brow shoots to her hairline. "Is everything alright?" She closes the door and moves around her desk, taking a seat while never once taking her eyes off me.

Out of the corner of my eye, the succulent blares like a beacon and I fight not to glance at it, as if a single look will cause the secret to spill out and I'll end up arrested.

"I, uhm…" My voice trembles as violently as my hands. Clutching them together until my knuckles ache, I clear my throat and try again. "I couldn't stop thinking about it. The body, I mean. And I just… I don't know, I have no one to talk to, and I thought I would go crazy if I just stayed in my apartment, so I came here."

As lame excuses go, it's pretty shitty, but luckily, I look as shitty as I feel and Sarah buys it. Her eyes soften and she nods, shrugging off her blazer and placing her mobile on the desk next to her keyboard.

"I understand. You've experienced something incredibly traumatic and it will take you a long time to heal. I can put you in touch with a therapist who can help you talk through a few things."

"I can't afford a therapist." I laugh dryly, amused by the fact that I'm *still* experiencing something traumatic. "I actually…"

I pause, and Sarah stares at me intently as she pours her coffee from the paper cup in her hand to the porcelain one on her desk.

This is my chance.

I should tell her the truth.

My lips part, and I expect Cormac to come crashing in through the window, as if he can tell what I'm about to say.

I need to tell her about him. About what happened to me last night and the threats on my life. But for some reason, the words don't come. They linger in my throat like hands, clawing their way back down into my gut instead of out into the open air where they belong.

"Evelyn?" Sarah prompts. Scrunching up the paper cup, she tosses it into a wastebasket that's out of sight under her desk. "Is everything alright?"

I want to tell her and yet I can't. Cormac's face bursts into my mind, mostly his look from earlier when he seemed so openly surprised that I would offer my sympathies. All he wants is to find out who killed his brother, and he's going to extreme lengths to do just that.

I can't imagine anyone loving me that deeply.

"Yes," I say weakly, and a sickly warmth flushes down the back of my neck. "I'm just very… tired. Actually, is there a chance I could get some water?" I pat my throat. "I'm so hot."

"Of course." Sarah stands quickly. "I'll be right back."

She hurries from the office, and I gasp desperately as if I'd been holding my breath the entire time. Sweat breaks out across my forehead and the floor sways slightly. I'm tired, thirsty, and haven't eaten since yesterday's breakfast.

Can you die from stress? My heart hasn't stopped pounding since I found the body and even now, it races up a gear when a light buzzing me alerts me to the fact that Sarah left her phone on the desk.

Exactly where Cian wants me to plant the other bug.

On the drive over, he explained that the smaller bug had to be placed next to the SIM card in her phone and that it was small enough to be undetectable.

I can't do it.

Fuck.

Come on, Evelyn. Do this, then go home. Do it.

Glancing over my shoulder to make sure the door is still closed, I snatch her phone up from the desk and pop the cute corgi phone cover off. Popping out the SIM card, my trembling fingers fuck up slipping the bug into place. My vision begins to blur from the strain of focusing on something so small, but eventually, it slides into place and I shove the SIM card back into her phone. As I pop the case back over, sweat drips from my forehead and lands on the screen so I have to wipe it away quickly. Then I set her phone back on the desk.

Or I try to.

I'd snatched it up quickly, and now can't remember exactly where it was sitting. She's sure to notice that it's moved, right? Everything about her office is so pristine. I bet she can tell when one of the keyboard keys has an extra layer of dust.

Tension snaps behind my eyes and a powerful ache spreads through my skull. It throbs in time to my pounding heart, and I set her phone back down where I roughly estimate it to have been. Once again, I've only just sat down when Sarah returns with a clear plastic cup of water. Her eyes widen as she hands it to me.

"Evelyn, what's the matter? Are you alright?"

"Yes, yes I'm fine, I just—" My hands tremble violently as I accept the cup and it slips from my grasp, bouncing on my knee and sending water over me and the wiry gray carpet below. "Shit, I'm so sorry!"

"Evelyn—"

"I'm sorry!" Lurching forward, I try my best to catch the cup, but by the time I do, the contents are soaked into me and the carpet. "I'm so, so sorry!" Flustered, I set the cup on the desk, knock it over, and then try to set it upright. On my third attempt, Sarah catches my hand and forces me still with her other hand on my shoulder.

"Evelyn. Take a breath for me, okay? It's just water."

"I'm sorry," I whisper, unable to look her in the eye. "Is there a bathroom nearby?"

"Down the hall and the third on the left," she says, squeezing my hand. "Are you alright?"

"I'm fine, fine. I just need to…" Without finishing my sentence, I lurch from the seat and sprint from her office, not stopping until I make it to the bathroom. Inside, the cool air against my skin is like the first bite of frost on a winter's morning, and it's as soothing as the sharp, cold water I splash on my face to try to calm myself down.

I almost fucked that up. What I've just done is surely illegal, and I don't know how much jail time you get for bugging a police station, but it's bound to be insane. And I did it for a strange man I don't even know.

Fuck.

Who the hell is that guy? Why me? Why did it have to be me who found his brother and not the night shift?

Clutching the cold sink, I stare into my dark reflection. My cheeks flush crimson, a stark contrast to how pale my skin has become, so it looks like I've been slapped across the face. My hair is a mess and my lips are pale, hanging open as I pant for air.

Nausea twists through me and an aching cramp follows, shooting through my gut like a punch. I spin around and fall to my knees in front of the toilet as my abdomen cramps. Gagging over the toilet brings nothing but another painful cramp through my gut, and I almost want to throw up if only so I can experience the relief afterward.

But there's nothing. I'm hollow.

I gag a few more times before the sensation passes and then I slump onto the cold tile floor, breathing heavily with tears building in my eyes.

What the hell is my life turning into?

I briefly close my eyes, but as soon as I do, all I see is the gaping wound across the throat of the body in the bath, so I snap them open again and force myself to my feet.

"You should have told her," I murmur to myself in the mirror. "Idiot."

I did it. Now I just have to get outside and hope Cormac will stay true to his word and let me go. Then I'm going home.

Or to see my mom. I'm not sure.

Splashing one more handful of water on my face, I quickly dry my hands and head out of the bathroom, only to run directly into Sarah who stands outside with her brows pulled low.

"Evelyn, are you alright?"

I nod, pushing some damp strands of hair away from my face. "I'm fine. Honest. Think I'm just really stressed, y'know? I think I'm going to go home."

"Are you sure?" Her look turns quizzical and she looks me over once, then sighs. "I wanted to let you know something. The body that you found? We identified him."

"Oh?" I say as casually as I can muster while my heart attempts to break free of my ribcage.

"Brenden Gifford. He was a very dangerous man, Evelyn. Neck deep in the Mafia."

All the blood rushes from my head, and an unsettling cool sensation grips my shoulders. "The Mafia?"

"Mmhmm. He and anyone associated with him are extremely dangerous, do you understand what I'm saying?"

I nod slowly.

"Has anyone contacted you, Evelyn? Anyone you don't know? If someone threatens you or makes demands of you in any capacity, then you have to let me know. Do you understand?"

I need to get out of here.

Nodding slowly, I lightly grip her arm as I move past her. "I understand. If that happens, I will definitely be in touch. Goodbye."

The Mafia.

Cormac is in the Mafia? No wonder he and his siblings were unfazed about asking me to bug the police station. It hadn't even crossed my mind until now how relaxed they had been.

Each step feels sluggish. It's like my knees aren't quite listening to the rest of my body so I have to use the wall for support as my mind races. First a dead body, then threats on my life that had me offering up my very limited life savings, and now I find out that this is all because of some Mafia net I've landed in.

It's the last overwhelming straw and as I step outside, warm air washes over my face and floods my lungs. I try to move forward but for some reason, the ground isn't there to meet me.

There's nothing but a dark abyss that I immediately fall into.

7

CORMAC

Evelyn drops like a rock right into my arms, and I sweep her up against my chest.

Cian said I was stupid for going to see what was taking her so long, but never have I been more relieved to be in the right place at the right time.

Her head flops against my shoulder and her arms dangle limply past my hands as I hurry her down the steps before anyone takes notice. Out of the corner of my eye, I spot Cian and Hank climbing from the car and rushing toward me as I carry her across the road and into the laundromat that sits on the street corner.

We own this place and run it cleanly as a way to keep an eye on the station and to deal with the cops on our payroll when they come in for their dry cleaning. As soon as I'm through the door, Cian is behind me, locking the door and flipping the sign to *Closed*.

I keep Evelyn close to my chest while moving through to the back of the shop, then I lay her down on one of the warm, empty tables and shrug off my leather jacket. Folding it quickly, I place it under her head and gently remove some of her hair from her face. For the first time since we met, she almost looks peaceful.

"Hank, get me some water and something sweet to eat," I order as Hank peers around my shoulder. He obeys me instantly. "Cian, check the bugs."

"You think she flaked?" Cian asks. "Ratted us out?"

I lift my head and fix him with a steely look. "Check the bugs."

Cian rolls his eyes and slumps away with his phone in his hand, leaving me alone with Evelyn. It did cross my mind that she would just spill the truth to that detective. I don't know anything about this woman other than that she was clearly terrified to be in our presence, so she very well could have handed us to the cops on a platter.

Wouldn't that be funny? The downfall of the Gifford Clan at the hands of a motel maid. Brenden would find that fucking hilarious.

The thought of him makes my chest squeeze, so I focus on Evelyn's wrist and check her pulse. It's a little weak but it's there. Her forehead is warm to the back of my hand but her fingers are cold to the touch. Hank appears a few moments later with a bottle of water and a chocolate bar. He presses them into my hands just as Evelyn moans softly, so I jerk my head and silently order him to disappear so Evelyn doesn't wake up to more than one person leering over her.

"Evelyn?" Cautiously, I touch her jaw.

She turns her head slowly into my hand, as if she's chasing the warmth of my touch, and then her eyes slowly flutter open.

"Evelyn? Are you with me?"

Her eyes close briefly and her lips press together. Her throat bobs and then her tongue darts out to sweep her lower lip. Then she opens her eyes and looks up at me. For a moment, I'm transfixed by the warm chocolate-brown irises holding me in place.

Then Evelyn's eyes widen and she lurches away from me with a cry. Her movement is so violent that she almost throws herself off the table, so I dart out my hand and catch her around the waist to stop her from falling to the floor.

"No!" Evelyn screeches, twisting in my grip, and fear bleeds into her voice. "Let me go!"

"Okay!" I throw my hands up and step back, watching her fall from the table at an angle and stumble as her shaky legs hit the floor. "I was just stopping you from falling. This is a stone floor." I stomp one foot against the floor to prove my point. "I was trying to stop you from hurting yourself."

Evelyn glares at me through tears, clutching at the table as she fights to maintain her balance.

"You collapsed," I explain. "I caught you, brought you here. Look, you need to eat something. Drink something." I point to the water and chocolate on the table. "Please."

"You," Evelyn gasps. "She told me what you are!"

It clicks in my mind like the snap of a puzzle and I lower my arms. "So?"

"So?" she screeches. "You're Mafia! You're the freaking—" She cuts herself off and sways to the side, clutching at the table. After a few seconds, she straightens up and snatches up the bar. "You are criminals, dangerous people. I see it on the news, in the papers. You're all just—" She pauses and takes a gigantic bite of the bar, then continues to yell at me through the chewing. "And you've pulled me into this terrible, terrible fucking mess. I'm just a maid, okay! I'm just a normal, regular person that likes wine and binge-watching TV shows and scouring adoption websites for pets I know I can't have. I'm not anything, okay? I was a nobody and I liked being a nobody until I found that body, and now—" She sobs, torn between crying and wolfing down the chocolate bar.

Her anger, while surprising, grows rather amusing. It's the first fire I've seen in her since we snatched her off the street, and it seems she is not as meek as I first thought. There's fight in her, a desire to live, which instantly soothes my concerns about whether or not she shopped us to the cops.

If she did, she wouldn't be here right now.

"I'm not a bad person! I've never harmed anyone, at least not to the levels of the freaking Mafia, okay? I'm a good person. I pay my taxes and shovel the snow off my part of the sidewalk, and I don't deserve to have my life derailed by a crime like this!"

"You're right," I reply quietly. "And my brother didn't deserve to die like this."

Evelyn glowers at me with her mouth too full to speak, so I continue.

"You're also correct in that we are members of the Irish Mob. I am the leader, the Captain of the Gifford Clan since my brother's death." Pain spears through my chest again, and I seek out the lighter in my pocket. It doesn't soothe me as much as I need, but I force myself to keep talking. "This is one of our laundromats. You see, we own most of the businesses in this part of the city, and we lend them out to struggling families and business owners who wouldn't be able to afford the property tax or rent otherwise. In return, we sometimes do business through them. The corruption in this state runs deeper than I or any of the other families can fix, so we take care of the little guys as much as we can."

Evelyn's angry chewing begins to slow.

"We're also in charge of the guns. You might think that it's ridiculous to flood the market with high-quality weapons, but let me tell you something. Those people out there who want guns? They will do anything to get them. So we match the supply with decent weapons that aren't rigged to explode in the hands of a teenager. If we don't do it, someone else will, so at least we can make sure the weapons are safe. And thanks to a deal my brother secured with the Italian families, we also have the market on pharmaceutical drugs so we can ensure that the same people we protect can get the healthcare they require without losing their homes."

All of that is my brother's legacy, and my mother's to an extent. It feels strange to list out our victories while the man responsible lies in the morgue across the street.

"So sure, we're criminals," I finish. "But we take care of the people better than any suit or cop ever will."

Evelyn swallows and scrunches up the chocolate wrapper in her hand. "Oh."

"Feel better?" I ask, indicating to the finished chocolate.

She glances down at her hand, and her realization is visible on her face as she nods. "Yeah… I guess."

"Your blood sugar was low. That coupled with stress is likely the reason you passed out."

"Breaking the law so an Irish Mafia man doesn't murder me is pretty stressful," Evelyn mutters, but the heat of her fury has died down somewhat and her shoulders slump. "Didn't know you guys worked like that."

"Not many people do. I don't speak for other families, only mine," I say. "We are territorial and loyal, and my brother, Brenden…" My throat closes briefly, and I swallow down the growing lump. "His death brings us on the brink of something terrible that isn't your concern. But you have to understand that he was what was best for this city and someone killed him, so I will do everything and anything I can to find out who the fuck did it. Including using you to plant bugs on the detective because apparently, money doesn't speak to her."

Sighing deeply, I drag one hand down my face and slide it around to the tight muscles at the back of my neck.

"And Brenden was my brother. I need to find out what happened to him. So I'm sorry that you are in a tough situation, but I'm not sorry for using you because he is—was—important to me. I loved him." I meet her gaze. "And I will do anything to bring his killer to justice."

"Wow," Evelyn says softly, reaching for the water bottle. "I can't even fathom that kind of love."

"Your family would do the same for you," I say, "if they had my means."

She doesn't reply. She merely drinks a few gulps of the water and then lowers the bottle. "Did you mean it?"

"Mean what?"

"That if I did this, I would be free to go? I want to go home."

"I need one more thing from you."

Her eyes narrow and her shoulders slope down. "What thing?"

Approaching the table, I hold her gaze and for a long while, she doesn't look away.

"I need to know why Brenden was at the motel."

"I already told you, I don't know him. I didn't see him and had no idea he was there."

"I believe you," I say firmly, and her eyes widen a fraction. "But I can't get into the crime scene. I need to get eyes in there to see if he left anything behind."

"Wouldn't the cops have it already if there were something?"

"Brenden is smarter than the fucking cops," I snap, fighting to keep the heat out of my voice. "I need my eyes in there. But I can't get in there. None of my people can. But you can because you work there."

Evelyn chews on her lower lip and glances away, crinkling the water bottle under her tightening grip. "I don't want to go back in there," she whispers.

"You don't have a choice," I reply flatly, but this time there's an odd bubble of static under my ribs at the thought of forcing her.

"Will you kill me if I refuse?" She lifts those big eyes back to me.

"Yes." And yet, that feels like a lie.

Evelyn drags a hand through her hair and sighs so deeply it's a wonder she doesn't deflate herself. "Fine," she mutters. "But this is the last thing, you understand? I'm not doing anything else and I don't care if you kill me for it."

8

EVELYN

It was a bold statement telling Cormac that I didn't care whether he killed me after this or not, because I do care. I don't want to die. My life might not be perfect, or even satisfactory at this rate, but it's still my life.

I'm instantly reminded of just exactly how shitty it is when I open the disconnected fire door at the back of the Sunrise Motel and ease myself inside. Glancing behind me, I catch sight of Cormac's car parked just at the mouth of the alley where he and Hank sit waiting for me. This is the last thing I need to do for them.

Then I will be free. Or dead.

The candy bar and water Cormac provided have significantly calmed the churning tightness in my gut. It never crossed my mind that I was feeling so nauseous because of hunger, and in any other situation, I would be embarrassed that I fainted. Here, though, there isn't time to be embarrassed.

Inside the motel, the familiar stench of stale piss and old smoke clogs my nose as I walk down the corridor toward the maintenance stairs at the back of the building. From there, it should be pretty easy to get up to the room cordoned off by crime scene tape. I just hope that Cormac will find the answers he's looking for.

The motel is silent, with most guests likely keeping to their rooms while the cops roam the place. I can't imagine how pissed off Gerald must be at having the police walking his halls, knocking on his doors and scaring off all the sleazy clientele he's spent so long building up. That man offers a space for people to do whatever the hell they want, and nothing burns his reputation faster than a heavy police presence.

I focus on him as a distraction from my trembling fingers and racing heart as I climb the stairs two at a time. I know this place like the back of my hand, so sneaking in was never going to be the problem. It's sneaking out that will be hard since the maintenance door at the top of the stairwell only opens one way. I complained to Gerald about it a few times, but in his opinion, it was necessary to stop people from sneaking past the cameras when they wanted to leave without paying.

I just hope I remember exactly where the cameras are to avoid them on my way out.

Reaching the top floor, I slowly open the door and peer through the crack. The corridor is empty. With my heart in my mouth, I step through and ease the door shut behind me. Metal creaks and wood clunks, sending a flash of fear crawling over my shoulders and arms. Luckily, no one is around to hear it, and I force myself to breathe slowly.

"Just pretend you're cleaning," I say to myself and then instantly regret it when my voice echoes too loudly in the silence around me. While walking toward the door sealed off with bright yellow tape, I pull my phone from my pocket and briefly mourn the cracked screen. When Cormac gave my phone back to me, he apologized and said the screen broke when it fell from my hand the night they kidnapped me. If we were on better terms, I'd demand that he pay for the repairs, but I can't get a read on him.

One moment, he's the scariest fucker I've ever seen and the next, he's feeding me chocolate and telling me all the secret good his family does for this city.

Maybe he's just one hell of a bullshitter to get what he wants.

Once outside the door, I dial the number Cormac gave me. It rings thrice, and each time my heart gives a more powerful beat in anticipation. Then Cormac's face fills the screen. The dark shadows in the car make the angular structure of his face all the more intimidating against the light from the call, but his eyes sparkle in an oddly distracting way.

"You get in okay?" Cormac demands. He doesn't sound as intimidating through the phone. I nod and turn the camera so he can see the door.

"You ready?" I ask softly, sinking my teeth into the inside of my cheek. My hands won't stop trembling, and the more I will them to calm, the worse it gets. In the end, I have to grip the phone with both hands.

"Ready," comes Cormac's reply.

I don't move.

Suddenly, I'm rooted to the floor and the prospect of going back into that room is terrifying. Logically, I know the body isn't in there anymore, but there's a scared voice in the back of my mind that wonders if it is.

Or what if there is something worse?

"Evelyn?" Cormac's confusion is audible.

"Sorry," I gasp. "I just…" I can't find the words because I know he won't care about my emotional turmoil. I know this because he's made it painfully clear how important his brother was to him and how he will go to any lengths to get answers. None of that compares to what I might be feeling.

"I just need a sec," is all I can manage, and I point the phone at the floor as the knots in my gut tighten.

I'd better have abs of steel after this shit is over.

"Take your time," Cormac replies.

"We don't have time," comes a quieter voice, likely Hank.

Silence falls while I stare at the door, mapping out the letters of the DO NOT CROSS words decorating the tape. I force myself to breathe in as I read each word and then breathe out at the end of each sentence, and it works to an extent.

"Alright," I say, and heat warms the back of my neck when my voice cracks. "I'm ready."

"At your own pace," Cormac replies, which is oddly understanding for a man who had a gun to my face about twelve hours ago.

Balancing the phone in one hand, I quickly rip the tape from the door and rush inside before my fear locks me in place again. Immediately, I gag as the coppery stink of old blood hits me like a slap in the face. Pressing the back of my wrist to my nose, I close the door and flick on the light.

"Show me," Cormac demands. "Show me the room."

I oblige, lifting the phone to show the motel room. It's mostly as clean as I remember, only now every surface is dusted in black powder from the cops collecting fingerprints. It's everywhere, even on the walls and around the plug sockets.

"Are there any vents? Or a ceiling fan?" Cormac asks. His voice is tight, like each word is being forced through a very narrow gap.

"No ceiling fan," I reply. "But there is a vent behind the bed and one in the—" I swallow thickly as my tongue weighs heavily in my mouth.

"In the bathroom?" Cormac prompts.

"Yeah." I glance at the closed door leading to the scene of the crime and coldness settles across my shoulders. I shiver sharply and turn toward the bed. "Is that what Brenden would do? Hide things in the vents?"

"Not exactly," Cormac explains as I get down on my hands and knees. "Something like that is too obvious, but if he had hidden something somewhere, he'd leave a clue in an obvious place that I could follow."

"Did you guys talk about this kind of stuff?" Reaching behind the bed, I use all my strength to start shunting it away from the wall enough that I can get behind it. "Like, what to do if you ever get caught by the cops or something?"

"Sort of. My mom had this kind of stuff drilled into us from a young age because you never know what's going to happen."

"Damn," I mutter, panting heavily by the time I've shoved the bed a few feet. "Must be nice to have a parent who gave a shit even when you were little."

"Doesn't every parent?"

I roll my eyes. How is a criminal a better parent than my Ivy League, honor student mother? All she cares about is how quickly I can start churning out babies with a man she approves of. Never once has she given me a talk about personal safety.

Maybe that's why I'm in this mess.

Behind the bed, I turn on the phone's flashlight and shine it at the vent. The surrounding screws are covered in the same black powder as the rest of the surfaces and luckily, whoever put this vent back together didn't do it properly. It takes only a few seconds to work the cover off the wall.

"What am I looking for?" I ask, coughing slightly as the dust from the vent clouds around me.

"Smears," Cormac replies. "It'll look like oil smears or some kind of lubricant. Something that looks like it should be there, regardless."

Shining the light into the vent, we come up empty. There's nothing but dust, a few dead bugs, and a balled-up piece of paper that's a receipt from two decades ago.

"Sorry," I murmur as I shove the vent cover back on. "I was really hoping there would be something there."

"Why?" Cormac asks.

"So you can focus on something other than me," I mutter. "Wouldn't that be better for both of us?"

Cormac makes a sound that almost sounds like laughter. "I just want a reason."

"A reason I don't want to die?" Does he really care?

"No, a reason Brenden died. I have nothing, so I need something, a clue or an idea of where to start."

I kick myself as a wave of foolishness washes over me. Of course Cormac wasn't referring to me.

After the bed is back in place, I puff out my cheeks and wipe some sweat from my forehead. If I get caught here, I'll have one hell of a struggle explaining why I'm helping this man. Twice, he's given me enough freedom that I could just tell the truth or run away, and both times, I've chosen to help him.

I don't even fully understand why. Maybe it's because he was tender with me back in the laundromat, or maybe it's because I sympathize with the loss of his brother.

Or maybe it's because I've seen more love in his family than I've ever experienced in my own life. I can't think of anyone, past or present, who would go to these lengths if I were found murdered in a motel.

"Where did you find the body?" Cormac's voice cuts through my thoughts and I turn toward the bathroom.

"In there."

"Show me."

Oddly, my heart begins to slow as I approach the bathroom. The frantic patters fade into slow, powerful beats that rattle my ribcage and make my head throb.

There's no body in there, not anymore. It's okay. It's okay.

Gripping the handle, I take a deep breath and hold it as I open the door.

No dead body. Thank God.

As I breathe out in a rush and step inside, the stink of copper and iron assaults my nose and I gasp painfully, then turn on the light.

In a second, the bathroom lights up and my heart breaks for the sight before me. When I discovered the body, I didn't register much about the place other than the body, but now it's hard to miss anything. Dried blood stains the tub, the floor, and the walls. There are splatters on the mirror and up the bowl of the toilet. It's horrific for me, and I can't imagine how painful it must be for Cormac.

He remains silent.

I want to turn the phone around and take a look at his face, but I can't.

"He was there," I say softly, and the urge to comfort him rises. "In the tub." A tremor shoots down my hand, and I wrestle with my own thoughts as the memory of his rigid fingers and that gaping wound burst into my mind.

Cormac still doesn't speak, and then Hank's voice comes across the call. "Check the vent."

I do as commanded, searching for the same clues that Cormac mentioned before, but again, there is nothing. With Hank's guidance, I search the room from top to bottom. We check the lining of the wallpaper for any disturbances, check for loose ceiling or floor tiles, pull apart the pillowcases, and even unthread some of the towels, but there is nothing.

The place is empty.

"Alright," Cormac says eventually, and my heart lifts unexpectedly to hear his voice again. "That's enough. Get out of there."

"Are you sure?"

"Yes. Meet us back at the car."

The call ends before I can turn the camera back around, and I'm suddenly left in the silence of the room. I'd really hoped we would find something that would give Cormac answers or a direction on how to get them, but instead, all I've given him is a first-hand look at where his brother was murdered.

Maybe he'll kill me just for that.

Defeat sits heavily on my shoulders as I slip out of the room and head down the corridor. It's not until I get to the second stairwell that I realize I feel oddly calm. The fear from before has simply faded away, replaced with the heavy sensation that I've let Cormac down in some way.

Why? I barely know the guy, yet I want to help him so badly, and not just to secure my own freedom.

Is it because he's attractive?

I immediately roll my eyes at the thought. It doesn't matter that he's attractive. What matters are his actions.

So caught up in my thoughts as I hurry through the motel, I don't notice that someone is standing in the side entrance to the parking lot until I hurry past them with my head down.

"Evelyn?"

I don't hear him at first, making a beeline across the parking lot while mapping out in my mind how to get back to Cormac's car. Suddenly, a hand grabs my arm and jerks me to a stop so sharply that a squeak of surprise escapes my throat.

"Evelyn!"

I spin around, trying to pull my arm free, and my eyes widen when I lock eyes with the culprit.

"Dillon?"

9

CORMAC

Nothing could have prepared me for the carnage in that bathroom. I knew the details of his death, to an extent, but seeing the blood stains in the bathroom and knowing my brother died there broke my heart. I couldn't breathe and ended up passing the phone to Hank just to get the world around me to stop spinning.

I'd climbed out of the car and paced back and forth along the length of the vehicle, trying to get my thoughts in order. Of all the places to die, he had to choose this fucking shithole. And to die the way he did? The only thing that makes sense is that it was someone he knew, someone who was able to get close enough to him to slit his throat. My brother was one hell of a fighter, and I know deep down in my gut that it was either someone he knew or someone with a lot of backup.

None of that made me feel better, so by the time I got back in the car and Hank confirmed that Evelyn had found nothing, I was back to square one.

The call ends and Hank places his hand briefly on my arm. "I'm sorry."

"It's fine."

"Dude."

"What?"

"Don't bullshit me. You need a minute?"

I tightly shake my head. "I'm fine."

"You look like you're about to explode. Got the same look on your face that Brenden got that time the Russians snatched you off the street, you remember?"

"Aye." I sigh deeply. "They were sore fucking losers."

"Made the mistake of taking Brenden's favorite sibling." Hank snorts. "Now that was a bloodbath if ever I've seen one."

"Why was he here, Hank?" I mutter, staring out through the dark windows to the peeling paint covering the shabby walls of this shit hole. "What on Earth would bring him to a place like this?"

"I don't know," Hank replies. "But I know it must have been important."

I grumble in agreement as my phone rings, and an unexpected tiny part of me hopes to see Evelyn's number. Instead, it's Cian, so I answer immediately. "What is it?"

"The bugs are good," Cian says. "We've listened in on a few calls from Detective Gogs but she hasn't discussed anything concrete."

"What about her computer?"

"Saoirse is working on that now. At a glance, it doesn't look like she has any leads. She's mostly been digging into us and you."

"Me?"

"Aye. Maybe she suspects you got tired of being second in command and wanted a fast track to the top." Cian snorts. "Either way, she's got nothing but bullshit."

"Alright. Keep a close eye."

"Will do. Anything at the motel?" There's such hope in Cian's voice that I want to lie and tell him we found something just so I don't break his heart further, but we have nothing.

"No," I reply shortly. "Not a fucking thing."

"Shit." Cian hangs up.

My head throbs. Closing my eyes, I pinch the bridge of my nose and massage in small circles. "Cops are as clueless as we are. Which isn't a fucking surprise, but what the fuck am I supposed to do now?"

"There's something out there," Hank says, trying to be as encouraging as possible. "I know it. We just have to find it."

"Aye, well, it's fucking impossible to see what it is. I want Brenden's accounts. I want to know where he was and what he was doing every second this past month, understand? Every dollar spent, every mile driven, I want it all. An entire fucking map of his life."

"Understood." Hank busies himself with his phone, and I glance at the clock.

Evelyn should have been back by now. The motel is right there.

Did she run? Did she finally decide she was sick of this and leg it out of here?

I call her, but there's no answer. It rings out long enough that Hank glances up from his phone and frowns deeply. "Evelyn?"

"Aye." I'm out of the car by the time the robotic AI voice tells me to leave a voicemail.

If she ran, I will hunt her down and drag her back for leaving here without my permission. And if the cops have her, then I will make them regret ever sticking their nose in my business. Pigs should know their place, and if they don't have helpful information for me, then I don't have the patience to deal with them.

Hank follows hot on my heels as we sprint through the motel searching for Evelyn. I don't care if the cameras pick me up or if someone sees me. All I care about is finding Evelyn. My lack of knowledge about this place gives me a small area to search, but as I sprint down one of the hallways, Hank barks out a noise. Turning, I watch him point out the window to a small side parking lot.

Evelyn.

She stands pressed against one of the cars with a tall man leering over her. He has both arms on either side of her shoulders, trapping her between him and the car, and they look close. Too close for my fucking liking.

My blood boils and I begin to suffocate in the heat. Is it anger that she didn't come right back to me or jealousy that there is someone as close to her as I desire to be?

Suddenly, the strange man whips his hand and slaps Evelyn right across the face. Her head snaps to the side and my blood turns red hot in the blink of an eye.

"Cormac!" Hank yells as I charge out the door, but I don't listen to him. Rage consumes me, pouring like lava through my veins. Evelyn and the stranger are blind to me as he grabs her by the throat and shakes her. Evelyn's hand flies out and she slaps the stranger, but it barely affects him.

"You!" I bellow as I charge toward them like a bull.

Evelyn's head turns and she looks at me with wide, tear-filled eyes. The strange man follows, but like every arrogant prick I've had the displeasure of facing, he doesn't back down. He immediately squares up to me with a roll of his shoulders.

"Who's this fucking cunt?" The man snorts.

"Dillon, don't—" Evelyn gasps, and it's the last thing I hear as I slam my shoulder into Dillon's chest and tackle him to the ground.

He has nothing on me, not in size or in strength, so he crumples like a wet paper bag. We hit the ground hard with Dillon taking the brunt of the impact. I ball up my fist and punch him hard in the face, and once I start, I don't stop. Fury consumes me. I punch him again. And again. His nose breaks under my fist, his jaw slams to the side, and hot blood sprays against my knuckles. My other hand locks onto the collar of his T-shirt, and I haul him upwards only to punch him back down into the ground again and again and again.

Finally, I have release. All the pain and wrath that's churned inside me since I got the call about Brenden finally has somewhere to go, and the outpour of rage is impossible to stop. A few more slams of my brick-hard fist into Dillon's face and his eye swells shut. He chokes and gargles on blood, but I hear nothing other than the rapid, fierce drum of my blood pumping in my ears.

I want to kill him. I want to feel his skull cave under my fist. I want to hear his dying gurgles and soak up his last tearful moment of regret.

"Don't you ever dare put your hands on her again. Do you understand me, you fucking sack of shit?" I roar, pulling my punches enough to haul Dillon up toward my chest. "You touch her, hell, you even breathe the same fucking air as her ever again, and I will rip your spine out through your asshole and make you wear it as a leash until your pathetic excuse for existence finally fails you!"

I punch him repeatedly until my shoulder aches from the repetition.

Dillon doesn't reply. By the time the cloud of anger finally dissipates, the man is a bloody, unconscious pulp and my knuckles throb from the impact. A white handkerchief appears at the corner of my eye from Hank, and I accept it while slowly climbing to my feet.

Breathing heavily, I begin to clean the blood from my fists. I lift my head and slowly turn to Evelyn, growing aware of how much I've likely terrified her even more. I have no explanation—none that I'm willing to share, at least—but when our eyes meet, it's not terror that I see in her warm brown eyes.

It's something else.

Curiosity? No, gratefulness?

Not quite.

"Evelyn, I—"

My apology that she had to see that, as weak as it would have been, dies because Evelyn throws herself forward and her plush red lips crash into mine in a desperate, heated kiss.

10

EVELYN

Never in my life has someone protected me. Not from the bullies at school who would make fun of my clothes, my shyness, or my good grades, not from the neighbor who would hug me for too long or make horrible comments even in front of my parents, not even from my sleazy boss who always felt one step away from forcing me to suck his dick to keep my job.

No one has ever deemed me important enough to protect.

Except Cormac.

In half a second, he had Dillon on the ground, beating him to a bloody—and deserving—pulp while Hank held me back at a safe distance. I expected Cormac to know Dillon from somewhere, considering how savagely he was beating him into the ground, but then Cormac spoke. He threatened Dillon to stay away from me, and my heart soared higher than it ever has before. The pain from Dillon's slap was instantly forgotten and Cormac morphed right before my eyes.

Gone was the terrifying Mob Boss with only revenge on his mind. Suddenly, he was a man who was protecting me, fighting for my honor and warning away the scumbag who couldn't take no for an answer.

So when Cormac stood up, sprayed in blood and panting heavily with his muscles bulging out of his shirt, there was only one thought on my mind.

A kiss.

His lips are surprisingly soft against my own. The ridge from the small scar on his lower lip presses into the corner of my mouth and the bristly fuzz from his facial hair stings across my jaw when he tilts his head, but I enjoy every second of it. Heat blazes from his skin, searing into my palms as I clutch at the sides of his thick neck. I have to raise to my tiptoes just to meet his mouth.

But it's worth it.

The copper tang of blood in my mouth vanishes the moment Cormac forces his tongue past the seam of my lips and into my mouth. In a single sweep, he removes the blood leaking from where my teeth cut into my cheek at the slap and turns my mind to mush with how he makes his tongue roll in a wave against my own.

His large, heavy hands clutch at my waist, drawing me in against his burning hot, broad chest, and my toes stumble over his feet. I can barely maintain my balance to keep the kiss up because each time his tongue curls and caresses my own, my knees tremble and my entire body feels weak.

Evelyn, what the fuck are you doing?

And why the fuck is he kissing me back?

A desperate need for air eventually forces us to part with a gasp, and my sluggish mind struggles to come up with an excuse or a reason as to why I did that. At least not one I can vocalize with Cormac looking at me like I'm the juiciest piece of meat he's ever seen in his entire life.

"Hank," Cormac says throatily. "I'll be needing the car."

"Sir."

I have no idea how we make it back to the car. One moment, Cormac pulls me into his arms. The next, he throws me down onto the cool leather backseat of the car and crawls over the top of me. His mouth collides with mine and a deep, rumbling growl vibrates against my fingertips as I slide them up his chest to caress his neck once more. His tongue invades my mouth while his hands skim under my T-shirt and stroke over my abdomen. One hand moves up to fondle my breasts through my bra, and the other slides around underneath my body. He uses that grip to shift me up the seat, and my legs fall open as I distantly hear the car door slam behind us.

Cormac takes up so much room that there's barely enough room for me to breathe, never mind move. With one leg braced on the floor, Cormac moves my other to hook over the headrest of the back seat and then his hips collide with mine. He grunts into my mouth, and I moan as the sudden weighted pressure of his hips between my thighs makes my core tighten so rapidly that it's almost painful.

My body flushes hot, my pulse races, and my skin tingles from every touch from Cormac. His fingertips are rough against my skin, likely worn and twisted from years of fighting and handling weapons.

"Fuck," Cormac growls into my mouth, and I ache to reply, but my mind is blank. All that exists is a focus on sensation. The leather quickly warms against my back and sticks to my skin as Cormac leans away and rips my T-shirt from my body so quickly that the fabric grazes my armpits. Then he's back on me, kissing me like I'm the very lifeline feeding him oxygen. His heavy hips roll down against mine, and the hard ridge of his cock becomes noticeable within seconds. My pussy clenches, and my mouth waters at the thought of exactly how much weaponry is hidden away in his slacks.

I slide one hand into his thick hair, wrapping the copper strands around my fingers and pulling tightly as I roll my own hips upward. Cormac moans deeply and breaks the kiss. His mouth lands on my neck. Teeth graze over my throat, and then his lips seal over my fluttering pulse. He suckles hard as if trying to reach the source of that racing pulse while his hands squeeze and fondle my breasts. I'm panting, unable to hold onto air for longer than half a second. My core clenches once more, and a familiar dampness soaks into my underwear while Cormac repeatedly rolls his hips down against me.

"Please!" I manage to croak, forcing the word past my kiss-swollen lips.

Cormac obeys instantly. His large hands drop to the waistband on my jeans. The zipper peels apart, and then he's roughly tugging the fabric down away from my hips, catching my panties in the process. I don't have time to be embarrassed or even wonder about what the sex is going to be like. It's been too long since someone last touched me, and I'm so hungry to feel those rough hands all over my body that I'll take what I can get.

There's a comical thirty seconds where Cormac wrestles with the denim clinging to my legs and he has to find the best way to remove my jeans in such a cramped space. By the time they fall free, I'm sweating buckets while Cormac rips his shirt free, exposing that gorgeous muscular chest. I slide my hands over the rises and ridges of muscle while he wrestles his slacks low enough to haul his thick, swollen cock out of his boxers. My fingers pause in the soft swirls of hair over his chest and my eyes widen.

"Holy—" He's huge. It makes sense, given how brick-lick this man is built, but seeing such thickness clenched in his fist is incredibly intimidating.

And fucking erotic.

"I'm gonna fuck the breath right out of you," Cormac growls, and his mouth collides with mine once more. Gone are the gentle waves and rock of his tongue against mine. His kiss is biting now, clashing teeth and dominating my tongue with such power that my eyes roll back in my head. He grasps one of my hands and locks our fingers together, then pins it back above my head to the seat just as he grinds his thick, naked cock against my soaked pussy.

Cormac grunts and breaks the kiss. "You're fucking soaked," he growls, writing the words against my lips as I chase him for another kiss. I slide my free hand up to cup his chin and jaw and meet his eyes.

"Do something about it, then," I gasp, arching my back into his body. We're so sweaty that the leather squeaks as my skin peels from the seat and Cormac makes a soft noise, then kisses me briefly. Each glide of his cock through my soaked folds slicks his cock up, and the hot sensation of his throbbing length dragging over my clit is a punch of pleasure through my body every single time.

I've never craved someone like this before. I need him inside me, on top of me, splitting me open and filling me so full that I bubble over.

A needy whimper darts past my lips with each breath while Cormac grips his cock and presses the thick, swollen crown to my entrance. He lifts his head and his eyes, currently inky pools of darkness, lock onto mine. And then he slowly presses his cock inside me.

The stretch is the right side of painful, and I clutch tightly at his hand while my other claws at his shoulder.

"Yes," I gasp, arching upward and pressing my hips down. "Yes, yes, yes!" Inch by inch, he pries me open, and I eagerly soak up every thick inch he gives me. My head tosses back and forth, my hair clings to my neck and cheek, and my core pulses as rapidly as my fluttering heart. Cormac thrusts inside me, then moves his hand to caress my cheek.

"I'm going to carve you open with my cock. No one and nothing will satisfy you like this ever again."

Then he starts to fuck me. Cormac fucks like he fights, with deep, powerful thrusts that would jolt me right out of the car if he wasn't keeping me pinned with his hand and his torso. Each thrust is like a punch, forcing the air from my lungs and dragging against every hidden bundle of nerves inside me. No part of me is left untouched, and the impact of his pelvis against my clit makes me see stars.

I am utterly and completely at the mercy of the best sex of my life. I grip his shoulders, scratch his back, and bite his lip as the pleasure grows quick and fast inside me, like a ball forming tight in my lower belly. Cormac fucks me faster, his hips slamming harder and harder into mine until we're both panting so much that we can't maintain a kiss.

His open mouth simply rests against mine, and we share air, locked in each other's eyes until his rhythm starts to falter and the ball inside me explodes and spreads tingling warmth all the way through my body.

He fucks my orgasm right out of me, and I come with a scream that he drinks down with the cockiest fucking smirk I've ever seen a man wear. Cormac comes a few seconds later, burying his thickness deep inside me and flooding my insides with his load. He thrusts three more times and then grinds against me, as if packing his seed as deep as he can.

Then he kisses me hard, our hands still locked together above my head.

Holy shit.

That's the best sex I've ever fucking had. With a dangerous man I barely know. It has to be the adrenaline, right?

Cormac kisses me softer, and his movements are gentle as he slides his cock from my pussy. He somehow manages to clamber into the front seat and passes me a bottle of water that I drain immediately. My throat is parched, and I've sweated so much that I may as well have been running a marathon.

My body aches and my pussy throbs like a pulse, but what affects me the most is the loss of Cormac's hand in mine. It was such a simple, small thing, but for some strange reason, it makes my heart heavy to no longer have it.

"You good?" Cormac asks, passing me my T-shirt and helping me redress the best he can from where he sits.

I merely nod. I have no words.

Not one.

I dress just in time as a second later, there's a knock at the steamed-up windows. Cormac pushes a button and lowers the window next to him, revealing Hank who hands him an electronic tablet.

"We've got something," Hank says.

Just like that, the air of sex vanishes and a more serious weight settles over the car. As Cormac studies whatever is on the tablet, Hank jogs around to the driver's side and enters the car, then he passes me an energy bar from the glove compartment.

As I lean over to accept it, I glance down at the tablet in Cormac's lap and my heart leaps.

On the screen are two pencil sketches of a man and a woman. Like a jolt of lightning in my mind, the face of the dead man in the tub suddenly snaps clear in my mind, no longer consumed by the wound to his throat.

I remember him. And not only that, but I also know he's been at this motel before.

"Who are they?" Cormac asks, enlarging the pictures.

"No clue," Hank states. "But it's a start."

"I know," I say softly.

Cormac whips around to face me, his brow knitting together. "What?"

"I've seen them before, here at Sunrise."

11

CORMAC

"Explain."

The tablet lands on the table with a clatter, bouncing once, then Evelyn catches it with her hands and settles it in front of her.

"I don't know how much help this will be," she says, wincing slightly as she shifts her weight back and forth on the seat.

The only thing keeping me calm is the lingering bliss from fucking her senseless in the back of the car. It was sudden and unexpected but close to the best sex I've ever had at the drop of a hat. The adrenaline rush from pulverizing that asshole and then spilling a load into someone so beautiful is a rush.

It's nice to know I've still got it.

"I don't know their names," Evelyn says, tapping on the screen to enlarge the picture of the woman. "I've seen her at the motel quite a few times with a lot of different men and women. She's an escort and goes by the name Peach. I've spoken to her maybe once or twice with room service, and she's always been very sweet."

"An escort?" Hank repeats, appearing at my elbow with an ice pack. He passes it to me, and I place the cold onto my swollen knuckles, biting back a wince of pain.

"Brenden was seen with her, apparently," I say. "At least that detective thinks so. Someone else in the motel gave that description because they bumped into Brenden and that woman in the elevator the night he died."

Evelyn's fingers skim over the drawing. "Her eyes are smaller and her hair is tightly curled, not wavy, but I'm pretty sure this is Peach."

"Can you contact her?" I ask, sharper than I intend.

Evelyn lifts her head. "No. I don't know her, I just know *of* her. Seen her around. I mean, you could try my boss, but he lets sex workers in without signing in. As long as he gets a lump of cash in his hands, you can do anything you want in those rooms."

Great. Another fucking dead end.

I press the ice harder to my swollen knuckles, ignoring Hank's concerned gaze as it drifts over me.

"But him..." Evelyn slides the first drawing away and brings up the one of the man. "I know less about him, but I definitely saw him with your brother."

Moving closer, I lean over Evelyn with my hip against the table. Every detail of her is sharper since I fucked her. It's like I'm truly seeing her for the first time now that I know what her lips taste like, how tight her pussy is, and how fast her pulse races when I'm inside her.

"When?"

"Two weeks ago, maybe? I'd forgotten because..." Her cheeks suddenly flush red and her voice grows quiet. "I couldn't remember what your brother looked like. Every time I thought about him, all I could see was his neck and the..." She waves her fingers over her own throat and then her dark eyes dart up to me. "I'm sorry."

I shake my head once. It's common to forget features when faced with such a brutal death. The first dead body I ever saw, I couldn't tell anyone a single thing about them other than their split open chest and the ribs protruding from the flesh.

"So he was with Brenden?" I press on, clenching my jaw to stop me from grabbing Evelyn and demanding the truth immediately.

"Yes. I remember because Dillon, that asshole you beat up in the parking lot, was asking me out. He was going on and on about how he was the only one who could treat me right and stuff, and my mind was wandering because he wouldn't take no for an answer."

The fucker definitely would now.

"And behind Dillon," Evelyn continues, "I saw Brenden with that man. They were having some really intense argument in the parking lot, and I didn't think much of it because there's always some sort of fight going on in that place. So it didn't stick out as important to me, but they were definitely arguing."

"About?" I demand sharply.

Evelyn flinches slightly and withdraws her hands from the tablet, dropping them to her lap. "I don't know. I didn't hear anything, and then Dillon was in my face demanding I go out with him, so I said yes. The only other thing I remember was Brenden grabbed the man by the collar and I thought they were going to fight one another, but Brenden shoved him hard and then they went their separate ways."

It's a lot and yet nothing at the same time. If I don't know who this fucker is, then what am I supposed to do about it?

Pushing off from the table, chunks of ice crush to dust in the bag under my tightening grip.

"Detective Gogs has some CCTV of this man," Hank says, taking the tablet from Evelyn and tapping the screen a few times. "It's blurry and distant, likely from across the street, but that's where they got the sketch from. Looks like he and Brenden were arguing with each other a couple of nights ago at the motel."

"That fucking motel," I mutter, pacing toward the window and glaring out across the city. "So what's the connection here? The motel? The woman?"

There are too many unanswered questions. The more I learn, the murkier the waters around Brenden's death become and the weight of it all returns to my shoulders like the slap of a heavy arm. So many people are waiting on me to work this out, to find my brother's killer and bring him to justice, but how am I supposed to do that with fucking breadcrumbs?

On top of that, there's nervousness in the smaller families about my capabilities in running this family and keeping the rest of them safe and prosperous. No matter what I do or say, none of it will matter if Brenden's killer still walks free.

"Boss?" Hank approaches me with the tablet in his hand and his eyes focus on my fist. "You really should get that looked at."

Glancing down, blood trickles to my wrist from where my angry flexing has reopened the wounds on my knuckles. It's nothing I haven't had before and likely will have again. I toss him the ice pack, deeming it useless now that my rising anger is dulling the pain, and pull out my phone.

"Cian," I say the moment he answers. "I'm sending you and Saoirse a couple of pictures. I want our best teams on tracking these fuckers down."

"You got it," Cian replies. "Was there nothing at the crime scene?"

"Nothing," I say, and the sight of that bloodstained bathroom flashes in my mind. "From the amount of blood, though, I'd say he went down fighting."

"Small mercies," Cian mutters, then he hangs up.

I tap the screen in Hank's hands and quickly send the pictures off to my siblings. "Hank, can you dig into the motel ownership records, as far back as you can? I want to know who, if anyone, has a connection there."

"On it." With a slight dip of his head, Hank hurries away, leaving Evelyn and me alone. My uninjured hand slips back into my pocket, seeking out the lighter that gives me so much comfort.

It's a small gift from my father. Each of us has one engraved with the family crest and name. When my father gifted these, they were small presents at Christmas, but somewhere along the line, they became important to each of us, even when they ran out of fuel.

The thought of Brenden's sitting in some evidence bag somewhere makes my stomach churn. I close my eyes and force a deep, calming breath. The chair behind me creaks and when I open my eyes, Evelyn stands beside me with a soft, sad look across her features.

"I'm sorry I couldn't find anything at the motel," she says cautiously.

I shrug. "He left nothing to be found. Not your fault. Not your responsibility." From the way Evelyn's brows pinch together in the window reflection, I suspect my words came across harsher than I intended, so I turn toward her. "Look. It's been a long couple of days and you need to take care of yourself. I'll get Hank to whip you up something to eat—something real—and then you should get some rest."

"Actually..." Evelyn's lower lip curls into her mouth and I'm struck with the urge to scold her. If anyone should be biting on her lip, it should be me. "I want to go home."

Home.

Right.

Of course.

That was the agreement. She does something for me and I let her go free. After all, she is still technically my captive.

"I did what you asked, I helped you as much as I can, but I have nothing else and you said you would let me go," she continues, speaking quickly as if she fears retribution for even asking. Given what she's witnessed, I can't blame her.

"I want to go home. Please."

She looks up at me with these gigantic eyes, and a different sort of ache wraps around my broken heart. I'm not sure what I expected, really. I kidnapped her, and even though I thought I felt something when we fucked, it was just sex with essentially a stranger.

She did as I asked, and I can't fault her for that—just like I can't fault her for wanting to get as far away from me and this mess as she can.

"Alright," I say after a moment of silence. "If that's what you want."

I catch the flicker of confusion in her eyes. After all, how could she want anything else?

"I'll call Hank and he will take you home."

Evelyn smiles—and it's the first time I've seen her do that. The corners of her eyes crinkle and her eyes light up with a warm glow as she reaches out and lightly clasps my wrist.

"Thank you."

As gentle as her touch is, it doesn't stop a bubble of disappointment rising just beneath my ribs.

12

EVELYN

Being home feels alien.

Cormac was true to his word and had Hank drop me home within the hour. He remained parked by the sidewalk until I'd let myself inside and closed the door, then he left and suddenly, I was all alone.

It's exactly what I asked for, but as I stand in the middle of my cold kitchen with three-day-old dishes in the sink threatening to become a biohazard, I suddenly hate it. The air is cold and the silence is too silent. I hadn't realized just how much I had enjoyed being around other people not related to my work for the past few days, even if it had been terrifying.

That has to be a trick of the mind, right? There's no way I'm missing being kidnapped. It was the most insane, surreal experience of my life. And yet, finding the body remains the worst part. Not the kidnap, not the gun in my face or Cormac's threat on my life, and definitely not the sex.

The sight of that body is going to haunt me for the rest of my life.

After lingering in the chill of my kitchen for a few long minutes, I retreat into the shower and dispose of the clothes Hank lent me. I briefly remember that they still have my work uniform, and my heart sinks. Gerald isn't going to be happy when I ask for a replacement.

In the lukewarm heat of my low-pressure shower, my mind spins over the events of the last few days. The body, the kidnapping, lying to the police, planting bugs on that nice detective, and then fucking a member of the Irish Mob. It's like someone else was living inside my body these past few days because never in a million years did I think I had the guts to do something like that. Maybe the threat on my life was enough to unlock this bold new criminal side of me.

Would a jury be sympathetic if I were caught?

I picture myself on the stands trying to tell them how terrified I was when I did those things, but then my pussy throbs as I move and I'm reminded of how easily I spread my legs for him. There's no denying how hot Cormac was, and watching him beat up Dillon was one of the hottest things I have ever seen. He did everything I wished I could do each time Dillon cornered me.

I slip a hand between my wet thighs and close my eyes, bringing up the memory of what Cormac felt like when he was over the top of me, buried inside me like it was where he belonged. No one had fucked me like that in my life and the ache he left behind was delicious. Temptation warms my core as I delicately stroke my clit, but it's just not the same.

Maybe he really has ruined me for anyone else, my own fingers included.

Dejected, I wrap up my shower and dress in my fluffiest robe then call for food from my favorite Vietnamese restaurant. It also makes me think of Cormac and how quickly he learned about my life. Did he think I was pathetic, seeing how little I actually lived?

The receptionist confirms my order as I drop onto my couch, and I'm about to spend the next twenty minutes scrolling through social media feeds that I stare at and never interact with when a message comes from Gerald.

You're fired.

Short. Sweet. To the point.

My heart plummets and a hundred questions flood my mind. What the hell did I do? Is this because I missed work for one day? Or did he see what happened to Dillon and deem me the cause? As much as my exhausted mind demands an answer, I don't have the heart to text him back.

At least I don't need to worry about the uniform anymore.

But it puts me in a precarious position. Without income, I won't be able to keep this apartment, never mind pay off my debts. I glance at my calendar and groan. Rent is due in three days and I can guarantee Gerald won't pay me on time, so there's only one person I can call.

My mother.

"Hello?" My mom always talks as if she has a hard candy tucked inside her cheek that she'd much rather be sucking on than talking, and no matter what age I am, it always makes my stomach drop out of my ass.

"Hey, Mom."

"Evelyn! About time."

"Huh?"

"Where were you? You were supposed to be here last night to help me with the delivery of my new closet. Now I have a wooden monstrosity stuck in my lounge because you couldn't honor an agreement with your own mother!"

Shit.

That completely slipped my mind.

"Mom, I'm so sorry. I was…" I pause. Can I tell her the truth? "Mom, something happened."

"I don't want to hear more about your reckless spending habits," Mom snaps.

"No, it's not that. At the motel where I work there was—"

"Did you get fired?" she barks. "I knew it. You can't commit to anything, Evelyn. I told you that you aren't built for the workplace. You need to find yourself a decent man, settle down, and start a family!"

My mind immediately turns to Cormac. He's clearly much older than me. Mom would have a heart attack if she knew.

"I wasn't fired," I lie smoothly. "There was an accident. Someone died, so I had to spend a lot of time talking to the police. That's why I couldn't come and help you."

Suddenly, my mom is incredibly interested. She begins questioning me with the enthusiasm of a crime podcast and we talk long into the night about the gory details. Part of me feels guilty explaining what I saw while knowing how much it pains Cormac, but it's nice to talk it out with someone who isn't involved. It's also the longest conversation I've had with my mother in months, and she goes for two hours without berating me in any way.

By the time the call ends, I'm full of my favorite dumplings and utterly exhausted. I collapse into bed and sleep for a solid sixteen hours.

Waking up alone in my apartment is strange. There's a strange new loneliness in my heart that I hadn't ever noticed before. As I go about my day—starting with asking Mom if I can borrow rent money, then poring over every job listing I can get my hands on—my heart lingers on Cormac.

He's the cause of my distress.

The way he spoke to me. The way he grabbed me and pinned me down as he fucked me like his very life depended on being inside me. The way he protected me from Dillon. In a few short hours, he showed me more love and dedication than anyone has ever shown me in my life, and instead of following that feeling, I chose to leave. So now I exist with this strange, new, lonely ache in my chest about what could have been.

And then I curse myself. It's not normal to want that, right? The man kidnapped me, for crying out loud. I should want to get as far away from him as possible.

If only I could stop thinking about him.

The next few days pass in a blur of job applications, promising my mom that she can set me up on blind dates in exchange for rent money, and drinking away the last of my savings. For two nights straight, sleep escapes me until I down a bottle of wine. Luckily, the wine sends me right off to sleep before I can act on the urge to call the number Cormac gave me back at the motel.

He's probably changed it by now. In fact, he's most definitely not thinking about me at all. A man like that wouldn't get this hung up on a random woman he met, and I shouldn't be either.

But he's like a drug, swimming around my thoughts just out of sight.

Friday night rolls around, and I breathe a deep sigh of relief as I send off my rent payment. That's one less worry for the next month. Unfortunately, none of the jobs I've applied for have gotten back to me, so with my last bottle of wine sitting next to me, I pull up countless job websites and begin the search for the umpteenth time.

After a few hours, I wonder if I can hire out my basic services as a bug planter. Crime pays, right?

Deep in thought, the sudden rapid, loud knocking at my front door makes me jump out of my skin. I glance at the clock. It's eight at night and I haven't ordered food. Who the hell is that?

Climbing out of the nest of blankets I created on the floor, I hurry toward the front door. It's impossible to stop my mind from leaping to the hope that maybe, just maybe, it's Cormac.

I can't think of a reason he'd come to visit, but he's the only person I can think of since I never get visitors.

The knocking comes again as I hurry down the hallway. "Hold on!" I call, pausing to adjust my hair and sort my clothes. Fuck. Well, he saw me at my worst when I was sobbing in that chair, so what I look like now is surely a huge improvement.

My heart races while I unlock the door, then I pull it open with an expectant smile.

My smile fades instantly.

It's not Cormac.

The man on my doorstep grins a gap-toothed smile and flicks a cigarette out of his fingers onto the step below. He stamps it out with crocodile leather boots and shoves his hand against the door before I can even contemplate closing it in his face.

"Hello, Evelyn."

My gut knots instantly. "Harry. What are you doing here?"

"Take a guess." He speaks slowly and leans in close so the last curls of cigarette smoke invade my lungs. I tighten my grip on the door, but Harry's already pushing it open wider so he can step inside.

"I don't have your money," I say tightly. My heart begins to pound, filling my ears with a strange pulsating sound. "I told you I'd call when I had it."

"You did," Harry says and with one last shove, he forcefully pushes his way into my apartment. I have no choice. Releasing my grip on the door, I stumble backward as he straightens up and fills my hallway with his tall, thin form. The front door kicks closed behind him. "But you haven't called."

Cautiously, I step backward, trying to keep distance between us, but each time I move, Harry mirrors it with a step of his own.

"I don't have your money," I say, cursing internally when a tremble slips into my voice. "Not yet."

Nine months ago, I was drowning in debt to more credit cards than I could keep track of. Bad spending habits plus a desire to feel loved through material means. The way store owners would light up when they saw me was a feeling I chased, as if any of their affection was real. When the banks repossessed my apartment because I couldn't pay and threatened me with legal action, I did the only thing I could think of.

I went to a loan shark. Harry gave me enough money to pay off my entire debt and get this shitty new apartment. Then I only had to worry about paying off one person rather than five. But I was naive. A loan shark was not the answer. The interest Harry piled on top was enough to make me sick the first time he mentioned it.

"Not yet." Harry tuts softly and sucks on his upper teeth. Suddenly, he flies forward and slams one hand around my throat while the other grabs a handful of my T-shirt. He uses that grip to slam me up against the wall, and fear lances through me like a knife.

"Harry—I'll get you your money!" I gasp, clutching at his narrow arm that tenses each time he flexes his fingers around my throat.

"Will you?" Harry growls, shoving into me. "Little birdie told me you've been spending a lot of time at the police station. You wouldn't be ratting me out now, sweetheart, would you?"

"No!" I gasp, fighting his tightening grip. I kick out my legs, but he shoves me higher up the wall so that I no longer touch the ground. "Harry—I wouldn't! Please!"

Releasing his grip on my T-shirt, Harry strikes me across the face. My head snaps to the side and heat explodes through my cheek and jaw. He strikes me again and again until my ears are ringing and my head is spinning.

"Don't lie to me!" he yells. "What the fuck were you doing down at the cop shop?"

"I'm not lying!" I beg while tears spring into my eyes. Warmth trickles down my cheek from my eyebrow and my gaze blurs. "I witnessed a crime at the motel and they were asking me about it, that's all!" Each word is punched out of me with a desperate gasp for air.

"You're lying!"

"No!" I weep as the sobs come. "Check the news—please, I need you, Harry. I wouldn't report you, you know I wouldn't!"

Harry strikes me again, and this time, he releases his grip on me so that the blow sends me crashing down to the floor with a yelp. He crouches down in front of me and grips my chin, then he tilts my head up to meet his eyes.

"You'd better not," Harry says, his voice back to an eerie calmness. "Because you don't want to find out what I do to rats, do you? A pretty thing like you? Credit card debt will be the least of your worries."

"I'll get your money," I gasp. A full-body tremble takes over me, and I dig my fingertips into my thigh to try and control myself. "I just need more time—"

"No. I don't trust you with the cops sniffing around. I've given you grace these past months, Evelyn, because I felt sorry for you." Harry pats my bruised cheek and smiles coldly.

"You've got forty-eight hours to get my money. Either you pay me when I come back here, or I'll kill you. Got it?"

13

CORMAC

I miss her.

She was only here for a few short days and we didn't exactly get to spend any kind of real time together, but her sudden absence in my apartment feels like something has been ripped away from me. As the days pass, I tell myself that it's just the lingering loss of my brother trying to settle into someone who's still alive.

I don't have time for romance. There's too much I have to do to get things in order with my Family and the world Brenden left me, and yet, through it all, I just can't get Evelyn out of my mind.

It's late one evening when Saoirse appears with coffee in hand. She sets it down on my desk in front of me, right on top of the latest contract I'm mulling over. Sighing, I pluck the paper cup off the desk and grumble slightly as a slightly damp ring is left behind.

"You know, putting coffee on my important shit isn't going to put me in a good mood if you have something to ask me," I say, setting the coffee aside.

"Cian says you're not sleeping," Saoirse replies, lounging in the leather seat on the other side of the desk. "So drink the coffee and shut up."

"I don't need coffee."

"Do too."

"Saoirse."

"Cormac." She narrows her dark-lined eyes at me, clicking her tongue against the roof of her mouth. "You think you're any use to any of us if you end up burnt out? Or worse, dead because you fell asleep at the wheel?"

"Hank drives."

"I mean figuratively." She tosses her head back and forth, shaking her auburn hair from her shoulders. "Killing yourself helps no one."

"Just as well that isn't what I'm doing." I don't look up at her. Instead, I try to find the sentence I was reading before she interrupted. "If that's all?"

"I'm worried about you." Her voice is softer. "Everything has gone to shit. Brenden is dead. Ma can't even handle a phone call without breaking down. The Italians are pressuring for answers and the Russians have their own bloodbath in the streets. Now, more than ever, we need to put on a strong front."

"You think I don't know what?" I snap, finally lifting my head. "I know exactly how restless the smaller families are. How no one sees a leader when they look at me. They all followed Brenden and I was happy being the underboss and getting my hands dirty. Now I have every single expectation on my shoulders to hold this family together, to hold the entire strength of the Irish together on top of making sure all of Brenden's hard work doesn't go to waste."

Saoirse, unfazed by my snapping, rolls her eyes. "So sleeping should be one of your priorities but instead, it's your second day in a row where you're just in here poring over paper."

"I can't sleep," I admit stiffly. "Feels… wrong."

"Why?" She leans forward, resting her forearms on her knees.

I stumble through a handful of thoughts, searching for the right words to explain this pit inside me. This grief that's swelling like a balloon with each passing hour that Brenden's killer walks free and the aching desire to see Evelyn again. As if her presence can make that balloon deflate even an inch. But no words come. I only stare at Saoirse until she finally looks away.

"Do you see him?" she asks softly, pressing her fingertips together. "I do. Every time I close my eyes, all I see are the crime scene photos. He was the best of us and he died like some dog in some disgusting motel, and we don't even know why."

My heart drops, and the responsibility of the Mob melts away. For a moment, we are just grieving siblings.

"I see him all the time," I reply, fighting to keep my voice level. "He's everywhere. His aftershave stains everything because he slept here more than in his own place. His plans are everywhere, his laughter is in the wind, his shadow is in the eyes of everyone who looks at me with expectation. Every time that door creaks…" I nod toward the office door. "I expect him to walk through. So… so no, I can't sleep. Not while his body is still cold in that morgue and his murderer still roams the city."

When Saoirse lifts her head, her eyes sparkle with unshed tears. "Can you promise me you'll find who did it?"

"Yes," I say firmly. "I won't rest until I do."

"You should rest," she says, sniffling as she composes herself. "Or should I go find you another woman to entertain yourself with?"

Just like that, the emotional moment passes and she's back to her regular self with that teasing curl of her upper lip.

"You think fucking will help me sleep?"

She shrugs. "I know what you did with that woman in the car." She laughs softly. "And Cian said you passed out not long after she left, so sure. Should I call her?"

Something about my expression must betray my desire for such a thing because suddenly, Saoirse's eyes narrow playfully. "You do, don't you? You want to call her."

"I don't want to talk about this."

"I do!" She rises from her seat and leans over the desk. "Don't tell me you developed a crush on the witness."

"I am thirty-two years old. I don't crush."

"Bullshit." Saoirse laughs. "You like her."

"I don't."

"Liar. It's all over your face. Y'know, I suspected because I couldn't remember the last time you showed interest in anything outside of work and then suddenly, you're fucking her in the back of your car. I told Cian it was just stress relief. Fuck. I could've made fifty bucks off him." She straightens up. "You should call her."

"No."

"Why not?"

"Because in case you forgot, she wanted to leave?"

"And?" Saoirse clicks her tongue. "She had no problems spreading her legs for you. Maybe she just wanted the choice considering you did kidnap her."

"With good reason."

"I'm not questioning that." She laughs. "Trust me, if snatching some hunk off the street is how I need to secure a man, then I'll do it. But she left and didn't go straight to the cops, right?"

"Right."

"So maybe you should call her. Get your dick wet and sleep. Maybe it's the grief talking and latching onto her because she's outside of this mess, but if it will get you to rest, I don't really care."

"Is that any way to talk to your Captain?"

"I'm talking to my brother," Saoirse corrects. "Or drink my shitty coffee. Either way, do something before you drop dead at your desk."

While her tone remains light, I catch the flash of deeper worry in her eyes as she turns away. I shouldn't give her cause to worry. I've been watching my siblings closely for any sign of them slipping, and it didn't fully occur to me that they would be doing the same. As Saoirse leaves, I make sure she sees me picking up the coffee.

I'll sleep later.

Unfortunately, returning to work proves impossible. My sister effectively knocked me out of my focus and now that my mind is wandering, all I can think about is Evelyn once more.

Saoirse was right about one thing. She would be perfect for relieving my stress. Unfortunately, she left. That was her choice, and I can't bring myself to invade her space more than I already have—not unless I want to risk misreading signals and send her right into the arms of that cop.

Discarding the contract, I sip Saoirse's terribly strong coffee and turn to my computer. In a few clicks, a map pops up with a glowing red dot showing Evelyn in her apartment. During her time here, I bugged her phone and every call, text, and voicemail that she's received in the past few days is logged on my computer.

I hit *Play* on the recorded conversation with her mother just to hear her voice and scan through her most recent texts. They're mostly related to job applications given her recent termination from the motel, with the others all being about food delivery. She hasn't left her apartment since she was dropped back there other than to collect takeout on the days she deems the cost of delivery to be too high. When I first heard her asking her mother for rent, I was struck with a powerful urge to pay that for her, but that definitely would have raised suspicions. I didn't want her to know I was watching her.

I just want to check in. Keep her safe.

That's also why I have one of my men, Dale, tailing her. Not that she ever goes anywhere so his job has mostly been sitting in his car for three days watching her apartment. I'm almost jealous he's so close and I'm not.

As I flick through her texts, I return to the list of old numbers that she hasn't contacted in more than six months. There was a period of time when she called the bank a lot, and even a lawyer, but there's no record of the calls for me to listen to. Other than her mother, her social circle is almost nonexistent. Even her social media is dead, other than a few likes here and there. She's as different from my life as one could get.

As I listen to her soft voice—and her mother's less-than-pleasant scrape of tone—my phone rings, and I patch Cian through at the touch of a button. "Hey, little brother."

"Saoirse still with you?"

"No, she left."

"Figures. I wanted to catch you both so I didn't have to say this twice."

"Out with it."

Cian takes a breath. "Alright. So this is mostly unconfirmed but I've had my ear to the ground. You know the Russians are a mess right now."

"Saoirse mentioned it, yeah."

"Since the death of the Pakhan, his daughter's been fighting like hell to keep her position over every other Russian bastard that thinks they can do it better. Anyway, there's rumors in a few smaller families that one of the middle families is claiming credit for Brenden."

"What?" Evelyn's voice fades from focus. "Who?"

"No name yet. Like I said, it's rumblings."

"If I have to carve through every fucking Ruskie to get to the truth, I will," I snap, shifting in my seat as heat lances down my spine.

"No," Cian snaps. "No reckless actions, you hear me? Like I said, it's a rumor. I don't know if it's an attempt to destabilize Anastasia's rule or if someone is just trying to direct us to the Russians and take out an already messy target."

Cian has a point. A rumor like this is dangerous to act on without proof. "Alright," I mutter. "We need to do this properly. I need to find out exactly what's going on. Can you get me a meeting with the Godmother?"

"Will do. And get some rest, will you?"

Rolling my eyes, I end the call, but before I can turn back to my computer, Dale's name pops up on my screen. I answer immediately.

"You need relief?" I ask, expecting Dale to be in need of a bathroom break or sleep.

"Nah, not until sunrise," Dale replies. "But we have an issue."

"Which is?"

"Evelyn had a visitor. A man. He arrived maybe an hour ago and I've been running his face through the Cops' database as well as our own to see if I can find out who the guy is."

A man? Does Evelyn have a man? Acidic jealousy fizzes at the base of my throat. "And?" I bark.

"I found him."

"And?"

"Boss, he's Russian."

14

EVELYN

Forty-eight hours.

My life is over. There's no way in hell I can get $250,000 in forty-eight hours. No bank will give me any kind of loan—if they did, I would just end up right back where I started—and my mom certainly doesn't have that kind of cash lying around. When Harry was still here, I tried my best to plead with him as he went around my apartment tearing through my belongings to make sure I had no money hidden away. He even forced me to strip partway out of my clothes to make sure I wasn't wearing a wire, then he left as quickly as he arrived.

After the initial shock passes, I seek out the bottle of expensive wine hidden under my sink. It was a gift from my mother at graduation but she made me promise not to drink it until my wedding night. In her grand plan, I was to be married within six months of graduation, but all these years later, I'm still single so the bottle remained untouched.

With a time limit on my life, I figure why wait?

Popping the cork, I trudge into the lounge and catch sight of my face in the hanging mirror on the opposite wall. Harry struck me so many times that he split the skin over my eyebrow, and my cheek is aching and purple. I turn the light off, sending me into darkness, and then sink down onto the floor between the couch and the table.

The first sip of wine is sweet and thick—it's definitely the good stuff. The second sip brings tears of hopelessness, and as I stare through the darkness of my apartment, defeat weighs heavily in my chest.

How has my life become this? As if everything with the Irish wasn't bad enough, my own mistakes with credit cards and loan sharks have brought me right to death's door. As a child, I envisioned my adult life to be something magical with a successful job, a home, and a couple of cats running around while I danced with the person I loved.

My mother's coldness and my father's death sent me careening off course, though it's easy to blame them in the darkness of my own hell. I sought comfort in the materialistic and now I'm paying the price.

Tears roll slowly down my cheeks as I sob quietly to myself, drinking mouthfuls of the wine each time I pause for breath. My mind sluggishly tries to come up with a plan, but there's nothing concrete. In the dark, I Google how to sell my kidney and how much money I can make from blood or plasma donation. Selling myself is the only thing I have left. Unfortunately, none of those are viable options for $250,000 in two days. Hopelessness washes over me like a suffocating wave.

What the fuck do I do?

Half a bottle of wine later, my mind drifts back to Cormac. If I'd stayed with him, Harry wouldn't have found me. He'd have come here, likely kicked down my door, and found absolutely nothing. I play the scenario out in my mind and then try to imagine how someone like Cormac would deal with Harry. The way he exploded at Dillon was incredible. Would he do that twice?

Or was Dillon only a target because we were at the motel?

It's wishful thinking, and my Google searches turn to more desperate measures, like how much an escort can make in two days. Nothing close to what I need, even if I advertised myself as having no limits.

I really am going to die—

An almighty crash explodes through my apartment, followed by a loud rumbling. Then, the door to my lounge flies open so hard that it hits the wall and immediately bounces back on the intruder. I scream, lurching back against my couch and kicking out at my table as if I can use it to stop whoever that is from coming closer.

The intruder lifts his thick arm, catching the door before it can hit him on the back swing, and then he strides further into my apartment.

Even in darkness with nothing but the streetlights pouring in through the blinds to illuminate the room, I recognize him. My heart pounds fiercely in my chest and I clutch the nearly empty bottle to my body, staring up at this panting, furious tank of a man.

"C–Cormac?" I gasp when I finally find my voice. "What... what are you doing here?"

"I should have known there was something off about you," Cormac snaps darkly. His voice is thick from anger, bringing out a sharp Irish twang to his words. "You just happened to be the one who found Brenden, right? And then the cops wanting to talk to you at the station instead of letting you go at the motel. Was it all part of the plan? Were you hoping I would scoop you up just so you could get close and find out what we knew?"

Cormac may as well have been talking a foreign language from how he wasn't making any sense. The wine made me bold and I roughly hauled myself to my feet.

"What?" I yell back. "What the hell are you talking about?"

"You!" Cormac points at me with a meaty fist. "You didn't think I would find out. Did you think I was stupid, huh? The big, muscular guy doesn't have a brain to figure it out?"

My mouth opens and closes, and I briefly register that there are other people in my apartment moving about in the dark behind Cormac. His eyes glint at me like the edge of a blade while my heart races and my thoughts struggle to catch up. Oddly, all I can focus on is the damage done to my wall.

"You—what?" I shake my head, trying to clear the alcohol fog from my mind. "Hold on, what the fuck?"

"Were you a plant, hmm?" Cormac stalks closer. "A spy? You Russians think you're so fucking sneaky, but let me tell you something. I won't blink if I find out you had any hand in killing Brenden, you hear me?"

"Russians?" I can't believe what I'm hearing. This is all so surreal that I start to doubt whether I'm really awake. Fear gives way to anger and I brandish the near-empty bottle of wine like a weapon. "I'm not fucking Russian! I'm American!"

"Birthplace doesn't dictate loyalty," Cormac growls.

"Loyalty?" A sudden burst of hot anger ignites in my chest, burning away the drunk haze and allowing me to see clearly for the first time all night. "No! You know what? Fuck you. Fuck you for bursting into my apartment like you fucking own the place and destroying my shit. Fuck you for throwing all sorts of accusations at me without talking to me first. Are you insane? Any other day, maybe I'd give you a pass for grief, but look what you did to my wall!"

I throw a hand toward the now very clear crack in the wall, which is illuminated by someone turning my kitchen light on.

"I'm not Russian and I had nothing to do with your brother. I don't know what you're on, but maybe switch dealers if it's making you so fucking delusional. I mean, take a look around, Cormac! I'm just me, okay? I'm just a regular woman who worked a regular, shitty job while dodging a regular, shitty guy and then all of a sudden, you came into my life and fucked things up. Most people don't get kidnapped after they witness a crime, but you thrust a fucking gun in my face and had me commit a fucking crime because you all live in this insane world where crime is as common as a fucking Starbucks. And not once, not once did you ever stop to think that maybe that's a shitty thing to do. And then you cast me aside once you're done with me, dump me back into the world like this, and I have to try and remember how to be a regular person, only I'm not a regular person anymore! I'm a witness and a criminal and a kidnap victim, and now you're in my fucking apartment destroying my shit, why? What possible fucking reason is there this time?"

I'm panting heavily by the time I pause my barrage of words that gave Cormac no window to respond. Not that he deserves it. I'm sick of this shit. I'm sick of people invading my home and my space, acting like I owe them the world when I'm just trying to live.

My worst crime is credit card debt. That's it. That's all I did, and that doesn't deserve Dillon trying to force his way into my pants, or Harry threatening my life, and certainly not Cormac and his men now going through my already fucked apartment.

"You can't lie to me," Cormac yells back, and his voice is much scarier than mine when he yells. "You were seen, okay? You had a Russian in your home and so soon after I let you go. Bit fucking suspicious, don't you think?"

"A Russian?" I can't believe my ears. "How the fuck would I know who is and isn't Russian? You want me to question every delivery guy that comes to my door to make sure they don't have any kind of gang affiliation, huh? And at that—" It hits me suddenly that if he knows someone was here, he must have eyes on me. "Are you stalking me? How the hell do you know who has or hasn't been in my home?"

"Harry Fox," Cormac recites, and my gut plummets like I've just been dragged off a cliff. "Name ring any bells?"

"If you'd opened with that," I snap, "instead of destroying my apartment. What was that noise, anyway? Did you kick my front door in, you psychopath?"

Cormac advances, but I hold my ground, clinging to this new rage inside me. Everything from the past week is piling up and it's too much. From the motel to Cormac to losing my job and Harry, what else am I supposed to do?

"Didn't want to give you a chance to run."

"Run?" I laugh humorlessly. "Where the hell would I run? If you're stalking me, then you should know I don't have anywhere or anything! I'm not a spy, you hear me? And Harry, I wouldn't fucking know what he is or isn't, okay? He's just a guy I have to deal with, and a very fucking unpleasant one at that."

"You expect me to believe that five days after my brother is murdered, you're shacking up with someone on the Russian payroll and that's just a coincidence?"

A wave of rage at Cormac's accusatory tone floods through me, drowning me from the inside, and I suddenly, can't breathe. The urge to lash out is too strong, so I turn and launch the wine bottle at the opposite wall.

"Fuck off with that bullshit!" I scream at him, enraged. "I don't know what the fuck you are talking about, okay? I'm just trying to pick up the pieces of my life after you and your brother fucked it, alright? So you know what? Go through my apartment for all I care. Tear this shit apart. Call my mother if you have to. I don't have anything to hide because I don't fucking have anything! I'm just me, but I don't have to stand here and explain myself to you in my own fucking home!"

It feels so fucking good to yell. It's more therapeutic than crying, and despite being breathless afterward, there's an odd freeing sensation across my shoulders. I force a deep breath and hold it as Cormac stares at me through the dullness.

"I'm just me," I repeat tiredly. "Do whatever you want. You won't find whatever you think is here."

I move around the table and push past Cormac, heading into the kitchen where I know there's no more alcohol, but there is water and I'm suddenly very parched.

Cormac follows me, his angry footsteps like a drum beat on the chipped tile flooring. "Evelyn," he snaps. "The evidence is piling up against you and I—"

He stops talking so abruptly that I half expect him to fall over when I turn with a glass of tap water in my hands. The anger on his face is so clear now in the light of the kitchen, but in a blink it fades and there's something else in his eyes. The same look he had when he stared at me after beating Dillon to a pulp.

"Your face."

He walks forward, and I brace for him to pull another accusation out of his ass, but instead, he lifts his hand and grasps my chin between a gentle but firm thumb and forefinger and tilts my head up into the light.

"He hurt you?"

15

CORMAC

The bruise around her eye, the split skin at her lip, and the split at her eyebrow weren't visible in the dull light of the lounge, but here, in the kitchen, it's as clear as anything.

It dampens my anger faster than any Scotch, and a different anger begins to curl in my chest. It's darker, heavier, and more dangerous than the rage I felt when thinking Evelyn was some kind of spy. Listening to her outburst didn't make the truth any clearer and all the evidence points to her being some kind of plant or mole. The Russian connection seen leaving her apartment is the biggest evidence of this.

Suddenly, it doesn't matter as much. At least not right now. The wounds are fresh and the bruise around her eye is still pink and purple. In a few hours, it will darken. Evelyn lifts one hand and attempts to push me away as she turns her head, but I don't move and I prevent her from looking away.

"Tell me the truth," I say firmly.

Evelyn rolls her eyes and jerks her chin out of my grip. "Oh, now you care about the truth. What does it matter what I say if you've already made up your mind about me?"

I catch her chin again, tilting her face back to me and studying the split on her eyebrow. It doesn't look deep enough for stitches but it still needs some kind of treatment. "Sit down."

"Don't tell me what to do in my own home."

"Sit. Down."

Evelyn finally relents with a grumble and she drops into the rickety wooden chair by her small, circular table. I move past her to the sink and rummage through a few cabinets in search of a medical kit, but there's nothing. I'll have to do this old school. As I'm searching, Dale appears at the door and clears his throat to catch my attention. I look him in the eye and he shakes his head just once.

He found nothing.

Shit.

Hank appears next, moving around Dale, and his eyes widen at the sight of Evelyn's beaten face then he looks at me. "You need anything?"

"Yeah. Go and get some food. She's been drinking heavily, by the smell of the place. And bring the kit from the car."

"I'm right here, y'know," she mutters grumpily, picking at some of the white paint peeling off her table.

"And Dale, I want eyes on Harry."

"On it." Dale leaves without questions, but Hank lingers.

"Hank. Go."

"Boss." He still refuses to move. "Leaving you alone wasn't part of the plan."

"I have a new plan," I say, setting the kettle to boil and finding some cotton balls in a top cabinet. "Go."

Hank's uncertain gaze moves to Evelyn, then he finally nods and disappears from the doorway. He's back a few minutes later with the medical kit and after another wary glance at Evelyn, he leaves.

"Does he think I'm going to kill you the moment he leaves or something?" Evelyn mutters, her tone still irritated, but at least she's not screaming at me right now.

"Probably," I reply. "Are you?"

"If I have to tell you I'm not a spy one more time, then yeah, maybe."

"It doesn't look good for you, Evelyn."

"Nothing else does. But God forbid we have an actual conversation. You've already got me at the gallows."

"Fine." Pouring the warmed water into a cup, I sit next to her at the table and fight back a wince as the chair creaks loudly under my bulk. "Let's talk."

Evelyn glares at me. "Maybe I don't want to now because you're a fucking asshole."

"Fine. I'll talk." I pull the kit toward me and pop it open while soaking some of the cotton pad in the hot water. Then I catch her chin in one hand and tilt her head to the side. She doesn't fight me, but she's visibly irritated. "Russians are claiming credit for Brenden's death. A man on the Russian payroll is seen leaving your apartment. A man you've had a lot of contact with these past six months. He was even a guest at the motel at one point."

Evelyn shifts under my gaze and winces as I start to clean the split wound at her eyebrow. "How do you know all that?"

"One I have a name and a face, there's nothing I can't find out."

She rolls her eyes but remains silent.

"Do you see how it looks?"

"Maybe," Evelyn mutters. "But I don't really care because you already decided I was awful the moment you kicked in my door." Evelyn groans. "Do you even know how much that will cost to repair? My landlord will flip out."

Dabbing gently at her eye, I clean away the dried blood around her eye, then down to her lip. We remain silent. Each stroke of warm cotton against her lower lip pulls the flesh slightly, parting her lips. It's difficult not to think about how good she tasted when I kissed her or how I'd happily leave a wound like that on her lips with my teeth.

It's different, though, knowing someone else did this to her.

"I'll fix your door."

"I don't need your help," she mutters darkly.

"You do. Because I'm not the only one who thinks you had a hand in killing Brenden. So you wanna talk yet or should I just continue down this path and kill you?" Releasing her chin, I turn to the medical kit and seek out antiseptic wipes.

"Does it even matter?" She sighs, pressing her palms flat together. "You already made up your mind despite everything."

"Everything being the fact that we've only known each other a handful of days?"

Evelyn blinks owlishly at me, then nods. She closes her eyes as I wipe at her wounds with the antiseptic wipe, and when she hisses in pain, my gut tightens with unexpected guilt.

"If I wasn't injured," she asks quietly, "would you have just yelled at me until you killed me?"

"Maybe. I don't know."

"Then why did you stop?"

"Same reason you stopped yelling at me," I say, discarding the antiseptic wipes. "I took a breath and my focus shifted. I don't know what would have happened if I didn't suddenly want to clean you up because I'm angry. Everything reads like you're secretly the enemy, and if you can't convince me otherwise, then I guess we'll find out."

Evelyn sighs deeply as if the exhaustion came from the depths of her soul. "I'm not a spy. I'm not Russian. I didn't even know Harry was, okay? He's just a loan shark and I owe him a load of money."

"You owe him money?" Selecting some butterfly stitches, I use my fingers against her jaw to encourage her head to the side so I can close the small wound on her eyebrow.

"Yeah. I…" Evelyn groans. "Suppose it doesn't matter now, does it? I was in debt. A lot of debt because I like credit cards. Stuff made me happy because I had nothing else. Anyway, my spending habits didn't match my income and I was losing everything to so many companies, so I just found a loan shark, borrowed some money, and then paid them off."

Evelyn is in debt. Is that really all this is? Everything points to something else—led by my anger, it seems. I struggle to wrap my head around it as I apply the stitches and she continues to talk.

"Only, Harry ended up putting a lot of interest on what I borrowed. Like, insane amounts of interest, and I was working it off slowly, but then he heard I was at the police station and he thought I was reporting him or something. He got angry and…" She waves one hand loosely up to her face.

The strange anger inside me grows as I place the last stitch. I'm going to find Harry, and I'm going to kill him.

"So I don't know anything about what you are talking about, okay? And you're a fucking asshole for not just coming here and asking me about it."

She's right.

It pisses me off, but she's right.

I get up slowly and clean away the blood-stained cotton and wipes, then stand by the counter and grip the edge with one hand. I got this wrong. So wrong. I was completely blinded by the thought that I'd fucked someone tied to Brenden's death and that the woman I was rapidly becoming infatuated with was the enemy. I almost wanted her to confess so I could attribute my feelings to grief, kill her, and move on.

But she's innocent. Harry's being on the Russian payroll could just be a coincidence, but it's almost too perfect. Who knows what else will go wrong if I take my eye off the ball now?

"So?" Evelyn asks as my silence drags on. "Aren't you going to say anything?"

I look over at her. "How much do you owe him?"

She winces faintly and looks away. "Two hundred and fifty thousand."

"Oh."

That's nothing, at least to me. A quick glance at Evelyn's apartment and that's likely more money than she's ever seen in her life, beyond her credit cards. "I…" Pausing, I search for the right thing to say. Maybe there is no perfect way to say it. "I understand. And I believe you."

"You're not acting like you believe me," Evelyn says with a pointed glance at the hallway leading to her broken front door.

"Harry being with the Russians and their trying to claim credit for the kill is…" I shake my head. "It's too much for me to get into with you, but if you really are as innocent as you say, then there's a chance Harry marked you."

"Marked me?"

"Yes. Brenden was at that motel a few times and you work there. Getting into debt with Harry puts you on a list of people they can use to get what they want. Maybe you were their way into the motel to get to him."

"But I–I didn't do anything, I swear. Harry never mentioned the motel and he's never been violent until tonight when he thought I was handing him over to the cops."

"Doesn't matter. It could have been something small you did that helped them unknowingly, or you were just a backup plan." Rubbing my jaw, my beard scratches at my palm as I try to decipher their plan in my mind. Without Harry, though, all I can do is guess.

"So you burst in here thinking I'm a spy, then patch me up, and now you're on my side?" Evelyn narrows her eyes. "I don't think I believe you."

"Then don't," I say. "I'm… sorry about your door. I was furious because I thought I'd let you get close to me when really, you were a culprit."

"Close to you?" She tilts her head in a way that reminds me of a curious puppy.

"Do you think I fuck everyone in the back of my car?"

Her cheeks flare pink immediately and she looks away. "I don't know," she mumbles. "I'm sure you fuck a lot of people."

"No." For some reason, it's very important to me that she knows that. "I've never fucked anyone in my car except you. In fact, I haven't fucked anyone in way too long."

"Really?" The coy way she glances at me suggests she likes hearing that, but given how I've interpreted things so far, I'm not sure I can trust myself.

"Really."

"Well…" Evelyn moves on her seat and brings her hands to the table, twisting her fingers together. "At least I got to see you again, one last time."

My full attention locks on her immediately. "What do you mean, one last time?"

She looks at me with those gigantic doe eyes. "I'm sorry for yelling at you. Everything just got on top of me and I got so angry at what you were saying. It feels like I'm out of control, and everyone is making these assumptions and choices about me without listening to me, and now—"

"Evelyn." I move to sit next to her and place my large hand over her clasped ones. "What are you talking about?"

"Harry wants his money now. As in, he'll kill me in forty-eight hours if I don't have it ready for him. And I don't have that kind of cash so…" She shrugs and her eyes sparkle with tears. "I thought drinking would help me feel better, but…" She trails off, shaking her head.

For me, though, this is perfect. "I'll pay for it."

"What?" Her head snaps up.

"I'll pay it. That's barely anything. Plus, it saves me from working out how the hell to get my hands on Harry before he runs back to the family."

Evelyn's mouth drops open. "You're not serious."

"Deadly," I say, then pull my hand away from hers. The contact is almost too much, like her touch is searing into me, and I can still feel it even as I rub my palm against my thigh. "Call him. Tell him you have the money and want to meet."

Despite the soft surprise across her face, her eyes narrow. "So that's it. I'm just a tool for you to use again."

"Does it matter?" I reply. "I'll pay your debt and get my hands on the little rat. It's a win-win."

Evelyn's face twists into a frown and she nods. "So just a tool."

"A debt-free tool," I joke, but it's clearly too soon for humor, so I rise and take a few steps away lest I get overcome with the urge to touch her again. "Evelyn, if you were just a tool, I wouldn't be helping you."

"Helping me gets you what you want," she replies, looking up at me. "So just a tool."

"All I need is a name and a face, and I already have that for Harry. I can get to him without you, so no. I wouldn't be helping you if you were just a tool."

"Then why are you helping me?"

I stare at her, and my mind goes blank as my heart skips a beat.

That is the one question I can't answer.

16

EVELYN

We rehearsed this countless times over the past few days, but as I walk toward the alley where I'm supposed to meet Harry with a duffel full of money over one shoulder, I forget everything.

Once again, I'm doing something that terrifies me while Cormac waits out of sight. Strange how familiar this is starting to feel. The only difference is that this time, this really will benefit me. Harry will get his money, and I will be debt-free, and maybe Cormac will finally get some answers as to whether the Russians really were involved in his father's death. I hope he does so that he can move on, and yet a tiny part of me hopes he doesn't so that somehow, we can run into one another again.

And again.

Is that selfish? Probably.

After our explosive argument in my apartment, things settled down and I slept for twelve hours straight, then awoke to Cormac cooking me breakfast while his men fixed all the damage in my apartment—including a cracked pipe Dale discovered under the sink. That was a nice surprise. Having Cormac look after me was also a nice, surreal surprise, although I'm not foolish enough to believe that there's something real between us. It's all circumstance. Cormac wouldn't look twice at someone like me in his regular life.

As I walk, I can feel his eyes burning against my skin as I cross the street and step into a puddle on the sidewalk. Another block and I'll be at my destination. Huddling into my coat, I tighten my grip on the bag and pick up the pace as a cold wind drags its long fingers through my hair. Cormac had listed off multiple scenarios I'm to look out for—Harry running and snatching the bag, bringing friends, refusing the money or adding more on top. All I have to do is keep him talking long enough for Cormac to get his hands on him.

Then all of this will be over for me.

I'll have a clean slate.

I close my eyes as the next gust of wind picks up dust and dirt from the street and a dark rumble thunders overhead. As long as the money doesn't get wet, I don't care how stormy it's going to be. As a child, I had always loved storms, and right now, the scent of rain on the warm ground and lightning in the air are the only things keeping me calm.

Then I'm at the mouth of the alley, staring down into a darkness where shadows melt together just beyond a cluster of dumpsters. Cormac told me it was important to make sure Harry doesn't block my exit so as I slowly walk down the alley, I keep a conscious thought on making sure Harry stays in front of me whenever he appears. I halt just before the dumpsters, eyeing them suspiciously as my heart begins to race. Walking here, I could pretend to be confident, but I no longer feel Cormac's eyes on me.

I'm alone.

"Harry?"

He appears suddenly from behind one of the dumpsters and his abrupt appearance makes me jump and step back.

"Evelyn."

"You scared me," I say, further tightening my grip on the rough straps.

Harry snorts. "Your face looks good. How'd you even afford a trip to the hospital?"

The gentle phantom touch of Cormac's fingers flares across my forehead and I lift my chin slightly. "I did it myself."

"Sure." Harry snorts. He shoves one hand into the pocket of his jeans. The other holds a lit cigarette, and he flicks some of the ash toward me with a slimy smirk. "You weren't kidding, huh?" His beady eyes lock onto the bag. "That my money?"

"Yup."

"All of it?"

"Of course." My racing heart becomes a blur, and I tense my thighs to stop my knees from knocking together.

"What did you do, huh?"

I narrow my eyes. "What?"

"Where did you get that kind of money in two days?"

"I have my ways."

"Really?" Harry snorts. "You got some golden cunt between your legs?"

My stomach rolls in disgust. "What is it with men and thinking the only thing a woman has of value is what's between her legs? You, my boss… fucking hell. There are other ways to make money!"

Harry snorts. "Sell a kidney?"

"So what if I did? It's my kidney." I keep my face as impassive as I can so Harry can't work out the truth, and it seems to work as he tosses his cigarette down onto the damp ground and waves his hand at me.

"Drop the bag."

The straps have embedded into my shoulder from the weight of the money, so I wince as pain flares upon removal. I drop the bag as close to Harry as I dare, then step back. "It's all there."

"I'll be the judge of that," Harry remarks. He drops down to his haunches and unzips the bag, then he pauses when the money comes into view. Releasing a low whistle, he picks up a wad of stacked bills and thumbs through them. "Holy shit. Golden cunt or not, whatever you did, maybe we should work together if it can get money like this so fucking fast."

"No thanks," I reply tightly. "So, are we good? You have your money and my debt is paid?"

"Hold on," Harry says, not looking up. "I gotta count it all and make sure you're not trying to pull one over on me. You wouldn't do that, though, would you?"

He glances up at me, but before I can reply, blood drains from Harry's face and his mouth falls open in shock.

"She wouldn't," comes Cormac's voice from directly behind me, and warm shivers dart down my back. "But I would."

I hadn't even heard Cormac walking up, but somehow, he's right here. He places a gentle hand on my lower back and guides me to the side as Harry stumbles upright and tries to flee.

He makes it two steps before Cormac is on him, lifting him by the collar of his jacket and slamming him down onto the top of the dumpster. Harry struggles and fights back, but Cormac subdues him with a couple of punches. By the time Harry's face is a bloody mess and he's panting, Cian has joined us.

My stomach flips and I take a step back to meet Hank.

He takes me by the arm and leads me toward the mouth of the alley. "You don't need to see this part," he says gently, and the kindness is unexpected. I don't know Hank at all, but at a glance, he seems hardened and mean. Given that he's clearly Cormac's bodyguard, it makes sense, but I got the impression he didn't think much of me so his kindness is nice. We stop near the mouth of the alley just as the skies split open and rain pours.

As Cormac and Cian beat sense into Harry, Hank shrugs off his coat and offers it to me to protect me from the rain. I accept it and hold it up over my head. Thunder rumbles overhead, and each flash of lightning gives me a sudden flash of the fight happening in the alley. Harry gives up quickly and ends up shoved against the wall by Cormac, who is panting heavily.

The rain soaks his shirt in seconds, and despite the danger in the situation, my eyes wander. His shirt becomes a second skin, so all I see are the long curves of his thick muscles and the way his hair turns blood-red when wet. Fear melts away just like it did when Cormac tackled Dillon. This man doesn't even know me, even suspected me for a time, and yet he's still doing what he can to keep me safe.

And it's so fucking attractive. My mouth runs dry and I can't take my eyes off him. Cian crouches down and quickly zips up the duffel bag to protect the money from the rain.

"The fuck?" Harry gasps through a bloodied smile. "The fuck are you guys?"

"I want to have a little chat," Cormac growls low, anger lacing his words. "About you and who the fuck you work for."

"What—" Harry's next response is snatched away by a roll of thunder. I watch lips move, but I can't hear them over the storm so I hope that Cormac is getting the answers he needs.

"You'd better have a better fucking answer than that!" Cormac suddenly yells during a lull of thunder. In a long flash of lightning, Harry drives his knee up into Cormac's crotch. He doubles over with a grunt and fails to avoid Harry's elbow crashing into the side of his face. As Cormac stumbles back, Harry starts sprinting toward me with Cian hot on his tail. Hank steps forward, pushing me back a few feet to maintain distance between angry Harry and me.

"You fucker!" Cormac yells, bolting after Harry like some kind of human bullet. I huddle into Hank's jacket, eyes wide, and step back a few more feet as Hank sprints forward. Harry is caught in a clash between Mob Boss and bodyguard and he hits the ground like a sack of bricks.

"Excuse me," mumbles a gentle voice to my left, making me jump in surprise.

I turn, alarmed to see that I've stepped out of the alley and am blocking the path of someone trying to hurry home in the storm. My lips part to apologize, but the hooded stranger shoves hard into me on the way past and their elbow catches me just beneath my ribs.

"Hey!" I snap with a gasp, stumbling back as they continue on their way down the street. "Rude," I mutter, glaring after them, then I turn back to the fight, only something is… different.

Where the stranger's elbow impacted me, a strange hot pressure begins to spread through my chest and down through my abdomen. My next breath in is tight, and the world sways when the alley lights up with another flash of lightning.

How hard did they hit me?

A wave of dizziness sweeps through me like a shiver, and Hank's jacket slips from my grasp. I don't hear it hit the ground. My focus is on the gradual pain growing through my body.

I open my mouth to say Cormac's name—or maybe Hank's—but nothing comes out. Instead, a hot spray of blood darts across the back of my tongue and the tang of copper is sickening. I step forward. Hank turns toward me. I watch his eyes widen and his mouth twists.

"Cormac!"

Cormac seems so far away, but I see him lift his head at the yell of his name. He looks at me and his brows shoot up to his hairline, then he abandons Harry to Cian and starts sprinting toward me. Despite how fast I can see his legs moving, he doesn't seem to be getting any closer. The next flash of lightning is dull as darkness spreads across my vision. I touch my abdomen, trying to understand why an elbow to the ribs hurts so damn much.

My legs weaken and I trip over myself, then look down.

In a flash of light, my hand illuminates red.

It's covered in blood.

What the hell?

"Evie!" Cormac yells at the top of his lungs, and yet he sounds so far away. I try to lift my head again but suddenly, every part of me is incredibly heavy.

I close my eyes and darkness takes me.

17

CORMAC

"Cormac?" Saoirse's hand lands gently on my shoulder, drawing me out from my slumber at Evelyn's bedside.

I lift my head, fighting back a yawn and immediately seek out Evelyn's unconscious face. She's been unconscious for the past couple of days ever since surgery to save her life, and the wait for her to open her eyes is long and painful. Many think I should be elsewhere rather than keeping vigil at the bedside of a woman I barely know, but nothing can drag me away. I have enough people that I can give orders from here and not have to worry.

After checking that Evelyn is still asleep and that nothing on the surrounding machines is cause for alarm, I glance up at Saoirse. She gives me a tight smile, then tilts her head indicating we need to talk and this isn't the best place for it. Easing myself out of the hard plastic chair, I follow Saoirse out of the room but keep the door ajar with my foot so I can maintain an eye line with Evelyn.

"What is it?"

"We lost McCullen's."

"The restaurant?"

"Aye. Burned to the ground."

"Russian?"

Saoirse nods. "Likely retaliation for that nightclub we raided last night."

Sliding my tongue over my upper teeth, I nod slowly. "Did we lose anyone?"

"Nah. Purely structural."

"Good." Evelyn's stabbing ignited a bloodbath in the streets, though openly, I deny that it has anything to do with her. The fact that she was attacked when we were meeting with that loan shark is the confirmation I need that she had been marked as a way into the hotel. Whether she was an initial target or a backup, it doesn't really matter. There's too much Russian blood involved in that motel for Brenden's death to be unrelated and I needed to lash out. War is brewing, and I'll burn down the entire city for Brenden if I have to.

And Evelyn.

But I can't say that part out loud.

"Cormac," Saoirse warns gently. "You know where this path will take us."

"Hmm?"

"You're starting a war before we've even spoken to the Godmother."

My eyes narrow. "What do you expect me to do? Sit around on my fucking arse while the Russians run free after what they did? I won't allow it. Not for a second. She knows where I am if she wants to fucking talk about it."

"I know," Saoirse says. "Believe me, I'm with you on this. Even since

Brenden—" Her voice tightens and she glances away. "I just want you to be sure. The last thing we need is a war with the wrong people."

"Okay, tell me how you see it."

Saoirse puffs out her cheeks, then places her hands on her narrow hips. "Alright, I see that the woman you have feelings for got stabbed on your watch and now you're tearing through the Russians like Cian tears through Scotch eggs at Christmas."

"It's not about her."

"Isn't it?" Saoirse's head tilts. "You really think a Russian loan shark is behind Brenden's death?"

"No."

Her eyes widen slightly. "What?"

"I don't think he had anything to do with it directly, but we know how the Russians work. We know that Brenden frequented that hotel in secret for some reason. We know Evelyn worked there and we know that those assholes always get some poor schmuck to either do their dirty work or to get them in where they need to be. Hell, it's what we would do if we needed eyes in a place we couldn't show ourselves."

Saoirse nods along slowly. "So you think they stabbed her to shut her up?"

"Why else?" I cast an eye back to Evelyn. "Either she saw something or she knows something they don't want her telling anyone."

"But what? I thought she told you everything."

"She did, and I believe her," I reply. "Which means whatever she knows, she doesn't know that she knows it. Or she's told me and I don't know how important it is yet. Either way, if the Russians want her dead, then that's good enough for me."

Saoirse sighs deeply, then lifts her hand and delicately rubs at her dark lined eyes. "Okay. I understand. I'm not questioning you, I'm just making sure I understand."

"I know."

"I feel like we can't even get a minute to breathe, y'know?" When she lowers her hand, her eyes betray the deep sadness inside her and I can't resist the urge to reach out and draw her into my arms.

"As soon as Brenden's killer is in the ground, we'll get that minute."

The hug is brief. Any longer, and I risk losing control of the lid, keeping my own grief buried and secure in the dark recesses of my mind. I can't lead if I'm unable to focus.

Saoirse says her goodbyes and leaves. Heading back into Evelyn's room, I close the door softly just as a dry voice reaches my ears.

"Cormac?"

My heart jumps. I'm by her bedside in an instant and it takes all my restraint not to grasp her hand. "Evelyn."

Her eyes flutter slowly as she wakes up, then she squints at me and presses her lips together. "What... What happened? Where am I?"

"You're in Queens Memorial Hospital." Hovering over her, I ache to touch her. Seeing her eyes open and alert brings me more joy than anything has in weeks. Each day she remained dead to the world, I feared another death on my shoulders and that whatever information she had in her would be lost. Fate, thankfully, has other plans.

"Hospital?" Evelyn repeats croakily, then she quickly dissolves into a flutter of dry coughing.

Using the jug of water by her bedside, I pour her a cup then guide a small straw past her parched lips. She drinks greedily, then sinks back into the pillows with a gasp. "What happened?"

"You were stabbed." Straight to the point seems like the best route. "Whoever bumped into you in the alley stabbed you with a thin, curved blade just under your ribs. That kind of blade is designed to kill. It was serrated. It tore into you and your lungs, which is why you went down so fast. You've had surgery to repair the tear."

"Some... Someone tried to kill me?"

It isn't until she whispers those words that it hits me—assassination attempts and brutality such as this are common in my world, but there's a look of horror and fear on her face. This isn't an everyday occurrence for her and my tactless way of delivering the news clearly wasn't the best.

"I... I'm sorry, Evelyn. It... Yes, someone did, but I promise you they will not get away with it. And I'm sorry. I should have protected you better."

Evelyn briefly closes her eyes, curling her fingers against the bedsheets. When she opens them, they're slightly shining with unshed tears, and she shakes her head. "It's not your job to protect me."

"It is," I reply immediately. "You're my responsibility and you're under my care. I didn't plan all the angles and I'm sorry, Evelyn. I promised you this would all be over once I got my hands on Harry, and instead, you got hurt. I'm sorry, but I swear to you this will never happen again."

It's unclear if it's my words or the painkillers she's on, but Evelyn gives me a lopsided smile and shakes her head again. "We can't play the blame game. Harry was my problem before I met you and I didn't stay close to Hank either."

"Don't." Without thinking, I reach for her hand. "This isn't an argument you will win. But I promise you that you will be taken care of. Hospital bills and everything."

Her eyes dart down to our hands and a sudden flush of heat warms between my palm and her knuckles, but I don't draw back. I won't unless she does first.

"You called me Evie."

"What?"

"I heard you. In the alley. You called me Evie."

Thinking back, I hadn't realized that had slipped from me. Nodding, my mouth twists slightly. "Did I? Must have been a slip of the tongue."

"Mmhmm," Evelyn murmurs. "I get stabbed and you give me a nickname."

"Sorry."

"No, s'okay." Evelyn smiles again. "I like it."

Evie.

The doctor arrives not long after to check Evelyn over, remove her catheter, and give her another round of painkillers. I give her some privacy through all of that and return an hour later with some food. She appears grateful for something to eat and much more awake than before, which is nice. She asks about Harry, and I quickly fill her in on how he's currently under lock and key at one of my facilities until we get some real answers out of him. She seems unfazed and only concerned as to whether he will still be an issue for her. Given the actions both I and the Russians have taken these past few days, I don't see her debt being much of an issue, but the money is there and ready, just in case. Then we sit in an amicable silence listening to music from her phone that drowns out the beep of machines around us.

Suddenly, her brow dips sharply and her face contorts. I'm on my feet immediately, ready to run for a doctor at the first sign of pain. "What is it? What's wrong?"

Evelyn meets my gaze. "I really gotta pee."

"*Oh.*" I snort softly with amusement. "Let me help you."

Evelyn's cheeks flare crimson immediately. "What?"

I stand over her. "I can carry you."

"I can walk."

"Fine, I'll help you walk."

"I don't need your help to pee," Evelyn says, unable to meet my gaze.

Rather than argue, I step back from her bed and watch as she slowly pushes back the blankets and slides her legs from the bed. As I expect, when she tries to stand, she lacks the strength and the balance to do so and immediately sinks back down onto the bed.

"Okay," she mutters. "Can you help me?"

"Here I was thinking you would remain too stubborn to ask me."

"If I didn't need to pee so badly, I probably would," Evelyn murmurs.

I scoop her into my arms with ease, mindful of the tubes attached to the drip stand, and carry her into the attached bathroom where I set her down near the toilet and hold her hand until she gets a grip on the porcelain. Once I'm certain she won't fall, I turn away and plan to leave to give her privacy, but within a second, the sound of her relieving herself fills the air.

"Sorry," Evelyn groans. "I'm too loopy to be embarrassed, but if you tell anyone about this then I'll... do something really scary, okay?"

For the first time in as long as I can remember, I laugh. I don't know if it's her attitude, the tone of her voice, or the amusing pink hue on her cheeks. Honestly it might be all of those things. She draws a deep laugh from me and then her hand curls into the back of my shirt and grips on.

"That's the first time I've heard you laugh," she murmurs, and it's my turn for heat to warm my cheeks. I can't think of anything to say so I let it slide for now.

"I won't tell a soul," I promise, keeping my back to her to maintain some air of privacy.

"Good, because you have a knack for putting me in danger and then saving me, so don't think I haven't learned a few things."

Ordinarily, such a comment wouldn't bother me so much given how dangerous this life is for myself and the people around me, but Evelyn is the last person I want to get hurt. Whether it's the asshole from the motel, the cops, or Harry, I don't want to bring harm back to her doorstep.

Which is why hunting down the bastard who stabbed her is my second top priority.

"I'm sorry," I say quietly. "If I could stay away from you, then maybe you would be safer, but for some reason…"

The toilet flushes, and I turn back around to help Evelyn get up.

"I just can't."

"It's because of my magnetic personality," Evelyn jokes as I guide her to the sink. "I'm a fucking charm to be around. I get it."

"You think I'm joking?"

Our eyes meet in the mirror as I lather soap onto my hands, then tenderly clasp her own cold hands and wash them in between my own. She nods, and the pink flush on her cheeks darkens.

"I'm not joking," I say firmly. "Hardly what you want to hear, though, I imagine, given everything that's happened."

Evelyn's eyes lock onto me. "You can't say things like that when I'm drugged up," she says softly. "You'll give me the wrong idea."

"Or the right one."

Soap rinsed, I carry Evelyn back to the bed and tuck her in as gently as I can. She gingerly adjusts herself under the sheets, mindful of the bandages around her torso, and then she settles down to rest. Which lasts all of five minutes before she's tugging at the covers and trying to bury herself beneath the sheets.

"Do you need anything?" I ask, fighting the wave of worry that fluctuates every time she moves. I don't want her ripping her stitches, but her restlessness is clearly worrying.

"I'm cold," Evelyn says, suddenly sitting up. "Can you cuddle me?"

The request makes my heart unexpectedly skip a beat. Helping her to the bathroom is one thing. That's a necessity. But hearing her ask for me to be close to her is another thing entirely, especially when I'm fully expecting her to want nothing to do with me as soon as those painkillers wear off.

"Are you sure?"

Evelyn nods and lightly bites her lower lip. "I can't curl up for warmth because of this." She presses one hand to her chest. "So can you help me?"

I don't need to be asked twice. Shifting out of my seat, I ease onto the bed and take up most of the room considering my bulk, but Evelyn doesn't appear to care. She immediately latches onto my chest and when I tuck my arm around her shoulders, she cuddles into me with the softest, most contented sound I have ever heard in my life.

Having her against me sends my thoughts running. There's a mix of anger and guilt at myself for letting her get hurt and not protecting her better when I was the one who put her in danger. Then there's a flurry of anxiety and a strange hyper-awareness of my body and where I'm touching her. I can feel her entire body against my own and every little shiver that runs through her sends a jolt of excitement through me.

I can't even try to explain away my feelings anymore, and it doesn't matter if they will never be reciprocated. I like her. A lot.

And no one will ever hurt her again.

"What does this mean?" Evelyn's cool fingertips suddenly brush against my neck, right over a black tattoo.

"It's a tattoo."

Her fingers become claws and she prods my shoulder. "Asshole. What does it mean?"

The tattoo is three interlocking triangles connected in a way that creates a single triangle with each outer edge. Her touch is gentle, yet focusing on that tattoo drags my heart into my gut.

"It's... each triangle is one of my siblings. There's one for Saoirse, one for Cian, and one for... Brenden. And then together, they make up my family."

"Oh." Her voice is soft. "I'm sorry."

"Don't be. It just means more now than it did when I got it done. It's all locked together because, as a unit, we're unshakeable. Or we were." I breathe deeply, staring up at the white tiles above.

"It's beautiful. Just like the flowers on your arm."

"Ah, now those are because of my home. Ireland and my actual home."

"Your apartment?"

"Nah, my real home." I tilt my head down to see Evelyn's eyelids drooping. "I'll show you sometime. After you sleep."

"Not tired," Evelyn replies stubbornly.

Within two minutes, she's fast asleep in the crook of my arm and the machines around me beep to the rhythm of her peaceful rest. I return my gaze to the ceiling and allow my mind to run.

Maybe taking Evelyn home would be a good idea.

It's unclear how long we stay like this, but as the world darkens outside the window, the door soon opens and Saoirse walks in. She doesn't bat an eye to see Evelyn and me cuddled together. Approaching the bed, she hands me a letter.

An invitation.

The Russian Godmother is requesting a meeting on neutral ground.

18

EVELYN

"You didn't have to drive me home." Placing one hand on the car door, I slowly ease myself out of the vehicle and bite back a wince as a dull ache shoots through my abdomen.

"I wanted to," Cormac replies, immediately offering me his elbow.

"Is this your way of making up for what happened?"

I loop my hand around his arm and clutch at him. Feeling the strength rippling through his muscles with the slightest shift gives me a warm sense of security. He might have been with me when I got stabbed, but he wasn't near me. Having him tower over me as we ascend the steps to my front door gives me a comfort that if something else were to happen, he would protect me.

"Maybe." He dips his head and when our eyes meet, he lifts his brow. "I would still prefer to have you at my penthouse."

"No, thank you. I need my own bed after trying, and failing, to sleep these past nights in that hospital." His offer had been kind and incredibly tempting, but I was exhausted. The last thing I want is to recover in a place that reminds me of my kidnapping.

"It's not safe," Cormac insists again, though he doesn't fight me when I unlock my door and let us both inside.

"You're here," I say easily. "I feel plenty safe."

"I can't be here all the time," Cormac replies.

"Ahh, so you were *teasing* when you said you couldn't stop thinking about me," I joke softly while releasing my grip on his arm. "I knew you were all talk."

"I wasn't teasing," he replies as seriously as if we were still discussing the details of my stabbing. "But they know where you live."

Reaching my kitchen, I set aside the small paper bag containing my medication and move to pour myself a glass of water. "Do *they* know where *you* live?"

"Yes." Cormac sighs.

"Exactly. Here has the benefit of my own bed and my own pillow. So here wins out. Sorry." Cormac doesn't strike me as the kind of person to make a face, but the way his eyebrows twitch suggests he would do that if he were ten years younger.

"Your logic is irritating."

"Just be thankful I'm on painkillers."

Just as I finish pouring myself some water, his hand appears over mine against the tap and he takes over turning it closed. "I'll be with you as long as I can tonight. Then Dale will take over."

"Dale?" I glance from our joined hands to Cormac's face. "The man you had tailing me ever since you let me go?"

He meets my eyes steadily, not a hint of shame in them. "Yes."

"You really aren't going to explain that?"

"What?"

"You had someone tailing me."

"Yes."

"*Yes?*" A dull spike of irritation rises, so I pull my hand away from him and turn to my medication. "No explanation?"

"I made myself clear," Cormac replies. "I couldn't stop thinking about you so I took steps to keep an eye on you until my interest died down."

"And did it?" Three pills land on my tongue and I chase them with several gulps of water, then I turn to face him. "Has your interest faded?"

Cormac holds my gaze. "Not in the slightest."

I should tell him to leave. The sensible part of me knows I should, but I can't. Maybe it's how warm his presence makes me feel or how small my kitchen feels with his bulk taking up most of the space. I want him here for as long as I can have him. Which might only be for tonight, and I'll wake up tomorrow with more sense in my soul, but right now, I'm still stuck yearning for him. It's been there, warm in my chest, ever since he cuddled me to sleep in the hospital that first night. And each night after until they discharged me.

"Alright," I say, coughing slightly as a lingering tightness clings to the inside of my throat after those pills. "Well, you do your protection thing and I… I'm going to go and shower."

Leaving the kitchen, I move through my small apartment toward my bathroom. Cormac follows.

"I don't need help showering," I say as I turn on the light.

Cormac lightly catches my wrist as my hand falls from the switch and he turns me to face him. "Maybe not, but you will need help wrapping your bandages so they don't get water damage."

He has a point but for some reason, his pointedness irritates me a little. Bathed in the bright light from the single bulb in my rundown bathroom, I clutch the hem of my T-shirt and pull the fabric over my head with only a tiny wince of pain. My upper abdomen and breasts are wrapped in thick, white bandages to protect the stab wound and my surgical incision.

Cormac barely even blinks and he doesn't break eye contact.

"Wrap me up, then," I demand.

He obliges. Using the remaining cling wrap from my kitchen, he tenderly covers all of my bandages to the point that I'm certain not even a drop of sweat is going to break the seal. Each brush of his fingertips against my bare skin sends a jolt of energy through me, like a bolt of lightning. He remains gentle even as he guides me to turn and lift my arms. It's so different to the last time he touched me when we fucked in the car, and part of me aches to return to that.

It would be the fastest way to chase away this heavy sense of weakness that's settled in my heart ever since I woke up in the hospital.

"There." Cormac steps back finally. "Now you're shower-proof."

"Thank you," I reply, and my heart flutters. If I didn't know any better, I'd say Cormac is blushing slightly, but it's difficult to tell in such a bright white light.

"Happy showering." Cormac steps out of the room, then he remains in the doorway with his back to me. He's really taking this protection thing seriously.

I don't mind at all. As I step under the lukewarm, weak spray of my shower, I finally have a chance to run through everything that's happened. From the motel until now, everything feels like some weird dream. I'm on a runaway train that's dragging me away from my normal life and I ache to return to it.

And yet, a growing part of me is enjoying it. It's the most excitement I've had in years, and somehow, my debts are paid—technically. I've no idea what happens next, and I should ask Cormac about Harry and the money, but I almost don't want to know—not when that detective could pop up at any moment and start asking me uncomfortable questions.

No, I won't ask. Not yet, at least. Right now, I'm going to enjoy having someone taking care of me for the first time in my life.

I finish washing away the grime and stink of the hospital and step out of the shower smelling like vanilla and berries, finally starting to feel like myself again. Wrapped in a towel, my heart leaps when I open the door and Cormac is right where I left him. He stands guard silently and only turns when I gently touch his back.

"Good shower?" Cormac asks, and this time he isn't subtle in the way he glances down my damp body.

"Amazing," I reply. "Well, as amazing as that shower can be."

"The pressure at my place is stronger," he replies.

I roll my eyes and move past him to the bedroom. "Like I said, my bed trumps everything at your place."

"Noted." Cormac lingers in the doorway, leaning against the frame as I make my way toward my bed and drop down onto the saggy mattress. As beds go, it's a bit shitty, but it has my own knitted blanket and smells like me. It's the only place I have that's warm and feels safe, like the blankets can act as some kind of barrier between me and the entire world.

"Are you going to stare at me the entire time I dry off?" I ask, suddenly shy about removing my towel.

"I need to take the wrap off," Cormac says. "If you will let me."

"Sure. Then can I sleep?"

"Sure." Cormac walks toward me, slowly rolling up the sleeves of his shirt. "Sure." As more of his sculpted arms are revealed to me, I become distracted by the beautiful, intricate ink on his arm. For a man so brooding and silent, so much color almost seems out of character, but the detail tells me he's spent *hours* getting it done. Which means it's important.

"May I?" Cormac sits next to me and touches the edge of my damp towel.

I nod, and my breath catches in my throat as he slowly pulls the cotton away from my naked body. Before my shower, I'd been tense with tiredness and slight irritation, but the painkillers are working full swing now, and the warmth of the shower and the scent of my body wash have soothed me. Suddenly, Cormac's presence is taking up my entire focus. As he looks down and works at removing the plastic wrap from my bandages, I look at him.

Really look at him.

His thick, auburn hair has grown wavy over the past few days, like he hasn't had time to brush it properly. His beard is thicker too, and the downturned corners of his lips betray the deep sadness hiding inside him. These past few days, he's been busy watching over me at the hospital and busy on his phone. I wonder when he last did something for himself.

Did a man like Cormac do things for himself? Did he have hobbies beyond fighting and kidnapping? Surely, he had regular, human desires outside of this Mafia life.

I study the wrinkles across his forehead, and each time he leans close with his movements, I breathe in the spicy peppermint of his cologne. My heart begins to race as my attention drifts down to his thick neck and the sexy slope of his collarbone. The top few buttons of his shirt are undone so I can see some gorgeous curves of muscle and a hint of auburn curls across his chest.

When we'd fucked in the car, I didn't have a chance to explore his body. Suddenly, I ache to.

"All finished," Cormac says suddenly, and his voice jolts me out of my distracted musings.

My eyes flick up and Cormac remains close, merely a few inches away from me. The sloped curve of his lips calls to me and a warm pull of muscle squeezes through my core.

"You know," Cormac says slowly, "when you dropped the towel, did you mean to drop it fully?"

"Hmm?" I glance down at myself. In my distraction of taking Cormac in, I had forgotten that, unlike in the bathroom when I removed my T-shirt, I am completely naked, and I hadn't attempted to cover myself. *Oh.* "I feel like I should be embarrassed," I say, glancing back up to those deep blue eyes. "But I'm not."

"Must be the medication," Cormac says softly.

"Maybe," I reply, sinking my teeth into my lower lip. "Maybe there's something wrong with me."

"Like?"

"Maybe I'm numb."

Cormac leans an inch closer. "You think you're numb?"

"Mmhmm. I feel nothing."

"Nothing at all?" His bushy brows knit together and he leans closer another inch.

"Not a thing," I whisper. My heart pounds beneath my chest and goosebumps race across my skin, bringing with them a chill that forces a shover across my shoulders. "Maybe we should test that, though. Before we call a doctor."

"Test how?" Cormac's heavy, rough hand lands firmly on my damp, bare thigh, and my heart leaps into my throat.

"You really gonna make me say it?" I whisper. He's so close now that his entire scent is the only air I breathe, and I can make out a few hidden flecks of green in his beautiful eyes. His hand burns with anticipation against my thigh, and I'm not even sure what I'm asking for at this rate. My mouth is running and my thoughts are leagues behind.

"Yes," Cormac replies softly. "You want it, you ask me for it."

"I don't know what I want," I reply honestly, placing one hand over his hot knuckles. "Just… something."

"Something?" Cormac presses.

"You."

That's the keyword, it seems, because no sooner has that sound left my lips than Cormac is kissing me deeply, and my needy mind goes blank in relief. All thoughts screech to a halt and the next rush of goosebumps across my body is warm.

"You're wounded," Cormac says, writing those words against my lips when he breaks the kiss. "I will be gentle."

And he is. Cormac lays me down on the bed and discards my wet towel, then he sits me up near my pillows for comfort. Through each movement, he kisses me and keeps one arm around my waist to help me move with minimal effort on my part.

My aching ribs thank him.

He kisses my chin, then kisses down to my throat, where he buries his face into the juncture of my neck and shoulder. Each needy drag of his lips and tongue over my fluttering pulse makes his beard graze against my skin, and it's almost painful. But it's nothing compared to when he kisses down my body and disappears between my thighs.

There, the drag of his beard against the sensitive skin of my inner thighs *is* painful, but it's a pain I enjoy. Like the heat from pressing cold hands around a hot cup. Cormac slides his arms under my legs, then curls his arms around to grasp my thighs and pull me closer to his mouth.

A pulse of nerves skitters through my chest and I almost ask him to wait.

Then he kisses me, a firm, lingering kiss against my vulva, then my head tips back into the pillows. I clutch at the blanket beneath me, and my toes curl as Cormac's tongue slides through the outer lips of my pussy and delves into my inner heat in one slow stroke.

I close my eyes and my focus narrows to his warmth between my legs. His tongue slides through my pussy, parting my inner folds and delving down to my entrance, then he laps back up where his tongue becomes a firm point that flicks over my clit. I gasp and lurch at the resulting burst of pleasure. His grip tightens on my thighs and he holds me in place.

I can't think, and with each slide of his tongue through my damp folds, I can barely breathe, either. Cormac isn't one of those men who thinks a few kisses and a touch of the other lips is all that a woman needs. He's a real man and he's buried against my pussy like it's consuming him. He laps, kisses, and suckles every inch he can reach, barely pausing for air. Each time pleasure causes me to shift and rock one way, he's right there with me and his hands are quick to guide me back into place so he has the easiest access.

The pleasure grows quickly, but when I try to close my thighs and rock into the sensation of his constant attention over my clit, Cormac's hands prevent that from happening. Being lightly restrained, even like this, sends a flurry of excitement through my body. Sweat breaks out across my skin and thin strands of hair stick to my neck when I toss my head back and forth. My nipples ache for contact, but they're trapped behind the bandages so all I can do is slide my hands over my own heaving abdomen. A light caress, then I stroke down to where Cormac's head is buried against me. The moment I grip onto his thick red hair, he thrusts his tongue deep inside me and seals his mouth against my pussy. He hums and sucks as his tongue thrusts into me, reaching deeper than I can even fathom.

Arching off the bed, I cry out even as tightness from my stitches flares across my chest and warns me not to go too far. Right now, it doesn't matter. Heat coils like a snake in my lower gut and my clit throbs in time to my pounding heart. Constant tingles sweep down my arms and legs. My toes curl and my thighs tense under his grip. His tongue swirls around my clit in circles, then zig-zags, and just as he presses it flat against me, my orgasm hits like a truck.

I arch forward with a cry and my entire body jolts like the crack of a whip. I squeal and moan, suspended in a rigid position for a few long seconds as pleasure pours through me like liquid gold. My core throbs under Cormac's tongue, then I flop back onto the bed, panting harshly.

"Holy… shit," I gasp.

Cormac is above me suddenly with one hand on my ribcage. His beard glistens from my juices and there's a soft look around his dark eyes. "Too much?"

"No," I gasp, lifting one hand and cupping his cheek. "Not at all."

"Are you sure?" His eyes dart back and forth as if he's taking in every detail of my face, then his lips twitch as if a smile sits just out of reach.

"So sure." My thumb skims over his cheekbone. "That was amazing."

"I'm not finished." Cormac leans down and kisses the very tip of my nose, then he vanishes from view and settles back down between my trembling legs.

He draws me to a second orgasm as the sun sets outside my window. He's slower the second time, taking his time and letting pleasure simmer in me until I'm desperate and begging to be tipped over the edge. Only then does he let me come, and it's the second-best orgasm of my life.

Sleep comes easily after that, once Cormac's looked me over to make sure our activities haven't affected my stitches in any way. I sleep soundly, completely at peace for the first time in months, and I don't wake until late the next day. Cormac is right there with breakfast and medication and then he stays with me the entire day. I mostly sleep, letting the painkillers do their thing, and each time I wake up, Cormac is there with a meal ready for me and a few light discussions either about the news or some random fact he wants to share. It's oddly domestic for someone so large and dangerous, but he means it when he says he's going to take care of me.

It lasts until late at night when Cormac wakes me gently and cups my face. "I have to leave," he says in a low voice. "But Dale is here and I have people stationed outside."

"Will you be back?" I ask sleepily, struggling to gather my thoughts through a painkiller-addled sleep.

"Yes," Cormac says, then his beard and lips brush against my forehead. "Sleep."

I do, and I dream of Cormac and I living in some nice house somewhere with a garden and a dog running around. My dreams last until pain from my surgical wound wakes me late the next morning. There's no breakfast to greet me this time, but Dale is there with a fresh pot of coffee and it will have to do.

"Where's Cormac?" I ask, accepting the steaming cup from Dale.

"Busy."

"He said he'd come back."

"He's not finished yet," Dale replies. "But he has a message for you."

"Oh?" My brow lifts slightly. "Which is?"

"Pack."

"Huh?"

"He's going to take you somewhere safe to heal."

"I told him I'm not going anywhere."

Dale smirks. "Trust me. You'll want to pack a bag. And bring your pillow."

19

CORMAC

"Cormac! Get your filthy boots off my chair. Don't make me come over there!"

The sharp, throaty tones of Hazel, owner of The Black Ox, drift over from the bar, and I immediately retract my legs from the chair on which they are resting.

"Sorry, Hazel!" I call. She shoots me a sharp look over the edge of the glass she's polishing and abruptly turns away.

"Careful," warns Saoirse. "You don't want to piss her off or you'll have more than just Russians to worry about."

"You remember when I chipped the bar?" Cian groans softly. "We kill people nearly every weekend and yet Hazel with a wooden spoon was infinitely scarier."

A soft chuckle rises from Hank who stands behind me, ever my vigilant guard. Hazel and her family have run The Black Ox for longer than anyone cares to remember. It's the only place in the entire state that can be called neutral ground, regardless of the family you are from. Many treaties and deals have been hashed out at these tables, along with the smothering of potential conflicts and even a marriage or two. The Black Ox is a legend, and anyone who is anyone in this line of work knows that Hazel and her bar are not to be messed with. If anyone dared, they would have the full might of every family crashing down at their door.

This is why this is the perfect place for me to meet the Russian Godmother. It's the only way I can guarantee I won't shoot her on sight before I get my answers. Leaving Evelyn alone with Dale and a few of my men is the best choice, even if every part of me aches to be back with her. It's a feeling I've never had to battle with before and it's a strange sensation, almost like loss. As if I left a piece of myself with her in that apartment.

Saoirse slides a beer over to me with a silent raise of her brow. She can tell I'm tense and she wants to relax me before the Russians get here, but beer won't help. Nothing will.

If my intel is right, my brother's killer is about to walk through that door.

I need every drop of my focus.

Twenty minutes later, the door of The Black Ox swings open and in stride two burly men clad in red shirts and black leather jackets. They're followed by a beautiful woman with poker-straight platinum blonde hair and striking green eyes. Anastasia Remizova is around my age but wasn't raised the same way I was. It was common knowledge how desperately her father was trying to marry her off to someone rich and successful to try and stop the great Russian flagship from sinking into obscurity. His assassination was the talk of the town for a few months until Anastasia herself became the news. She refused to bend to the will of the generals in her family and then had them all killed for questioning her.

In one night, Anastasia proved herself to be tactical and ruthless, even if she's still fighting for power within her own ranks. Which makes it even more believable that she would act out and come after Brenden.

Despite this, she has the same look of apprehension on her face that I feel in my heart. Being thrust suddenly into power carries a certain weight that's hard to grow accustomed to when everyone is suddenly looking at you for direction and answers.

"Ana!" Hazel greets her with a smile. "Are you drinking tonight?"

"No," Anastasia replies with a tight smile, and her Russian accent is sharp to the ears. "Business only, I'm afraid."

"A shame," Hazel replies, and her eyes dart to mine with a warning. Peace is the only currency here.

Anastasia approaches my table, and I wait until she's a foot away before I stand. My brother and sister were on their feet the moment she entered, but I'm not here to keep relations smooth. Not if Brenden's blood is on Russian hands.

"So." Anastasia sits across from me and crosses one leather-clad leg over the other, resting her long red fingernails against her knee. "You've been causing me a lot of trouble, Cormac."

"Not enough," I reply shortly, sitting. Saoirse sits down, but Cian remains standing, squaring up to one of the Russian bodyguards who steps too close. Tension clogs the air as Anastasia and I hold one another's gaze. Cian refuses to back down despite the Russian having at least sixty pounds over him.

Then Hazel appears and slams a bucket of ice down onto the table, making everyone flinch. "Don't make me go over the rules," she states sharply. "No blood, you hear?" She glares at me, then Anastasia. Then she departs after an affectionate pat on Saoirse's shoulder.

"You killed Brenden," I say as the Russian guard steps back and Cian relaxes a fraction.

"No," Anastasia replies.

"Yes," I snap, and anger ignites like a hot flame in my chest. "The only thing keeping you alive right now is Hazel, do you understand? You kill my brother then dare sit across from me and deny it?"

Anastasia tilts her head and presses her dark lips together. "I have no interest in war with you Irish," she remarks. "You are misinformed."

"You're a liar!"

"Look." Saoirse cuts me off quickly and leans one arm on the table. "We know Russian hands caused the death of our brother. We have a witness. She was being scouted by a loan shark on your payroll, and he was a frequent guest of the motel where Brenden was murdered."

"And?" Anastasia raises one sharp brow.

"When we confronted him, our only witness was stabbed," I say, curling my hands into fists beneath the table. I want to reach across the table and punch that smug look off her face, then force her to tell me exactly who killed Brenden and why she thought she would get away with it. The rules of this place are the only things keeping me still, but my blood runs hotter with each passing beat of my heart.

"Name?" Anastasia asks.

"Harry Fox." Saoirse slides a thin paper folded toward Anastasia. "He was very forthcoming about who he works for after Cian was finished with him."

Anastasia opens the paper and takes in the information gathered on Harry after Evelyn was stabbed. Cian beat him until Harry spilled everything and anything about who he worked for, but none of it was any use. So we'd let him go.

She purses her lips and then passes the paper to one of her guards. "He is one of mine," she admits.

I lurch faintly in my seat. Under the table, Saoirse's leg knocks into mine.

"But I have more important shit to be dealing with than trying to make a move on the Irish. As soon as you started on our territory, I had some of my own people look into why you would make a move against me. Imagine my surprise when I was able to trace my own men to the cause." Anastasia snaps her fingers, and the second guard behind her pulls out a phone and taps the screen. Ten seconds later, a third bulky Russian enters the bar dragging a badly beaten Harry with him.

I glance at Cian who subtly lifts one brow. Cian had given Harry a good once-over, but it wasn't as bad as this.

Harry coughs up blood and immediately gets a meaty fist to the face because of it. "I told you," the new guard spits. "Don't bleed on Hazel's floor."

Anastasia straightens up in her seat. "Listen to me, Cormac. I have a lot of respect for the Irish. The work your mother did was magnificent and the few times I met with Brenden, he was a gentleman. I was… saddened to hear of his passing. Yes, technically, Harry works for me. He's a low-level loan shark who's nothing more than a handful of numbers at the bottom of one of my columns. He works for a nothing family that works for another family that works for me. Do you understand? He's nothing."

Her voice is level and her words strong, but it does nothing to calm the heat simmering beneath my skin. I'm boiling alive on the inside as seeing Harry just reminds me of Evelyn dropping like a rock right in front of me.

"You expect me to believe you?" I bite out through clenched teeth.

"I'd say I don't care what you believe, but I don't have time for a war with you, so yes, I do expect that. Harry certainly doesn't have the smarts to make a play against your family, and the people he works for don't have the balls to talk back to me, never mind make a move against you. Isn't that right, Harry?"

Harry nods quickly, clutching at his bloodied shirt, and he looks at me with fear in his eyes. "It's true. I ain't never had orders about any Irish, sir. Evelyn was a nobody. She was just someone who sought me out because she needed money, and I obliged 'cause that's what I'm paid to do!"

"And the man who stabbed Evelyn?"

"I have no idea, I swear. I always work alone. I didn't know she was messed up in any gang shit, I swear. I never would have put her on the books if I knew she was Irish!"

I don't correct the assumption that Evelyn is Irish. Instead, I turn back to Anastasia. "You can say what you want, but I wouldn't ever expect truth from the mouth of a Russian."

"I'm not my father," Anastasia snaps, and it's the first time there's a hint of something human on her impassive face. "I have enough trouble stabilizing the internal mess my father left behind without tackling a family as big as yours. Especially one with the Italians on their side. It would be suicide for me, don't you see that? I'm trying to build something up, not crush what little I have my hands on."

I glance at Saoirse who gives me a small nod, a signal for me to keep listening.

"I don't expect you to be concerned with the inner turmoil of the Russians. We're hardly allies. But you must believe me that the death of your Captain is not on my hands, nor on my orders. I don't know if someone is trying to make me look bad or is counting on your taking me out in blind revenge, but Cormac. This was not me. I'm balancing a family on broken stilts right now. War? Conflict? I may as well swap my antidepressants for cyanide."

As much as I hate to admit it, Anastasia talks sense. What little I know of the Russian hierarchy is enough to make me believe her words, even if her intentions remain clouded. Indeed, this course of action, with proof, would result in my annihilating her and everyone associated with her. Instead, she's here talking to me.

The anger inside me stalls and flares in my chest, suffocating me for a few long seconds. It had nowhere to go, and I was so desperate for some kind of outlet, even at the risk of Hazel's wrath. Instead, I'm forced to squash it down once more, so I bite my tongue and sigh.

"Fuck."

"Fuck indeed," Anastasia murmurs, then she lifts one hand. "Hazel, I'll take that drink now."

As Hazel appears with some bourbon for Anastasia, I accept the beer Saoirse offered me earlier and pop the cap quickly. Three gulps later, I have a better grasp on my rage.

"I think we can help one another," Anastasia says. "I'm not here for a war, you understand? I am here because I can't afford one and someone is working really fucking hard to make it look like I'm out for Irish blood. I don't care who they are, but I want them dead. Even if it's someone in my own ranks."

I study her face, seeking out any hint of a lie, but she appears to be honest. And I'm growing inclined to believe her. Whoever is behind this has made it seem like Russian hands took my brother's life. If I'm wrong here, then his killer walks free.

"Alright," Saoirse says. "We have two people we're looking for. One we know is a sex worker, but other than her name, Peach, we know nothing else. The other person is a mystery."

Cian leans over Saoirse and hands Anastasia two photographs of the police sketches. Anastasia glances them over, then passes them to the guard she gave the paper to. "I don't recognize them, but I will have someone dig into it."

"That's all I ask," Saoirse replies.

We fall into a strained but amicable silence where drinks are shared and Anastasia's guards eventually take a seat. Cian remains standing, despite Saoirse's persuasion, and even Hazel swings by to make sure we're not secretly at each other's throats. Through it all, my mind drifts to Evelyn and the man who stabbed her. If I take Anastasia at her word that the Russians really aren't behind this, then who is the person who stabbed her? And how did they find her?

We drink until the early hours until one of Anastasia's guards gets a call. They pass the phone to Anastasia, and she listens intently for a few long minutes, then she hangs up and sets the phone aside.

"Well?" I prompt.

"I know this looks bad," she says tightly. "But Peach is one of ours. We're in contact with her pimp and in the process of tracking her down."

I'd let Harry slide as a coincidence, but Peach being on the Russian payroll as well makes Anastasia's defense crumble around her. Every muscle inside tightens like the snap of a belt, and I slam one hand down on the table.

"You've got to be kidding me."

"The man isn't known to us and will require some deeper research," she says, meeting my gaze. "This doesn't change what I said."

"Yes," I say, standing so abruptly that my chair clatters back. "It does. You better find that woman, Anastasia. And that man. Or I will stop at nothing until I have wiped you and all of your kind off the face of this fucking Earth."

20

EVELYN

"You're not serious!"

The words are barely out of my mouth when Cormac opens the car door and offers me his hand. As I reach for my small suitcase that sits at my feet, Dale is one step ahead of me and has already taken it out from the other side. I take Cormac's hands and let him guide me out of the car. The second I step onto the tarmac, my heart begins to flutter.

A few feet away sits a gorgeous black jet with gold ink swirled across the wings, making it look like some kind of golden butterfly. As the sun beats down from above, creating a slight shimmering hue across the tarmac, I tighten my grip on Cormac's hand. When Dale told me Cormac was taking me somewhere safe, I thought he meant a hotel.

"What?" Cormac asks innocently. "Never been on a jet before?"

I shove at him slightly as we walk toward the jet. "You know I haven't. I don't even have a passport!"

"Don't need one," Cormac replies. "We're not going international."

"Are we going somewhere that's within driving distance? Because this feels like a huge effort if we're just going to the other end of the city."

Cormac snorts softly, amused when we reach the bottom of the steps leading into the jet. "No, Evie. I promise we're not going to the other side of the city. So can you please get inside?"

My mouth twists as I debate the risk of climbing onto this jet with Cormac and his team—family? It can't be any more dangerous than the last few weeks and I'd be lying if I said I wasn't excited. A private jet suddenly makes all the drama worth it.

"Fine, but know that the environmentalist in me is protesting."

"Protest away." Cormac sweeps an arm to the side and steps back, allowing me to climb the stairs at my own pace. I remain slow, forever conscious of how even the simplest of movements can pull at the muscles of my abdomen and thus, my stitches. You never realize just how everything is connected until something hurts.

The pain fades the instant I step into the jet and the beauty takes my breath away. Large cream seats offer the highest level of comfort regardless of the length of flight. Each comes with its own table where glasses rest and are secured with rubber bands. The sparkling black curtains wink at me as I walk cautiously over the plush gold carpet. Dark wooden paneling runs parallel to my eyes as I walk, and I glimpse my suitcase disappearing behind one of the slats as Dale tucks it away.

"Wow," I breathe, turning to face Cormac. He's watching me intently. "This belongs to you?"

"Yup."

I shake my head. "I can't even fathom having this amount of money."

"This isn't even the expensive jet."

"How many do you have?"

Cormac lightly grasps my shoulders and slides my jacket from my shoulders. "Four."

"Four?" My eyes widen. "Care to donate to a girl in need?"

Cormac snorts softly, draping my jacket over one of the chairs then indicating for me to sit. "You want a private jet?"

"If I had the money, I'd definitely have four," I say, sinking down into one of the chairs. It's like resting my ass on a cloud and I sink into it until it feels like every inch of me is perfectly supported. "Y'know, it's a huge risk for me to get on a plane with someone I barely know."

"Is that a complaint I hear?" Cormac asks, taking the chair next to mine.

"Maybe," I say, closing my eyes in bliss. "I can be persuaded to just… roll with it."

"Rolling with it is good," Cormac replies. "Besides, isn't this more exciting? You have nothing to tie you down, so why not enjoy some reckless luxury?"

I crack open one eye and watch as Dale passes and sets a glass of scotch down on Cormac's table. He places sparkling water on mine and winks—it's bubbly, so drinking it from the fancy glass will give me the same experience without messing with my medication.

"I have stuff to tie me down." I crack open the seal on the water and pour it into the fancy champagne glass as the steps are retracted and the door closes with a soft hiss.

"Like what?" Cormac prompts.

"My mom. And my job."

"You lost your job." Cormac watches me steadily over the lip of his glass. "Hardly tying you down."

I pause with the glass halfway to my lips. "How do you know I lost my job?"

For the first time since we met, Cormac almost looks embarrassed. His eyes flicker and then the faintest hint of a smile crosses his lips. "I kept an eye on you."

"Clearly," I scoff. "Some people would call that stalking."

"Is that what you would call it?"

"I dunno." Even the water is the freshest, crispest water I've ever drunk in my life, and two sips become several gulps as if I've just stumbled in from the desert.

"I did tell you I was keeping an eye on you, so it shouldn't be a shock."

"Dale outside my apartment, you mean?"

"Among other things."

"Other?" I shift in my seat, drawing one leg up to my chest. "Did you bug my phone like in the movies?"

Cormac doesn't reply.

"Holy shit, you did!"

Again, that faint hint of a smile appears on his lips. I've never seen him smile. Even his laugh is like a bark of air rather than real softness. "I protect my assets."

"This is insane. I shouldn't be on the plane," I joke. "I need a new phone."

"You'll have to wait until we land."

During our conversation, somehow, the jet took off without my noticing. I turn to stare out the window and am greeted with fluffy white clouds, an infinite blue sky, and the city stretching out like a toy model. It's stunning and my stomach lurches faintly. Maybe I should have told him I've never actually flown before. It speaks to the luxury of the jet that the engines are so quiet and I never even felt us leave the tarmac.

"Holy shit," I breathe out in a whisper. "This can't be real."

"The plane? The view?"

"All of it," I say softly. "How is this my life?"

"Worth getting stabbed for?"

I turn back to Cormac and laugh. "How many times before you just give me the jet?"

The flight is smooth, and after I finish my water, I'm confident enough to get up and walk around. It's surreal to be moving about while being thousands of miles up in the sky. The rest of the jet is just as phenomenal as the front, and Dale shows me the entire drinks cabinet, a fridge stocked with food, and even an entertainment system with every game or movie I could possibly think of. Dale tells me he'll warn me before we land, and I find myself half-hoping that we will never do so.

This little bubble of luxury gives me the same high as spending obscenely on my credit cards with the bonus of knowing I don't have to pay anything at the end of it. After exploring, I return to my seat and find Cormac buried in his laptop. There's a strange pull of yearning in my chest as I stare at him, wanting him to look at me and give me attention. Unfortunately, he's completely drawn into whatever he's looking at so I boldly try a new tactic.

"Dale?"

"Yes Ma'am?"

"You make me feel so old saying that."

"It's only in respect, I promise."

"Can you make yourself scarce?"

Dale looks at me with confusion in his eyes, but when I waggle my brows, he seems to get the hint immediately. With a small smile and a nod, he stands. "I should check on the pilot."

"Good idea."

Cormac seems oblivious to the entire exchange and doesn't look up as Dale moves past us to the cockpit, then vanishes behind the security door.

Perfect.

I give it a few minutes just in case, by some terrible stroke of luck, there is an issue with the pilot, and then I stand and step across the aisle. In one move, I close Cormac's laptop and drop into his lap just as he looks up with a deep frown across his forehead.

"Evelyn."

"Ooh," I tease, pressing my fingertips against his chest. "No Evie this time?"

"I'm working."

"And you should be looking at me."

His eyes dart from my eyes down my body, then back up. "Are you telling me you desire my attention?"

"Do I need to spell it out for you?" I don't know if it's the wonders he worked yesterday with that devilish tongue of his or the excitement of the jet and the lavish air I'm surrounded with. Being in Cormac's lap makes me hot and I want to feel his hands all over me just like before.

"Maybe," Cormac replies. "I'm illiterate."

"Oh, really?" I chuckle softly, amused. "Well then." Adjusting myself in Cormac's lap until I'm straddling him, I lean forward and bring my lips to his ear while rolling my hips down against his crotch. "I want you to fuck me."

Cormac's hands land on my waist and grip. "You're still injured."

"And?" I lean back, rocking down slowly. "I know my limits."

"But I do not," he says, his voice growing husky. "You think you can give me a taste and expect me to stop?"

A hot thrill shoots through me and I bite my lower lip, continuing to roll my hips down. It doesn't take long until I feel his cock swelling beneath me.

"You think once you start fucking me, you won't stop?"

"I know I won't," he says, his palms flexing around my waist. "So be very careful about what you do next."

His warning doesn't pause my hips, and my pulse quickens as his eyes grow darker with every passing second until his pupils are so blown with desire that all color has vanished.

"I think," I say softly, drawing out the words, "you need to just sit there and let me do what I want."

"You think?" he asks.

"I do. Because I'm the one with the stitches, I'm in charge."

Cormac's hips twitch upward and a coy smile forms across my lips. He doesn't strike me as a man willing to give up control, but the prospect clearly excites him.

"And if I can't let you be in charge?"

I place both my hands on his shoulders and push him back against the chair. "Then I'll go back to my seat and finger myself instead."

Cormac's grip becomes like iron and a red flush sweeps up his throat. His Adam's apple bobs hard when he swallows, and I can see the debate raging behind his eyes. Then he nods.

"Fine. Your rules."

I kiss him hard, finally giving in to the heat rushing through my body with every rapid flutter of my heart. My core clenches and I grind my hips down, riding the thick ridge that's grown rapidly beneath me.

Never have I known a man to get turned on so quickly by me, not without the promise of a blow job, at least. A few seconds and Cormac hungers for me.

Back in the car, he told me he'd ruin me for anyone else and he's right. After something like this, how can anyone else compare?

His hands roam over my back, pulling me close and tugging at my shirt so he can slide his hands underneath. When his palms slide over my bare skin, I shiver and allow his tongue to slip into my mouth while my mind turns south. He keeps his touch to beneath my bandages, and I busy myself with undoing my jeans. Rising only to my knees, I deepen the kiss and keep him pinned there. Thankfully, he helps me out of my jeans with his strong hands as I clutch at his bulging arms, and I'm back in his lap within moments.

My world narrows to just Cormac. We kiss like each is the air the other desperately craves. His hands roam my body, and I tear open his shirt to expose his gloriously sexy chest. Soft curls of hair brush against my fingertips and a softer, needier moan escapes him when I roll my panty-clad hips down on his slacks.

I need him.

I need him now.

Cormac's teeth snag on my lower lip, and he cradles the back of my head with one hand while I unzip his pants, fight with the fabric, and draw his thick cock out for me. The crown glistens with pre-cum and my pussy clenches eagerly. Knowing he's already bursting for me and I've barely done anything is enough to send my mood sky high. I smile against his mouth and stroke his thick cock with one hand. Dampness soaks into my panties so when I next roll my hips down against his bare cock to tease him, Cormac's head thumps back against the seat.

"Holy shit," he gasps as I kiss his lower lip then nuzzle against his fuzzy chin. "You're killin' me."

"In a good way?" I tease, lifting myself up until we're face to face and pulling my panties to the side.

He cups my face with one hand and the other cradles my hip. "The best way."

That's what I want to hear as I line his cock up with my entrance and slowly let my body weight take me down. The first touch of his crown against my pussy makes us both whimper, then my mind runs blank as his impressive thickness slowly pries me open inch by glorious inch.

Both of Cormac's hands move to my waist, but he doesn't force me in any direction. He merely guides me while panting heavily. My lips part and my eyes roll back as he stretches me wider and wider, reaching deeper and deeper inside me. It's not the first time I've felt his cock, but I almost forgot just how delicious it is to feel him reach every single inch inside me.

By the time I'm fully seated, it feels like his cock reaches right under my ribs, and I press one hand over my abdomen, panting. "Holy shit," I gasp weakly. "I feel so full."

"Your insides won't be the same after," Cormac says breathlessly, and I laugh then cup his face.

The moment we kiss, I start to move. Rising up onto my knees, the movement pulls a long, low moan from the depths of my soul as his length strokes my walls and caresses my G-spot, sending a flurry of pleasure shooting through me like sparks. They ignite along my skin and by the time I rock back down onto his cock, my skin is on fire. I need to feel him everywhere, need to feel his cock as deep as it can reach, and I need Cormac imprinted on my body.

He holds me as I begin a slow rhythm that gradually picks up as my body relaxes and eases around his cock. Each stroke and slide becomes easier until I'm openly panting and moaning, riding him for all I'm worth. My hands sink into his hair as he kisses my chest and throat, lavishing me with attention while keeping his hands around my waist to support me. Pleasure consumes me, clouding my thoughts and my senses. All that matters is using Cormac to chase my orgasm. Faster and faster, I fuck myself down onto him, using him for my pleasure until Cormac drops one hand between us and teases my clit.

Pleasure jolts through me like a bullet and I cry out, tightening around his cock. I come with a scream of delight, pulling on his hair as I ride him rapidly to catch every delicious, sweet drop of that powerful orgasm. Cormac comes a moment later, grunting out his pleasure and sinking his teeth into the meat of my shoulder. We remain like that for a few moments, suspended in the onslaught of pleasure. Once it passes, I collapse into his arms, panting heavily, and Cormac presses one hand over my bandages.

"You're okay?" he asks, his voice husky.

I nod against his chest, smiling, and wipe a few beads of sweat from my upper lip. "I'm amazing. Promise."

It's sweet that even post-orgasm, his thoughts immediately turn to making sure I'm okay, and I hold onto that for the rest of the flight after Cormac helps me clean up. I end up falling asleep curled up in my chair and wake in the late evening to a warm setting sun streaming through the windows and a blanket over my shoulders. I blink groggily and yawn, then sit up to see Cormac rising from his seat.

"We're here," he says and he offers me his hand.

"Where is here?" I ask, taking his hand and rubbing the sleep from my eyes.

Cormac guides me through the jet and then ushers me in front of him when we reach the door. I squint in the sunlight and walk out onto the first step, then pause.

Stretching out for miles around is more greenery than I've ever seen in my life. There are miles of forest surrounding countless fields of crops and animals, and in the distance sits a gigantic ranch house that glows amber in the setting sun.

I breathe in, and the sharp sting of cool, clean air bites at my lungs. An array of scents follows, and I can barely decipher them while trying to take in every beautiful sight before me.

"Where are we?" I ask when Cormac's warm hand presses against my lower back.

"Home."

21

CORMAC

There's a beautiful sense of wonder written all over Evelyn's face as she descends the jet and takes in the beauty of the Gifford Family Ranch. This Ranch has been in our family for generations, an offset from the farms back in Ireland, and it's the one place in the world where I know it's safe to be me.

Being back here after so long comes with a few unexpected weights. I need to see Ma, but I'm not ready to face her. The pain that I'm sure to see in her eyes will make it all the harder to keep a lid on my own.

So instead, I choose to focus on Evelyn. She holds my hand tightly as we walk from the airfield and she declines the offer to take a cart and drive to the Ranch house. Instead, she wants to walk in the crisp air and take in everything around her, so I stay by her side. We walk past fields of freshly planted crops, although I can't tell her what they are as it's been too long since I was part of the farming side of things. The next few fields have some cows and horses that make Evelyn's eyes go so wide it's a wonder they don't pop out of her head, and she gets the giggles when a cow comes charging down the field to greet us at the fence.

Her shyness in reaching out to pet the animal's muzzle is just as cute as her delight at finally reaching to scratch the cow's nose. Today is a lot of firsts for her. By the time we reach the ranch house, the sun has turned the entire world a warm, burnt orange and Dale has already delivered our suitcases up to the rooms. My mother is nowhere in sight, though, so as much as I'd like to collapse into bed, I know I have to greet her.

Evelyn stays by my side, staring in awe all around her as we head to the nearest barn. This late in the evening, there's only one place I can think Ma will be and her telltale sharp tones dart through the air as soon as I haul open the door.

"Wesker! Get off your sister! Don't think I won't exclude you to the other coop, you little rat!"

A flurry of squawks answers her, followed by the sound of scattered seed hitting the ground. Suddenly, my palm is clammy and my calm heart turns up a notch. We cross the straw-covered floor, and Evelyn's hand tightens in mine, then we turn past the last wall and my mother comes into view.

She's dressed in jeans and a checkered shirt, with her crimson hair scooped into a bundle atop her head. Numerous chickens dart about at her feet and she occasionally uses her boot to push back some of the more rowdy girls. A basket sits under one arm, and she gathers a handful of seed from it, then scatters it down to the noisy chickens.

"Greedy fuckers, the lot of ye'," she grumbles.

"Hey, Ma."

She freezes, then turns so abruptly that a wave of seed is ejected from the basket. The chickens go crazy for the extra food while my mother stares at me with open shock on her face. She blinks, and her eyes shine.

"Oh, Cormac," she snaps. "You're so late I thought you weren't coming!"

"Sorry, Ma."

She dumps the basket aside, then charges toward me at an impressive speed for someone so short. As soon as she reaches me, she grabs me by the collar and drags me down into a hug so tight it's a wonder I'm able to breathe. "Come here, you big lug," she mutters, and emotion clogs her voice. "About time you came home."

"Sorry it took me so long," I reply. "You know how it is." For a second, I'm twelve years old again, burying in my mother's hair after a rough day at school or hiding in her arms after a nightmare. No matter how old I get or how dark the world is, she remains a pillar in my life. I circle my arms around her and cuddle her tightly, and for a long moment there's nothing but the stuffed clucks of fat hens and the occasional creak of the barn.

"Alright, let me look at you." She pushes me back and brushes her hands down my shirt, looking me over with a sharp eye. "You eating right? Drinking enough?"

"Aye, Ma."

"Don't Aye me if you're bullshittin'."

"I ain't."

"Good." Satisfied, she turns to Evelyn who resembles a deer in headlights. "And who is this?"

"Ma, this is Evelyn. Evie, this is my Ma, Clodagh."

"It's nice to meet you, Mrs. Clodagh," Evelyn says in her politest voice. She holds out her hand to shake, and then her eyebrows fly up to her hairline when Ma swats her hand away and pulls her in for a hug.

"We don't do that shite here," she says with a hearty chuckle. "An' call me Ma. It's lovely to meet you! Thought I'd be dead and buried before Cormac brought a girl home."

The urge to correct her rises, but when Evelyn merely blushes and ducks her head, I choose not to. The circumstances are odd, to say the least, but considering Evelyn my girl, even for a little while, is nice.

"It's lovely to meet you too." Evelyn laughs softly, and her cheeks are crimson by the time the hug is over. She seems stunned at being greeted with such warmth, and I'm briefly reminded of her phone call with her own mother.

"Look at you. When was the last time you had a decent meal, hmm?" Ma asks, looking Evelyn over.

"She was stabbed," I remind Ma. "So be careful."

"I'm always careful," Ma snaps, nudging Evelyn with a wink. "Don't worry, chick, there's not a soul around here that hasn't been on the wrong end of a blade."

"Ain't that the truth." I snort, amused.

"Anyway…" Ma ducks and snatches up her dropped basket, rubbing her forehead as she watches the last of the spilled seed be consumed. "These damn birds. I better see extra eggs tomorrow!"

Basket in hand, she begins to lead the way out of the barn. "Cormac, Saoirse tells me you met with the Godmother."

"Aye."

"And?"

I grimace. "It's not looking good."

"It's not been looking good since…" She trails off, unable to say Brenden's name. Outside the barn, she breathes deeply and when she turns to me, her bright smile is back. "We're feasting tonight because we have a special guest, so make sure you wash that jet stink off you before you come to dinner. You too, dear."

With a wink at Evelyn, Ma turns and strides away to the ranch house with impressive speed.

"Wow," Evelyn breathes. "Your mom is amazing."

"Yes." I nod. "She is."

"I thought she was going to yell at me at first." Evelyn laughs awkwardly and presses the back of her hand to her flaming cheeks. "It was kind of scary."

"She's the scariest, nicest person you will ever meet," I reply. "She'd feed the enemy a good meal before killing them just so no one can say she's a bad hostess."

"Wow." Evelyn shakes her head in awe. "What about your dad?" She looks around as if expecting an Irishman to sprout from the ground and introduce himself. "Is he just as scary?"

"He was," I say quietly.

"Was?" Evelyn's head snaps to me, her eyes wide. "Oh, is he…? I'm so sorry."

"Nothing like that," I assure her, then I offer her my elbow. "He's not dead."

"Oh." Evelyn loops her hand through my arm. "So he's…"

"He's in Ireland," I say, ignoring the familiar twang of loss that rises at the thought of him. "We lost him a few years ago to Alzheimer's. It was so rapid, it was sort of hard to believe. We tried everything to soothe him, including sending him back to his homeland in the hope of easing his mind. It soothes him, but not in the way we hoped. I think we all thought as soon as he was among the Irish moors again, he would remember us and be cured. Instead, he's happy and lost."

"Oh, Cormac." Evelyn's voice is soft. "I'm so sorry. That's awful."

"It was tough but…" My jaw tightens and I pet her hand. "There's nothing we can do."

"I never imagined someone like you growing up in a place like this," she says quietly, changing the subject as we walk toward the house.

"What, not enough flannel?"

"No." Evelyn laughs. "This is just so... all this open air and the animals, the nature and everything. You seem like you're cut from city stone, that's all."

"Well, fertilizer is a great front for getting weapons across international waters," I tease, and Evelyn laughs loudly.

"I can't tell whether you're being serious or not."

"No one wants to dig through shit, that's all I'm saying," I reply, leaving her in the mystery of the truth.

Her laughter forces away the ache in my heart, so I focus on her happy, smiling face and briefly tighten my hand over hers. Despite everything, she remains light and it eases my heart.

"Enough of that, though. You've got a ham to carve."

"What?" Evelyn stops in her tracks. "In front of everyone?"

"Yep. House rules, I'm afraid. Guest carves. Come on, it won't be that bad."

22

EVELYN

Never have I seen a dinner table so full of food. It resembles an advert I'd see splashed across my television during Thanksgiving, surrounded by a happy and wholesome family. Cormac and his family seem to fit that idea to a T, and it's strange to see people so dangerous acting so homely.

If I didn't know what I knew, I'd assume they were just like every other ranch family sitting down to a hearty meal at the end of a long week. There's a roast ham at one end, and I eye it suspiciously as I take my seat next to Cormac. His mother, Clodagh, sits at the head of the table while Saoirse and Cian sit across from Cormac and me. Between us sit three kinds of potato, grilled veg, steamed veg, some chicken legs, a basket full of homemade bread, and several sauces and jams that fill the space. It's a far cry from the two-day-old Thai food I surely would be tucking into if my life were moving on its normal path.

"Come up here, dear," Clodagh says, waving her hand at me. "Guests carve. It's tradition!"

Cormac shoots me an I told you so glance and then sits back as I stand and approach the head of the table.

"Don't fuck it up," Cian teases.

"Shut up," Saoirse snaps, elbowing her twin. "Honestly, Evelyn, just cut a slice and then we can dig in."

"I've never carved anything before," I admit, unsure why such a thing makes me feel so shameful. It can't be a regular skill, can it?

"Don't you worry," Clodagh soothes me instantly, pressing a long fork into my hand. "I'll take you through it. Stab the ham just about here. It will give you a decent grip on the meat."

As I oblige, Cormac stands and begins filling the empty glasses with wine and juice.

"Now this knife is sharp," Clodagh warns. "So if you feel like you're going to slip, then stop cutting and adjust your grip."

"Although I've worked with sharper," Saoirse comments as she sips her wine.

"We're not carving bodies here," Cormac remarks. "Although you butchered that last Christmas turkey. I'm surprised anyone lets you near a blade."

"Oh, really?" Saoirse glares over her wine. "There's a reason they call me and not you when they want real information."

"And you're both shite at getting the real answers first try," Cormac replies, settling back in his seat. "Maybe you should both go back to training on birds."

"Scared I'll out carve you?" Cian's eyes flash.

"You can't even outrun me, little brother." Cormac barks out his laugh. "I ain't scared."

"Oh, really? You wanna race right now? I'll kick your ass all the way to the barn."

"Prepare to get shit on, little brother—"

"Sit down," Clodagh barks, placing her hand over the top of mine holding the knife. "This food isn't going to waste because you two want to piss up the creek, alright?"

Cian and Cormac share a good-natured glare, and relief pours through me as Clodagh helps me carve my first perfect slice of ham. It's not as difficult as I expected, but my next two slices without her help are definitely lacking. With a chuckle, she takes over and sends me back to my seat where Cormac grips my thigh under the table.

"Nicely done," he says in a low voice.

"Thanks," I murmur, and his praise sends a pulse of warmth through my chest.

Dinner is a wonderful affair. Plates are piled high with food, and there is only the occasional clash of spoons when two people want the next scoop of potato. Everything is cooked to perfection, and despite how heartily I eat, I keep going back for more. I've never tasted anything like this before, and it has to be because it's homemade. My mother's version of home-made was from freezer box to plate, and there was a distinct lack of love there, especially after my father passed. This table is like a whole other world and I am here for it.

Just as I swallow my final bite of corn and tell myself I can't eat another bite, Clodagh pulls out a cheesecake and cheers rise around the table. Everyone has room for dessert. As memories are shared and the twins reminisce about the one time they tried to make their own cheesecake but failed because their father was a terrible cook, something about Clodagh's being away for work caught my attention.

"I'm sorry," I say as I cut through the laughter. "Away for work, is that code for something?" Everyone else is so open about their life and work in the Mob, but the phrasing about Clodagh catches me off guard.

Cormac frowns slightly, then he nods quickly. "Sorry, force of habit around guests, I think," he says. "Ma was the Captain."

A crumb of cheesecake goes down the wrong way and I choke softly, quickly grasping at my glass of water. His mother was the Captain? Suddenly, my casualness around her feels very rude and I drown my embarrassment in several gulps of water.

"I'm so sorry," I gasp.

"Why?" Confusion washes over Clodagh's face.

"I just… I thought you just worked at the ranch and stuff," I explain quickly.

"I do." Clodagh nods. "I always did, technically. Ask anyone who ran into this family and my husband's name will leave their mouth before mine ever would. But you needn't fret. There's no special rules here about ex-Captains."

"Sorry," I whisper. Cormac takes my hand and squeezes.

"You're fine."

"That's amazing, though," I say once I'm over my surprise. I'd subconsciously viewed her as this homey ranch mother without a clue that she was just as powerful and as dangerous as Cormac. "I didn't know women could…"

"Lead?" Clodagh prompts. "It's not uncommon, but there can be pushback. The Russians, for example, have a woman in charge now, and you would think we are still in the fifties from how some of those generals acted." She tips her glass back and forth. "In a way, my husband was my mask. I noticed pretty quickly that people defaulted to him, so I used that. He turned up and showed his face with my orders in his ears. Some families were more understanding and I could deal with them directly, but when we started building the weapons business, I had to be more careful."

"Careful how?" I ask.

"Well, the Mexican Cartel and the Japanese Yakuza refused to deal with women. They are definitely a boys' club. But I needed them in the beginning. Securing deals with them was key in gaining the foothold we have today, but it wouldn't have happened if they knew they were dealing with me and not Conor. But it was a necessary sacrifice for the success of my family. It's different now, though." She drinks deeply and smiles. "These days, no one cares. The Italians, especially, are famous for their dangerous women. And my very own Saoirse has a reputation of her own."

Saoirse ducks her head, her cheeks pink. "I'd rather talk about Cormac dating the woman he kidnapped," she says, trying to throw the attention off her.

Cormac snorts and squeezes my hand. "Any complaints?"

"None," I reply, then I tilt my head. "Though… dating? Are we?"

Cormac rolls his eyes as his mother laughs.

"To think they say the Giffords have egos when my own daughter deflects a compliment so expertly." She chuckles. "Romance in this world is precious. I trust Cormac knows what he's doing."

"Kinda winging it, Ma," Cormac admits. "Like Da."

"Aye." She smiles warmly. "I'm proud of you. Who would have ever foreseen me raising four amazing…" She falters suddenly at her slip of the tongue, and suddenly, it's like the two empty chairs at the table have become large and loud. They suck up all the air and silence falls.

Cormac's hand tightens over mine.

The two empty chairs. Conor, his father, and Brenden.

Clodagh drains her glass and firmly sets it down. "I…" Her voice quavers. Cian and Saoirse exchange a glance. In all the happiness, Brenden's absence wasn't touched on, and it was surely intentional to try and keep everyone's spirits up. But grief comes in waves and there's suddenly no avoiding it.

"It's alright, Ma," Cormac says, half rising out of his chair as if to comfort her.

She waves her hand and touches her napkin to her mouth. When she blinks, her eyes are like glass. "For a moment, I forgot." She shakes her head. "Every day, I forget. Just for a moment, y'know? I'll be doing something or I'll see something, and I'll think to tell him and then I remember, and it's like being hurt all over again."

I look around the table. Everyone shares the same sadness and pain, and my heart aches for something to say or do that can ease that pain. But this is beyond me. I place my other hand over Cormac's in silent support.

"When the police cremate his body, I want him returned to Ireland." Clodagh stands suddenly. "It's where his ashes belong."

A soft murmur of agreement moves through everyone, then Clodagh quickly excuses herself. After a second, Cian and Saoirse follow. When Cormac stands, I expect him to do the same but instead, he pulls me up with him.

"There's something I want to show you."

We talk in silence away from the ranch house, cashing the fading sun toward one of the larger barns out the back of the ranch. As the air grows cold and the sky turns dark, I huddle into Cormac's arm, half for warmth and half to let him know I'm right here. The man is a locked box when it comes to anything outside of hunting Brenden's killer and protecting me. Any time I've been close to seeing what makes him tick, he's closed down quickly, and it's happened again at the dinner table. I can tell he's grieving, but he avoids it like I avoided my repayment letters.

"Where are we going?" I ask softly.

Cormac doesn't reply. He just keeps walking in large strides so I have to hurry to keep up with him, two steps for every one of his until we reach the barn and he hauls the door open. Slipping from my grasp, he strides inside, and I follow as the sharp scents of hay and manure tickle my nose. Inside, there's a farm hand who vanishes the moment they see Cormac, leaving the two of us alone.

Well, four of us if you count the horses.

There are numerous stalls in the barn, but only two of them currently hold horses. One is absolutely gigantic, with silky black hair and a long mane that disappears behind the stall door. It hangs in crimped waves, and the horse neighs sharply and starts to fuss in its stall as Cormac approaches.

He grabs a strap of the halter and pulls the horse's head down to his own. They bump foreheads, and it's the first time I've seen Cormac look small.

"This is Parsley," he says. "My horse."

"Wow," I breathe out. "She's stunning."

"She's a Percheron, a breed of draft horse. And that's her brother, Angus." The horse in the stall across is of a similar build but with a silver coat rather than black. "That's Brenden's horse. They're best friends."

"Oh."

"We raised them together. They were inseparable, just like us. Kinda made us feel better, I think, after Cian and Saoirse were born. Twins have a special bond and we wanted one too." He strokes Parsley's nose and she huffs happily, nudging repeatedly at his shoulder and nibbling along the fabric.

"They're both so beautiful," I say, and my chest tightens like a band. "You must miss him," I add softly.

Cormac grunts in his usual way, as if waving off my words, but something is different. His stance falters slightly, and his hands fall away from his horse. "You've no idea how much," he says, and his voice shatters like a fragile vase. "I think… I think it might kill me."

Never have I seen a larger man suddenly grow so small as grief consumes him. He sinks down to the straw-covered ground and sobs. They're loud and open, raw pain pouring forth like a river, and the tears come so swiftly that it sounds like he can't breathe. My heart breaks for him and I crash to my knees, joining him on the floor.

"Oh, Cormac," I say sadly. "I'm so sorry."

"I miss him." Cormac chokes. "I miss him so fucking much."

23

CORMAC

"You're laughing at me," Evelyn gasps breathlessly as she slides down from her third failed attempt to get into the saddle. "This is harder than it looks!" Her hair catches in the gentle breeze, lifting away from her face and making her wide smile even more prominent.

My heart squeezes.

"Yes, tell the experienced rider that getting on a horse is harder than it looks." I chuckle.

Evelyn pouts and crosses her arms over her chest. "I'm not built for this. I'm a woman who likes cars and maybe, at a stretch, bikes. Horses are a whole other deal." She casts a nervous look toward the gentle filly I chose for her first ride.

Marie is an old horse and usually the one we give to children when they're about to embark on their first grown-up trail ride, so I thought she would be perfect for a ride with Evelyn. It seems she's more awkward than I first realized, though, and things aren't going to plan.

Not that I'm concerned. After breaking down in Evelyn's arms in the barn yesterday, I've been trying to shake this foolish feeling that drapes over me like a shawl. A ride with Evelyn feels like the perfect cure. We deserve to be out in nature, exploring the ranch and spending time with her with a few treats I've gathered in the bag hanging from Parsley. If Evelyn can get onto the horse.

"Do you want to try again?" I ask as she readies herself for another attempt, but there's defeat clinging to her brows, and I'd rather not start this day off with disappointment. "Or ride with me?"

Evelyn's eyes light up, even as she chews slightly on her lower lip. "Your horse can take two of us?"

"My horse can take me," I point out. "You will barely be felt."

"Okay." She doesn't even try to hide her eagerness.

I laugh and offer her my hand, which she takes, then I lead her across the paddock to where Parsley stands, chewing lazily on the grass at her feet.

"You ready, Parsley?"

She lifts her head and snorts softly, pulling slightly at her reins. I keep one arm around Evelyn and then lift her up bridal style to set her right down on the saddle. She lands with a squeak and immediately clutches at Parsley's mane. I pull myself up behind her and scooch forward until I'm mainly on the saddle and Evelyn is in my lap, then I take the reins in one hand and keep one arm around her waist.

"Oh!" Evelyn squeals as I nudge Parsley into movement. "Don't let me fall!"

"You won't fall," I assure her, murmuring low in her ear. "I promise." I tighten my grip around her waist to show her that I have her, and the ride starts—after I call to Ma that Marie can go back to the stables.

The ride is everything I need it to be. Evelyn is tense at the start of the journey, so I ensure Parsley keeps a slow, steady pace through the ranch and toward the forest. As Evelyn relaxes against me and grows more comfortable on the horse, I pick up the pace until we're trotting comfortably along the trail toward the lake. The air is thick with the scents of pine, floral mixtures, and dirt warming in the early afternoon sun. Birds chirp, trees whisper and creak in the wind, and a few squirrels chitter over the branches above us. The stress of the city melts away, and suddenly, I'm a teenager again, just exploring with my horse. Nothing else matters. I keep Evelyn close to me, and she's mostly silent, except for a few gasps of awe and murmurs of how cute the other animals are.

When we reach the lake, she's much more vocal.

"Holy shit." she gasps as I slide from the horse and then help her down from the saddle. "This is beautiful!" Evelyn takes a few steps away and then winces, clutching at her thighs. "Oh, my God, ow."

Laughing, I unhitch my bag and then firmly secure Parsley to a nearby stake in the ground. "Sore?"

"So sore," she whines. "What the heck?"

"Welcome to horseback riding."

"Oh, my God." Evelyn waddles down the path toward the sandy beach that lines the beautiful, deep blue lake that stretches out as far as the eye can see.

There's a scattering of boats in the far distance, but we're secluded enough that I don't mind. Following her, I remove a picnic blanket from my bag and toss it down onto the sand.

"Sit and rest," I instruct, moving toward the water's edge. As Evelyn situates herself, I gather water for Parsley as well as some feed, then take it back to her so she can eat her fill while we relax. Parsley snuffles in gratitude, and I pet her nose, then kiss her. Moving back to Evelyn, some of the other items in the bag are the ingredients to a gorgeous picnic, and Evelyn's aching pain is quickly forgotten.

"You did all this for me?" she asks between bites of cracker and camembert.

"Life's about embracing the little things," I say, popping a tomato in my mouth. "Plus, you deserve it."

"Wow. Mr. Scary Killer Mafia Man has a soft, romantic heart involving horse riding and picnics. Whatever must your enemies think?" Evelyn teases, rolling her eyes slightly. "If I didn't know any better, I'd say there's two different people in that head of yours."

"It's not like that, Evie," I reply, catching the way she blushes slightly at the nickname. "The city makes us hard. You have to do what you have to do, and my mother's legacy is important. But I won't forget what I enjoy in life. Besides…" Brushing crumbs from my leg, I move closer to her on the blanket. "This is all for your benefit."

"Mine?" Evelyn lifts one brow. "What did I do?"

"You need rest, and there's nothing better than the air of real nature to get you back to a hundred percent."

"I'm already a hundred percent," Evelyn teases with a smirk, and she cups my face with one soft hand. "That private jet did wonders."

"Is that all it takes?" Closer and closer we get. "Some luxury and your batteries are recharged?"

"If I were at home right now, I'd be eating four-day-old corn out of a can and pretending it was popped." She groans. "Trust me, luxury is healing."

"What about this?" I close the last inch and kiss her gently. "Is this healing?"

Evelyn glances away in exaggerated thought and hums. "I don't know, I might need a bigger sample."

Another kiss and she winds an arm around my neck, drawing me in. I follow the movement, and each kiss gently pushes her down flat onto the blanket. "How about now?"

"Jury's still out," she murmurs against my lips. She runs her fingers through the shorter hairs at the nape of my neck, sending shivers down my spine, and when she moans, my heart skips a beat.

"Well, the jury can take all the time it needs. I'm not finished. You should look in the bag." I break away from kissing her lips and move down to the warm juncture of her neck. I lavish her pulse point in soft bites and gentle kisses, and Evelyn hums softly as she reaches for my nearly empty bag and rummages around for the last treat inside.

When she finds it, she gasps and pushes at my shoulder. "You didn't…"

I pull back and smirk. "Too intimidating for you?"

Evelyn's eyes narrow and she pulls out one of the toys I brought with us. It's a coral-blue clitoral stimulator. Holding the box up, she taps the edge. "Do I want to know where you got this?"

"You really should have looked deeper around the jet," I reply, kissing across her collarbone. "I have a whole collection."

"Wow." Evelyn laughs. "Are you a bit of a slut, Mr. Gifford?"

I pause my kissing and lift myself over her, bracing on one arm. "Why, are you a bit of a prude, Miss Morris?"

Evie's eyes twinkle up at me and she pops the tab on the box. "Not at all."

"Excellent."

We dissolve into deeper kisses this time after removing the toy from the box. My entire focus becomes Evie and everything else melts away. I let my mouth lead, mapping a path over her body and slowly removing her clothing, allowing me to kiss over her breasts, suckle on her nipples, and gently kiss the freshly healing scar beneath her ribs.

Each kiss draws a breathless noise of joy from Evie. Her hands fist in my hair, caress my jaw, and even vanish to clutch at the blanket as I make my way lower and lower. Her pants come off swiftly and her underwear joins the heap until she's a gorgeous, writhing, naked beauty in front of me. A blush creeps over her abdomen, sweeping her ribs in the moments I just admire her, and when our eyes meet, she smiles almost shyly.

"What?" Evie asks, and she shifts as if to cover herself up.

I catch her thighs in my hands and immediately spread her legs wide, pinning them lightly to the blanket so I can gaze down and admire her glistening pussy. "You're beautiful."

"Don't—" Her hands shoot to her face. "You're gonna make me explode."

"Why?" I ask softly. "Can't handle a compliment?"

"No..."

"Is it because I'm admiring you? That you're completely naked and I can hold you like this and see how wet your pussy is? Or is it that I've got you on display and I can feel that you're not even resisting me?"

Evelyn whimpers behind her hands, and her abdomen concaves slightly as she pants. Suddenly, her thighs tense as if she's trying to close her legs but she's not strong enough to break my hold.

"Lower your hands, Evie."

The blush on her body deepens and a burst of slick drips down from her pussy lips. She is turned on from this, and I haven't even done anything yet. She doesn't lower her hands, though, instead trying to shift on the blanket and roll over.

"Evie." I lower my voice and deepen my tone. "Lower your hands. Let me see your face."

There's a moment of silence with only the birdsong and lapping water at the lake for company. Then Evie lowers her hands to show her deep red blush.

"Good girl."

"Oh, God," Evie whines and she instantly hides her face. "Don't."

"Don't what? Do you not like it?"

"No, it's… I do. I don't know why, though."

"Evie. Hands."

She obeys again and drops them from her face.

"Not everything that makes us tick needs an explanation," I say softly, holding her gaze. "Sometimes, something clicks and it just… is."

"I've never had someone do this before," she whispers. "Just… look at me, I mean."

"Then they missed out on a work of art," I say. If she rolls her eyes, I miss it because I've left her waiting and wanting long enough. Leaning down, I release my grip on her thighs so I can settle between them and bury my face in her gorgeous pussy. The first contact of my tongue against her core makes her moan loudly and her thighs close quickly around my head. Her fingers bury in my hair, and I lose myself in my favorite activity, eating her out.

From her clit to her entrance, no inch of her goes untouched. I lick and suck for all I'm worth, scarcely coming up for air because she is my lifeline. Every slick fold of skin is lavished in love. I write my desire for her in patterns across her clit and then thrust my tongue deep inside her to taste her most intimate corners. Her moans and gasps are music to my ears. I give her free rein, letting her writhe and twist above me while I chase her toward her orgasm, and when she comes with a scream, pride swells in my chest.

But I'm not finished.

While she's still in the throes of her orgasm, twitching and gasping through the wave of pleasure, I take the toy and slick it with saliva and her juices. Then I slide the stimulating mouth over her clit and turn the toy on as I pin her left thigh with one hand and her right with a gentle press of my knee.

Evie screams, her eyes flying wide open, and she reaches for me but can't quite make contact.

"Holy fucking shit!" Arching off the blanket, her body makes a beautiful bow shape as she twists and writhes against the sudden rapid onslaught of pleasure. Her stiff nipples could cut glass from how they stand out, and I can't resist leaning down to take one in my mouth and bite.

"Cormac!" She moans my name like a prayer while her hips jolt and rock, trying to escape the toy, but I make sure it doesn't move. Through pure clitoral stimulation, I get the privilege of watching her build up and then explode from a second rapid orgasm. The full-body blush seems to ripple over her skin like crimson waves, and she comes so hard that her eyes roll back and her body is rigid for the better part of fifteen seconds.

By the time she comes down, she's panting harshly, and I ease the toy away. Then I lean down and drag my tongue over her swollen clit. She whimpers and moans, then sighs blissfully.

"Wow," Evie murmurs. As I set the toy aside, I kiss my way lazily back up her body but pause at the scar. It's so fresh that one wrong touch and it could re-open, and such a sudden thought makes my chest ache.

"I promise," I say, kissing her ribs. "Nothing else will hurt you, understand?"

Evie cups my face as I slide up her body, and she kisses me breathlessly. "I believe you."

"I swear it."

"But you…" She wets her lips, and her eyes dart back and forth between mine. "Do you see a future here?" Her voice is wispy. "Or is this just a bit of fun for you?"

I kiss her deeply, sliding my tongue into her mouth and consuming her until the need for air forces us apart. "I don't have fun," I say simply. "Look at what you've witnessed with me. Have I ever half-assed anything? When I commit, I commit."

She smiles so widely that her cheeks dimple, and she moans softly, closing her eyes. I move to rest next to her, cuddling her close, and when she opens her eyes again, I see a cheeky twinkle in them.

"You brought other toys, right?"

"Mmhmm."

"Any you can leave in while we ride back?"

24

EVELYN

It was a flirty, sexy suggestion at the time. Let Cormac slide the other toy, a purple vibrator, inside me and leave it there for the ride back to the ranch. In my mind, nothing could go wrong. Being held in his arms, feeling his muscles at my back while being stuffed and teased after two mind-blowing orgasms, and then we could fall into bed together, and all that build-up would make for some incredible sex.

It was a good plan.

Until we made it back to the ranch and others had a different idea. By the time I slid from the horse, I was sweating and horny after being on the edge of another orgasm for so long. The vibrations weren't enough to get me over the edge and I was trying to hold off so that Cormac could make me come again, but two steps toward the ranch house and his mother appeared with requests for us to wash down the horses, feed the ones in the stables, and then go and feed the chickens. Cormac had the most devious smile on his face when he agreed, and none of my desperate looks were enough to sway him.

Two hours.

It took two hours to wash down the horses, feed them, set up hay for the night, make sure they had clean water, clean the tack, and then head over to clean out the coop and feed the chicken. Having a toy buzzing away inside me, teasing all the right nerves with each step, was torture, and I was very nearly at my wit's end by the time we wrapped up and finally headed back toward the house.

Until Cian strolled out with a fishing rod in hand and a desire for Cormac to join him in catching tonight's dinner. If he'd agreed, I might have exploded on the spot. Cormac stopped and talked to him for a while but eventually declined the invitation and led me inside. Each step toward our bedroom was torture. I barely had the strength to keep the toy inside me anymore, but somehow, we made it and the moment we did, Cormac began laughing.

"Oh, shit," He chuckles, running one hand through his hair. "I thought you were going to pass out in the barn."

"Oh, my God," I chant, pulling my clothes off my too-hot body. "I can't breathe. I feel like I'm on fire everywhere!"

Cormac continues to chuckle, watching me with dark eyes. "Still turned on?"

I moan softly when I lean over to drop my pants and kick them away from my sweaty legs. "You have no idea!" Just as I reach for my panties, eager to remove the toy, Cormac suddenly catches my wrist and prevents me.

"I don't think I'm over this yet."

"Huh?" I whine desperately. Heat blooms across my shoulders and the fire inside my core flares hotter. "Please. You've no idea what this is like! I've had this inside me for hours now and I'm pretty sure one touch and I'll explode."

"I like seeing you desperate," Cormac replies. "You get this antsy look in your eye like you're about to do something reckless, and I like that."

I arch a brow and try to pull my hand away, but he keeps me in place. It sends a thrill through me, and my pussy clenches around the buzzing toy. "Please," I gasp. "I can't stand it much longer."

"Maybe," Cormac says, spinning me in place and grasping my other wrist. He pins them together at the small of my back with just one of his hands. His other seeks out the remote in his pants and with a click of a button, the toy inside me suddenly ramps up in speed and force.

"Oh, fuck!" My legs give out, and just as I sink to the ground, Cormac drops the remote and slides his hand between my legs to keep me upright and the toy buried deep inside me.

"Beg me," Cormac whispers in my ear. There's such power in his voice despite his speaking so low, and a curl of desire throbs through my chest.

"Please let me come," I whimper as tears of overstimulation flood my eyes. "Please, please, please. It's been so long and I can't… I can't. I feel like I need to rub against everything like some kind of cat or something, please!" As I beg, my hips roll against his hand and there's a delicious moment when my clit rubs against the heel of his palm. That stronger, more focused burst of pleasure is nearly enough to send me over the edge but Cormac catches on to what I'm doing and immediately withdraws his hand.

In one sweeping move, he tosses me onto the bed and then he's over me, pinning my wrists to the bed and locking his thighs in against my knees so my legs are spread but have nothing to grind against.

"Look at you," he grows softly. "Your body's all flushed, your panties are soaked, your nipples are so fucking hard…" He leans down, catching my left breast in his mouth. I arch into the heat of his tongue, whimpering as he sucks hard and pleasure pulls across my core, but once again, he backs away just in time.

"Please, I've been good," I gasp. "I really want to come, please. Please just let me, just one more time, please!"

"You're so close to saying the right thing," Cormac murmurs, tightening his grip on my wrists. "So close. Try again, sweetheart."

Something about that soft pet name makes my heart ache in a different way, and if I wasn't so strung out, I'd try to focus on why. Instead, all I can think about is Cormac. His deep voice and how it vibrates through me, the strength he has to pin me down with such care, the thickness of his thighs keeping me spread and the darkness of his gaze as he looks me over.

"Please," I beg, racking my brain for what I need to say that I missed. "Please let me come. I did everything you asked, and I helped with everything, and I'm so turned on. Please, you've been so good to me. Just one last time, please, please, Cormac. I'll suck your dick dry, I'll let you fuck me as hard as you want, and I—"

Cormac smiles, and suddenly, it clicks what I'm saying wrong.

"Please!" I gasp louder. "Fuck me! I want to come on your cock, not some plastic toy. Please fuck me like you own me. Make me see stars, please, Cormac. Please, I'll give you everything, just please fuck me with that massive—"

I can't speak anymore. He removes the toy and thrusts inside me with such efficiency that it's a blur, and I forget everything—how to speak, how to breathe, how to move. All that matters is the delicious, satisfying stretch of Cormac's hot cock sliding so deep inside me that I'm certain he's about to pry me apart.

"Good girl," Cormac growls. "I knew you'd get there."

"Oh, my God," I gasp, my voice raw. "I—"

Cormac thrusts once, and I come with a noiseless cry. My entire body locks up and my pussy clams around his length like it never wants him to leave. Pulse after pulse of heat shoots through my core and the lava in my veins reaches boiling point as an array of sensations explodes like fireworks across my skin.

And Cormac doesn't stop. He places his hands on my thighs, forcing my legs apart, and fucks me with his gaze down at where he's sliding rapidly into me. There's something so dirty about knowing he's watching his cock slide into my pussy that turns me on more than I can understand. He's definitely unlocked something inside me that I never knew was there.

"Kiss me," I beg as he fucks the very air out of my lungs. "Please!"

Cormac doesn't hesitate. He kisses me so hard that his beard scrapes my skin, and I'm obsessed with the feeling. If I could, I'd wind my legs around his waist, but I'm utterly boneless, and he fucks into me with such power and speed that everything is a blur.

"Fucking hell, you're so fucking hot," Cormac grunts. "So fucking wet."

"Just for you," I gasp against his lips. "Only you!"

He kisses me hard, a clash of lips and teeth as his hips pound into me, and in the rippling waves of my last orgasm, there rises another. Somehow, Cormac manages to find it inside the depths of my exhausted soul and it sweeps up so quickly that I have no chance to say anything about it.

I come for the fourth time as Cormac finally buries deep inside me and floods my core with his own orgasm, grinding against me like he's trying to lock us together for eternity.

"Mine," Cormac growls against my lips as he kisses me deeply, cuddling me in his thick arms.

Absolutely. Never in my life have I been more cared for or made to feel more desired than this.

I've found my future.

25

CORMAC

"Evie?" Moving into the kitchen, I expect to see her up to her elbows in soap subs helping wash up from the gorgeous lunch my mother prepared for us, but she's gone. My mother is by herself buffing dry a casserole dish, and she flashes me a smile when she sees me.

"I sent her out to feed the chickens," Ma says. "They've been oddly enamored with her since she arrived, and I'd rather not get pecked by their disappointment."

"Oh." I snort softly. These past few days have been close to domestic bliss. Cian and Saoirse returned to the city to resume work, but I remained here with Evie as the mountain air seemed to be doing wonders for her recovery. We've eaten well, drunk well, and Evie has picked up a thing or two about life on a ranch.

Not horseback riding, though. That still escapes her.

"Is it too early for me to pry into what your plans are there?" Ma asks, setting the dish aside.

"My plans?"

"With that girl." She tosses the tea towel at me with silent instructions to take over the drying.

"I don't have plans."

"You always have plans."

"Not this time."

"Cormac Aaron Gifford, you'd better not be stringing that girl along for some entertainment!"

The use of my full name makes sweat prickle across my shoulders as I quickly dry some glasses. "That's not it, Ma."

"It better not be."

"I just mean… I don't have a plan because she's unexpected. She was a witness and then she was just suddenly…" Words fail me, and I resort to a silent shrug until Ma pokes me hard in the arm. "I couldn't stop thinking about her, and then I wanted to help her, and now she's here."

"Good heavens," she murmurs. "To think our future rests with a man as dim as you."

"What?" I move on to the cutlery.

"A woman like that doesn't just drift. Look at the situation you are in. You kidnapped her and yet she has no problem being here with you, letting you take care of her."

"So you think she's relying on my feeling guilty about how I treated her?"

"You are my pride and joy," Ma says wistfully. "Where did I go wrong?"

"What?"

"She's not relying on guilt, you big lump. She likes you. And if you're not careful, you'll be dumb enough to let something like that slip right through your fingers."

She likes me.

Evie likes me.

Given her words at the lakeside a few days ago, the signs are there, but I'd presumed she was simply talking like that because I made her feel so good. How I feel about her is complicated but incredibly strong. In some odd way, she makes me feel safe. Like I can be myself and she will accept me for all of it. The thought of her leaving my side hasn't crossed my mind because it's not something I want to allow, but is she really choosing to stay because she has true feelings for me?

My thoughts are derailed by my phone once again bringing me right back down to reality. Abandoning the tea towel, I answer Cian's call and move into the lounge.

"Hey, little brother. You're calling with good news, right?"

"You can view it that way," Cian replies. "We've found her."

"Who?"

"The mystery woman from the sketch. Anastasia wasn't kidding when she said she wouldn't rest until that woman was found. I hear she went all the way down to the streets and spoke to her escorts in person until she found her."

"Shit. You think she did that because she's determined to prove her innocence?"

"Maybe. Saoirse says it's a woman thing and we would never understand." Cian snorts, then he yelps. "Ow! Okay, okay, I'm sorry! Saoirse also says it's important that we understand that women talk to women because men are scary shits."

"It's fucking true," Saoirse murmurs faintly in the background. "You catch more flies with honey than shit."

"I respect Anastasia for doing the leg work herself." It definitely appears like Anastasia is doing everything she can to avoid further conflict with me. In an ideal world, such actions are perfect, but if she's acting like this from a true place of innocence, then I'm back to square one with Brenden's murder.

"Any news on the cops? Have they released Brenden's body yet?"

"No." Cian sighs, and there's a sharp edge in his voice. "From what I can tell, they're refusing to until one of us collects."

"So what's the problem?"

"Soon as anyone they want walks through those doors, there'll be cuffs on our wrists before you can say backgammon."

"So send someone else."

"Cormac, they won't take anyone else. Trust me. The only way they're releasing that body is if Brenden's killer walks through the doors and hands themselves over with video evidence of the crime."

"Fucking bullshit." I rub at my eyes until I see stars. "Alright, see what you can dig up on that cop. I don't care how far back we need to go, but I want something on her, understand?"

"On it."

"When can I speak to the woman?"

"Anastasia says she's yours as soon as you land."

* * *

Evie sits across from me with her legs crossed, tapping her foot in the air in time to the music playing through her earphones. She'd been very amicable about our need to return to the city, but a lump of sadness formed as I watched her pack up the few belongings my mother had gifted her during her stay. She'd been recovering so well at the ranch, and now we have to return to the city where nothing but darkness lurks.

My mother's words swim in my mind as we fly, but I can't bring myself to act on them. In the sun-warmed coziness of the ranch, romance was easy. In a blink, I could envision a life with Evie, and telling her the truth of my feelings was the sweetest thought in my mind.

Not now.

Being back in the city brings the walls back up. A thousand eyes are back on me, Brenden's killer still walks free, and I'm one wrong decision away from war. I can't afford to rest in my feelings. The only thing I know for sure is that I want Evie to stay with me.

That remains a single goal.

"You look pensive." Evie speaks up softly, removing one of her earbuds. "Are you nervous about going back to the city?"

I roll my eyes and push slightly back into the seat, briefly casting my attention to the passing sky. We'll be landing soon, and I need to make sure the mask is back in place. "I don't get nervous."

"Sure you don't." Evie rolls her eyes and nudges my leg with her foot. "You're something. You're acting weird."

"No, I'm not."

There's a flash of uncertainty in Evie's eyes and she straightens up in her seat. "Yes. You are. It's like you're…" She trails off and tilts her head.

"Like I'm what?"

"I don't know." Evie looks away. "You just seemed softer at the ranch, that's all. You put that suit back on and you're a different person."

I self-consciously adjust my tie. "I'm me. I'm always me."

"Sure." Her tone stiffens. "So what, the ranch was just some dream bubble? Now that we're going back to the city, you're back to being Mr. Ice?"

"Evie, I'm not Mr. Ice. But things in the city are different. You know that."

"Yeah, I guess." She sighs deeply. "I wish we could have stayed."

"Brenden's killer would have loved that," I mutter, not missing the flash of hurt in Evelyn's eyes. I know that's not what she meant, not really, but I don't have time to soothe her as the pilot announces our descent into the city. I'll have to make it up to her later.

As we land, the air around me grows thin. This woman Anastasia has found is the only lead I have. For too long, I've been chasing ghosts in this damn city trying to track a murderer, and she is the first concrete lead I have. I can't fuck this up.

Unfortunately, Evie will have to wait.

We land smoothly, and I exit the plane first to find several cars waiting with my men. I approach one car, then glance back to see what's taking Evelyn so long. As she descends the steps, her brow pinches in worry as she stares down at her phone. When she reaches the bottom, she answers a call, and I'm unable to figure out what she's saying as she lingers near the steps.

My fingertips buzz. I don't have time for this.

I'm so close to answers, so close, and each second I'm forced to wait makes my pulse quicken until it's a furious drumbeat in my ears.

Finally, Evie ends the call and hurries up to me.

"I have to go."

"What?" No.

"I need to visit my mother. Something's happened. She wasn't very clear, but she needs my help."

I think back to the last time Evie spoke to her mom and the conversation about moving furniture. If that's her mother's idea of an emergency, then I don't have much belief that this is serious. But if it will split Evie's focus then it's likely useful for us to deal with this first.

"Fine." I sigh, opening the door for her. "We'll swing by your mother's first."

"You don't need to come with me," Evie says, hesitating. "Don't you need to follow up with your siblings about that woman?"

"I do," I say. "But I need you there too. You're the one who's seen her before, and I don't want you worrying about your mother while we're interrogating this woman."

"But…" Evie squints at me, and I can't decide whether she's surprised or relieved to hear that I am concerned for her. "I'm quite capable of seeing my mother by myself, and you have the drawing. You don't really need me."

I'd suspect Evie is trying to slip away but I understand she's trying to remove herself from the situation after I snapped at her on the jet. "Either we go together or not at all. So where are we going first?"

She tilts her head to the side and a silent debate battles behind her eyes, then she lowers her shoulders.

"Alright. Let's see that woman first. I don't want you to wait any longer."

26

EVELYN

"**A**nswer me!" Cormac slams his hands down on the table, causing the chain connecting the woman's handcuffs to the table to jump at the force. She flinches but glares at Cormac through tear-soaked eyelashes

"No," she replies through gritted teeth. "I'm not scared of you."

"You should be, Holly," Cormac mutters. "I'm the only thing standing between you and an entire army of men wanting revenge on the one responsible for killing Brenden."

"You think I'm the one that killed him?" Holly scoffs sharply, her voice thick from the tears she's cried since she was snatched. "You're so fucking stupid."

I nearly step forward, but Cian's hand lands on my elbow, holding me back. It's tough to watch. Cormac's angry and it oozes from him like some kind of smoke, somehow filling the room we're all standing in. Holly's upset, and my heart goes out to her. I've faced an angry Cormac, and it's not easy, although Holly is handling it a lot better than I am. That piques my interest.

How many men like this has she faced in her line of work that makes Cormac look like just another bulldozer? Part of me can barely stomach to watch, but I feel like I need to. Holly holds answers that could set us all free—release Cormac from his grief, release his siblings from their anger, and me from this constant fear about who is coming for me next. I want to stop seeing a corpse each time I close my eyes.

"Do you need me to say it in a different fucking language?" Holly snaps, drawing me from my distracted thoughts. "I have nothing to say to you, and your big ogre act isn't doing anything, so if you're just going to kill me, then get it over with! Maybe I'll have a nice conversation with Brenden when I get to the other side. How the fuck are you two even related?"

"You fucking bitch—"

"What are you gonna do?" Holly taunts. "Hit me?"

Cian suddenly darts forward, reading something I miss about Cormac's stance. Within a second, he's next to his brother and dragging him away from the table.

"Walk it off," Cian orders in a low voice. "Take a fucking breath, Cormac." He drags him out of the main room and into the warehouse office behind us.

I glimpse Cormac's face, which is twisted with rage and pain. Such a look turns my blood to ice, and I understand it. He's so close to discovering the truth, but Holly taunts him instead of helping him. And I can't blame her, given the situation. Given her line of work, it's no surprise she gets defensive when faced with aggression, even aggression as understandable as Cormac's.

Holly slumps back in her seat and sniffles, tilting her head back to let stray tears leak down her face. Her fingers flex in their cuffs, tapping against one another.

Suddenly, I'm walking forward before I can stop myself. When I reach her, I pick up the bottle of water from the table and unscrew it, then offer it to her. She glares at me.

"What are you, the good cop?"

"Not exactly," I reply. "You've been crying since you got here and I know how much that fucks with your head. So have a drink. You want a smoke?"

Holly's fingers suddenly stop tapping. "You got one?"

I glance over my shoulder to the nearest guard, who approaches me with an uncertain look. He digs out a packet of cigarettes from his pocket and hands them to me, along with a lighter. I flash Holly the brand. "Good enough?"

"Honey, right now I'd take a stick if you had it. Could you do the honors?" She lifts her hands in their restraints. "Little tied up."

"Can we take the cuffs off?" I ask the same guard, who shakes his head. "Why not? You really think she can take all of you on and escape?"

A sheepish look washes over the guard's face, and he looks at one of his companions, who shrugs. Cormac and Cian are still in the other room, so I still have time.

"Exactly," I sigh, removing a cigarette from the pack. "So take them off."

The guard finally complies, and Holly hisses at him, sucking on her teeth while massaging her wrists. I hand her the cigarette, and she sets it between her lips, then gazes up at me from beneath her clumped lashes while I light it for her.

"You're not one of them," she says, taking a slow drag. Her eyes close briefly in bliss. "Are you?"

"Not exactly," I reply, taking the seat across from her. "Not so long ago, I was on your side of the table."

"Same accusation?"

"Not exactly. I found Brenden's body, so they did suspect me for a while."

A strange look moves over Holly's face, and she tries to hide it by drinking the water. It's the same look Clodagh had on her face when looking at the empty chairs at her table.

Pain.

"That must have sucked," Holly says, taking another long drag. "I've seen some fucked up shit, but never a dead body."

"It's left a mark," I murmur. "I saw a lot of shit working there, but that's top of the list."

"I can imagine."

"Cormac isn't going to hurt you."

"Let me guess, you won't let him?" Her eyes flash.

"I won't. But also, he won't. He's not like that."

"And how do you know?"

I shrug. "I just do." It's a gamble because, in truth, I don't fully know what Cormac is capable of. I've seen him pulverize men, but I don't think he'd do the same to a woman. In fact, I know he wouldn't. A man raised by Clodagh isn't that stupid.

"You have a lot of faith in a man who accused you of murder."

"He saved my life," I reply. "So I can forgive him for that."

She looks me over, dragging in slow puffs, then she flicks the cigarette off to the side. "I remember seeing you around the motel. Was the boss really as sleazy as he looked?"

I nod with a snort. "Honestly, I think he wanted me to offer sex with each free clean. Creepy fucker."

"I got that vibe." She smokes slowly. "He adds a different kind of tax every fucking time I'm there, but it's the closest place to my route that doesn't ask questions." Holly shakes her head and rubs at her nose. "What a mess."

For a moment, her walls shift and I see her, really see her. The glimpse of upset that leaked through earlier is suddenly more prominent and I recognize a deeper sadness in her eyes. A sadness that also lingers in Cormac's eyes.

"I know you didn't kill Brenden," I say.

Holly freezes. "Maybe I did."

"No." I speak softly. "You didn't. You cared about him."

Footsteps shuffle behind me and Holly glances away, her eyes hard at presumably Cormac behind me, but I keep my attention on her.

"Holly." I draw her back to me. "He was your friend, wasn't he? You two were seen together a few times, and I know in your line of work, that could mean anything, but you're sad. I can see that. You're really sad that Brenden is gone."

Holly takes a much longer drag on her cigarette, and the amber flares in her eyes. Then she blows out the smoke and sighs deeply. "Yeah," she says shortly. "He was a good guy."

There's more to it, but I force myself to approach it carefully. "He was, from what I've heard. He had a good heart. Worked to make sure everyone was taken care of. Cormac's trying to do the same thing, but it's hard knowing the killer is out there. We share a common goal there, I think."

Holly's eyes flick behind me once more, and she straightens slightly in her chair. "He didn't deserve to go out like that," she says finally. "Brenden was—" She chokes up and tries to cover it with a cough. "He was different. He was good."

"So maybe you can point us in the right direction?" I tilt my head. "You're not the only one we want to talk to. There's someone else who was seen with both you and Brenden, but we don't know who he is. If you could help us, maybe it will help put us on the right track, y'know?"

"I see a lot of people," Holly mutters, then she pauses. "You think one of my clients killed Brenden?"

"Maybe. Or they know who did. All we know is that he and Brenden had some disagreements and we want to talk to him about it."

Holly's gaze drops away, and she smokes silently until the cigarette is nothing but a stub. As she flicks it away, I offer her another, and it takes all my strength to keep my hands from trembling. I feel like I'm close, but I'm also winging the shit out of this.

"You got a picture?" Holly asks eventually.

I nod and as I turn, Cian slides the second drawing onto the table.

"Even if you don't know his name," I say as Holly takes the picture. "If you happen to know what Russian family he belongs to, that would be amazing."

Holly's face changes in an instant and anger pulls her brows tight. "This guy?" she snorts. "He's not fucking Russian. This prick's Italian."

27

CORMAC

Italian?

The urge to call Holly a liar rises like vomit, and I clench my teeth in order to prevent it. Seeing Evie talking so casually to Holly almost had me dragging her out of here for fear that Holly was somehow a danger. I'm still a little stunned that Evie has managed to get her talking, and it's lucky that Cian was a bit more level-headed about this than me.

"Italian?" Evie asks. "Are you sure?"

"Hundred percent," Holly says bitterly as she lights up another cigarette. "Fucker's as Italian as they come."

"You know him well?" Evie presses gently.

I grip the back of her chair, biting my own tongue to remain quiet. There's so much I want to say, so much I want to demand, but I know one word from me will cause Holly to clam up.

"Too well," Holly mutters. "He was a client, and then we used to date for a while, but he couldn't shake the jealousy of my work. Although I was always pretty clear about my reasoning for this work."

"Money?" Evie asks.

Holly snaps her tongue. "Got it in one. And a pimp whose name is on everything I own so I have nothing and no one. So yeah, Noah and I dated for a little while, but I broke it off with him six months ago."

Behind me, Cian darts out of the room with the information. I stare hard at Holly, trying to find a lie in her words. Could this be a Russian trick to shove blame onto the Italians? Or have I been looking at the wrong family this entire time?

"I'm so sorry." Evie reaches for Holly's hand. "I can't imagine what that must be like, living like that. Is there anything we can do for you?"

Evie offers help like it's hers to give, but I find myself following her lead. Her way is working and at this point, I will give Holly anything just for the truth.

"Ironic," Holly murmurs around her cigarette. "Brenden said the exact same thing."

"What?" I can't keep quiet this time, as much as I kick myself for speaking. "What do you mean?"

Holly flicks her cigarette. "I met Brenden not long after I broke up with Noah. It was a complete accident, but we met at a cafe near that motel and he took my coffee. We argued, sort of, until he drank it to prove me right and his black coffee was my vanilla latte." Holly smiles wistfully "He was quite the dramatic actor. Anyway, I won't bore you with all the details."

"You loved him," Evie says suddenly, and my heart stalls in my chest.

Holly nods and she gives a sad smile. "I did. We started dating not long after that, and we—"

"Liar," I bark out, moving past Evie to the edge of the table. "Don't you dare say something like that!" If Brenden was dating someone, I would know about it. We shared everything. He was my confidant and I was his, and if he had found love, I would have known.

"You think?" Holly moves to put her hand in her bra, drawing the attention of every gunman in the room. She pauses, raising her other hand palm upward, then rummages in her bra. She withdraws something and opens her hand. On her palm sits a gold lighter, and the sight of it makes my heart drop down to the dark pit in my stomach.

Brenden's lighter.

I know it because it's the exact same as my lighter. "Why do you have that?" I ask thickly.

"Brenden gave it to me. He told me it was to prove he loved me," Holly replies. "I told him not to be such a sap and so he told me it would be a symbol of my safety." When she blinks, her eyes shimmer and she shakes her head. "What a fool he was."

"Safety?" Evie prompts. "What do you mean?"

Holly sniffles and returns to her cigarette while my mind reels from the revelation. These lighters are precious to us and they would never leave us. But to an outsider, they look normal and if Holly had stolen it, there's no way she'd know the importance of it. But since she does, Brenden must have told her.

She's telling the truth.

"Brenden was sweet. He didn't shy away from my work and recognized how badly I wanted out of it, so he was helping me get out of a life filled with sex work. He was helping me pay off debts, had worked out a deal with my pimp and everything. Then he went and got himself killed." She shakes her head. "I should have known he was too good to be true."

"What about Noah?" Evie presses, tapping the picture. "How does he fit into this?"

"Noah was jealous when he learned I'd moved on," Holly explains. "But then suddenly, it didn't matter because when he met Brenden, he was pissed for other reasons."

"What reasons?" I demand sharply.

Holly rolls her eyes. "I don't know. They were butting heads over some old deal that apparently screwed Noah over. They argued about it a few times. And…" She looks from me to Evie. "The night Brenden died, he… he was supposed to be with me. He was there for a while, but then he left because he said he needed to talk about business with Noah. He said he was sorting things for good this time and then he'd come back and we'd be together."

Holly's voice changes suddenly, and the same pain that exists in my chest suddenly pours from her as she starts to cry properly.

"But he never came back," she weeps brokenly. "I waited at the cafe for hours and he never showed. I called him and got nothing and then the next day, I found out he was dead. My future just vanished."

Evie rises from her seat and moves around the table, hugging Holly tightly. She flashes me a distressed look, but I'm too distracted to focus on her right now. I sent a quick text to Cian and Saoirse. This Noah just became the last person to see Brenden alive, which makes him public enemy number one. With only a first name, it'll be hard to track him down, but now we can stop wasting time with the Russians.

Holly provided a lot of info, but frustration still simmers underneath my skin. Every step closer feels too small, like there's something wrapped around me, constantly pulling me back no matter how close I get to the truth. A change in target doesn't make much of a difference if I still don't have that fucker's throat in my hands. As Evie comforts Holly, I stride away to gain some breathing space.

Brenden was in love. So in love that he gifted Holly his lighter. He was doing everything he could to help her until he butted heads with Noah. But what deal was he talking about? We've been at peace with the Italians for years and to my knowledge, there hasn't been any shift that would require fresh deals to be made. I send a text to Ma just to check there isn't anything I'm missing, then I head out of the warehouse.

The cool night air is refreshing. I hadn't realized how much my skin was burning inside until the cold breeze kissed my neck and forehead. Several deep breaths later and the tightness across my chest eases. I take another deep breath and hold it as I gaze up at the stars.

Noah.

Wherever the fuck he is, his days are numbered.

"Cormac?" Evie appears beside me, keeping some distance. "Are you alright?"

"No," I say shortly, puffing out my cheeks. Then I catch myself. "Sorry. It's a lot."

"I can imagine," she says softly. "Did you know that your brother was…?"

"In love?" I glance at her. "No."

"He never said anything?"

"No."

"Okay." She nods quickly. "That lighter is the same as yours."

"Yeah."

"So you think she's telling the truth?"

"Maybe."

Evie grunts softly. I can tell she's trying to reach me, but right now, everything feels far too heavy. I need to process before something inside me snaps. Suddenly, Evie's hand slides into mine and despite her warmth, a strange cooling sensation washes over my shoulders. The tension in my chest eases like the pull of gum, and my next breath is easier.

"I'm sorry there wasn't an easy answer," she says carefully. "I can't imagine what this feels like."

"I don't know how to explain it," I reply. "The truth changes nothing about Brenden. I know this. But I want to hurt someone. I want to look in the eyes of his killer and make them regret everything."

"I know," she whispers. "A name is good, right?"

"It's a start."

"What will happen to Holly?"

"Well..." I glance back at the warehouse. "If she's telling the truth and Noah exists, then I will honor Brenden's attempts to save her. Whatever deal he made with her pimp, I'll secure it. He clearly loved her, and I will take care of her."

"That's a good thing to do." Evie smiles.

Before I can reply, a screech of tires pulls my attention toward the parking lot where Cian's car has just returned. He flies out of the driver's seat and sprints up to us, panting harshly.

"Easy, little brother. What's wrong?"

He holds up his phone, displaying a message. "The Italian Don. He's pissed. As soon as Saoirse started asking about Noah, he took personal offense and demanded proof of Italian involvement. So of course, she gave him the CCTV and he says it's too blurry. He wants watertight proof that Italian blood is involved or he's taking the accusation as a personal insult."

"What the fuck? He said he would help us," I snap. "This isn't fucking helping."

"Nah," Cian pants. "But it screams guilty."

"That it does. Did you tell him we have proof?"

Cian glances at Evie. "I did. And he wants to see it."

"But he can't," Evie says, her grip locking onto my hand. "I can't prove what I saw."

"No," Cian agrees. "But you can prove it's Noah you saw. Picking him out of a lineup should be easy, right?"

My heart jumps back into my throat. Evelyn's eyewitness account of that argument is the best we have outside of the police sketch.

"What if I say no? What if I don't want Evie anywhere near the Italians?"

Cian looks at me and winces. "I don't think we have a choice," he replies. "Without her, these accusations are against the Don and he's made it pretty fucking clear he's taking it as a personal insult. If Evelyn refuses, that puts us at war with the Italians. And that's not a war I think we can win."

28

EVELYN

"I don't mind speaking to the Italians." The words are barely out of my mouth when Cormac reaches across the car and takes my hand, half his attention still on the road as he drives us to my mother's house.

"I can't ask you to do that," he says. "You've already done so much for me, especially with Holly. Besides, I'm not going to hand over the only witness to the people who might be behind this whole fucking thing."

"You'll protect me, though."

Cormac's grip tightens around my fingers. "I will. But I'm not going to walk you into the wolf's den. Not until I know exactly what's going on."

I settle back in my seat and stroke my fingers over Cormac's knuckles, watching familiar streets flash past the window. He insisted on driving me to my mother's house, taking a simple car so that we could drive without being noticed. His guards sit back in the car behind us so if I squint, I can block out most of my thoughts and pretend that we are simply a real couple out for a drive.

We learned so much from Holly, but it all fades from my mind when we reach my mother's apartment. She'd been blowing up my phone since we landed and it's been tough to balance that and Holly. I hadn't planned on Cormac ever meeting my mother, but I don't have time to tell him to wait in the car. As soon as I climb out, he follows and the front door opens before I reach the steps.

"Evelyn!" My mother squawks from the doorway. "Where the hell have you been?"

"I'm so sorry," I say, hurrying up the steps. "I was traveling, and I got caught up… it doesn't matter. I'm here now. What's the emergency? What's wrong? Are you alright?"

"Would you even care if I wasn't?" she snaps, looking me up and down. "Why do you look so filthy?"

"What?" I glance down at my T-shirt and jeans. "I look… normal?"

"Hardly. I don't hear from you in weeks, you bail when I need you, and you take hours to come to me when I call you. What if there was a fire?"

I fight not to roll my eyes. "Was there a fire?"

"No," she snaps. "But my apartment has lost all power! I have no heating, no hot water. I can't even make a hot meal. I've been living with my flashlight and not even my own daughter can come home and help me."

"Mom, I'm sorry, can we—"

"Maybe I can help." Cormac stands at my back, drawing my mother's attention. Her eyes widen and she glances between the two of us.

"Who are you?"

"This is Cormac." I introduce him with a smile.

"Your block still has power, so I'd guess this is a fuse issue. Where's your box?"

Mom looks at him with narrowed eyes, then points down the dark hall with her flashlight. "At the end."

"Excuse me." He slides past us with impressive agility for a man of his bulk and heads down the hall. I stare after him until my mother catches my wrist and pulls me inside. The door slams and she jerks me into the lounge where a few battery-powered lights litter the shelves.

"Is that why you are late?" she scolds. "You were playing with a man while your poor mother lives in the dark. To think I was worried about you and instead, here you are flouncing around with a man."

"I wasn't flouncing," I say, feeling my stomach twist into knots. "You refused to tell me what was wrong, so I came as fast as I could."

"Not fast enough. I fell, you know!" As she barks at me in the dark, the light suddenly blooms above as Cormac fixes whatever is wrong with the fuses. We both blink quickly at the sudden change, then my attention drops to my mother's ankle. She winces and sits immediately, rubbing at her apparently fine ankle.

"Mom," I sigh softly. "Why didn't you call 911?"

"Why on earth would I waste time doing that?"

"Because you lost power and you fell," I reply, hurrying into the kitchen for the medical kit. Locating it, I bring it back through and kneel in front of her. "Calling 911 would have been the best thing."

"Are you calling me stupid?"

"No, I—"

"You think I can't think for myself?"

"No."

"Then why do you say these stupid things? I will not waste the time of others when I have a daughter who is supposed to take care of me!"

She clicks her tongue sharply when I apply a cold compress to her ankle.

"There's no swelling," I say. "How long ago did you fall?"

"I don't know," she replies shortly. "It was dark."

"An hour? Two?"

"I don't know, Evelyn."

It wouldn't be the first time she'd be lying in order to lay the guilt on thick, but strangely, I don't feel as guilty as I usually do. So often, she would reduce me to tears trying to reach impossible expectations, but something about her tone doesn't quite hit the same now. Maybe it's because of everything I've been through or because Cormac is somewhere nearby. I'm not sure, but when I apply a compression bandage to her ankle, none of her comments about my cold touch faze me like they used to.

"I've done all I can." I pack up the kit. "But you should call a doctor tomorrow."

"It wouldn't have even happened if you'd been here."

"Maybe, but if you fell in the dark and the dark was your emergency, there's no way I could have gotten here in time."

"Of course not," Mom scoffs. "No time for your mother. You brush off responsibility like a duck brushes water. And then you bring strange men into my house!"

"Cormac isn't strange," I reply defensively. "He's my…" Boyfriend? Partner? No word seems right to describe him. "I don't know. But he's not strange."

My mother's eyes suddenly light up. "Tell me, is he to be your husband?"

"Mom…"

"I told you to be careful, didn't I? That no one would like you as you got older."

"I'm only twenty-four."

"Past your prime." She sniffs with disdain. "But if he can look past that, then I will make sure you don't let him go!"

"I thought you didn't like strange men."

"Well, you can't afford to be picky at your age, so what can I say?" Mom rests back in her chair. "You're already running out of time."

Standing, I fight the urge to sigh deeply and instead clutch at the back of my neck. "Please call a doctor tomorrow, okay? Get your ankle looked at. And I'll call the building super about your fuses."

"Is that it?" Mom glares at me. "You're leaving already?"

"I have to," I reply. "I have things to do." That and I just want to crawl into bed and sleep. Holly was more draining than I expected, and time with my unhappy mother always takes years off my life. "But I'll call you."

"No you won't."

It takes me an hour to leave my mother. Each time I try to slip away, she comes up with another thing to nit-pick about my appearance or lifestyle and always ends with a guilt trip about leaving her all alone in her apartment. In the end, Cormac is the one who pulls me away because it's so late, but he promises to send someone tomorrow to take her to the doctor. She's so shocked at his offer that we're able to slip away, and I don't breathe until we're back in the car.

"Wow," Cormac groans as we start driving. "The way she was talking, I thought she'd make me inseminate you right on the coffee table."

"I'm so sorry. She's convinced I'm too old and that I'm wasting my life by not being married and having kids. She's... old-fashioned."

"Or backward." Cormac snorts. "I didn't think people still held those views."

"I'd try to say she's traditional, but she didn't exactly embrace the role of mother." Facing her after a lovely few days with Clodagh just highlights how cold and empty my childhood was. Is it any wonder I turned to material things for love?

Maybe it's why I'm so enamored of Cormac. He's shown so much care for me in such a short time. By comparison, his actions are more loving than my mother's ever were.

"I'm sorry you had to grow up with that," Cormac says gently. "I can't imagine what it was like to experience that."

"That's kind of why I didn't want you to come," I murmur. "It's embarrassing."

"Evie, there's nothing—"

"Cormac!"

We see the lights too late. As Cormac pulls out of the intersection, a horn blares and a gigantic truck runs the red light. I clutch at Cormac's hand for a split second, then the truck collides with us with an almighty crash and scream of metal. My head whips to the side, cracking into the glass, and then darkness takes me as warmth trickles down from my hairline.

"Cormac!" I jolt awake, my head pounding and my vision swimming. Everything is bright, too bright, so I close my eyes again and groan softly. My throat is so dry that the groan catches and I immediately start coughing.

"Easy," says a voice, and a cool hand lands on my bare arm.

I crack open my eyes once more and lock eyes with someone above me. Someone who makes my confused heart sink.

"Evelyn," says Detective Cogs. "You have some explaining to do."

29

EVELYN

"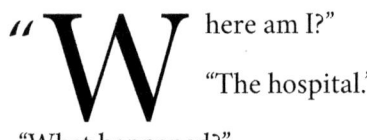here am I?"

"The hospital."

"What happened?"

"You were in a car accident. The vehicle you were in was T-boned by a delivery truck."

It comes back to me slowly. The conversation with Cormac in the car, the comforting smile on his face, and then the blinding headlights of a truck we had no hope of avoiding. My head swims and I close my eyes, swallowing around my tongue that feels like cotton.

I'm alive.

Somehow.

When I open my eyes again, Detective Cogs remains beside me, her thin brows pinched with worry. As my sluggish thoughts catch up with my wakefulness, Cormac fully enters my thoughts, and I struggle to sit up. "Am I okay?"

"Mostly." Sarah sighs. "Some bruised ribs and you sustained a head wound from the side window. Luckily, the driver was already trying to brake when he hit you. Your driver took the brunt of the impact."

My driver.

Cormac.

Thinking of him with a detective right next to me is more sobering than being dunked backward into ice water, and stress chases away the last lingering sluggish fog clinging to my thoughts. I see Sarah as clear as day, and the hospital room I'm in is less fancy than the one I woke up in after the stabbing. It seems when Cormac is awake and able to care for me, he ensures more than a regular room.

"Is he…?" I'm almost too scared to ask about Cormac's condition, and cold fear grips me like a vise.

What if it was terrible and he's dead? What if I've lost the first man I've fallen in love with? The revelation makes my stomach churn, and something about my face must have given me away because Sarah quickly reaches for the dish nearby and holds it near me. No vomit comes, just a cramp in my gut.

"If you're asking me if the driver of your car is injured, then yes, he is. He's alive, but like I said, he took the brunt of the impact being in the driver's seat and hasn't woken up yet," Sarah explains. "Which is why I'm here to question you."

"Question me?" I take the dish from her as another uncomfortable roll of tightness moves through my abdomen.

"I've been trying to get in touch with you for a few days," Sarah says. "I went to your apartment and you were gone. Your neighbors hadn't seen you. So imagine my surprise when I get a call from the cop in charge of this crash and learn that you are here in the hospital. After being dragged from a car wreck, the same car that Cormac Gifford was dragged from."

My heart leaps into my throat while I stare at Sarah. Her face twists slightly, as if she knows everything and she's just waiting for me to trip up so she can catch me in a lie. Cormac never explicitly told me not to talk to the cops, and Sarah felt like she was on my side since the murder. But right now, she's looking at me like I'm a suspect and I have no idea how to navigate this.

Do I lie? What if Cormac dies? Who will be in my corner then?

Do I tell the truth? Would the cops be on our side?

Thinking back to the bugs I was forced to place, I already know the answer. If she were on our side, I wouldn't have had to do that.

"I don't know what you mean," I say softly. "What's wrong with Cormac?"

"You want to play it like that?" Sarah sighs. "Really, Evelyn? Playing dumb isn't a good look for you."

"I don't know what you're talking about." My head swims again, and an ache pulls like a hot band through my skull. Lifting my hand, I'm met with gauze across my forehead.

"Cormac. The man you were in the car with? Are you telling me you didn't know he is the brother of the man whose body you found?"

"Oh, no. I knew that," I reply as casually as I can. "But I don't understand what your issue is. Shouldn't you be talking to the person who hit us?"

Sarah's eyes narrow. "Who is he to you?"

"Cormac?"

"Yes."

"He's... just a guy. He came to find me and explained who he was. His brother just died," I say sharply. "He was pretty broken up about it."

Sarah scoffs in disbelief but doesn't speak.

"He had a couple of questions for me, but I didn't know anything, and then we had coffee and I guess became friends." It's a version of the truth. Technically.

"What questions?"

"The normal questions. Asked if I saw anything, if I knew anything about his brother. I told him I didn't."

"And you didn't think it was strange that he found you?"

I shrug and immediately regret it as the bruises on my ribs complain painfully. "I figured you guys told him. It's not like I'm a suspect or anything."

Sarah suddenly stands and moves closer to the bed. "Evelyn. I want you to know that you are safe here, understand? There are cops all over the hospital and if you feel threatened in any way, you can tell me. I can help you. Do you understand?" Her brows lift slightly. "I can protect you from anyone. So if you feel like you're in danger or that your mom is in danger, then I can help you with that."

It clicks suddenly. She thinks I'm lying because Cormac is threatening me and she's offering me help. I shake my head. "I'm fine, I promise. I don't feel threatened at all. Why would I?"

"Cormac is a very dangerous man, Evelyn. The fact that he found you is incredibly concerning. More concerning is that you were in the car with him."

"If he's dangerous, shouldn't you be watching him instead of questioning me? I don't have anything to tell you and it sounds like the crash was an accident."

Sarah straightens up and her lips press into a thin line. "He is dangerous. It's in my nature to recognize people caught up in things they shouldn't be."

"Wait." Something Sarah said suddenly resonates with me. "You said there are police all over the hospital?"

"That's right." She nods, then frowns. "Why?"

My defensiveness toward Sarah begins to thaw. I remember the conversation between Cormac and Saoirse back when I first met them. The whole reason I needed to plant those bugs was because Sarah couldn't be bought, and they didn't have many other cops they could trust. But other families did.

If Sarah can't be bought, then maybe she can actually help.

"I read once that criminal organizations in the city often have cops on the inside," I say as casually as possible, not breaking eye contact with Sarah.

"What are you—"

"Is that true?" I stare harder. "Is it true that other families and organizations have plants within the police to give them information?"

"That's just a rumor." Sarah scoffs, but she's nodding slowly.

"Cormac introduced me to an Irish Coffee once. Very strong. But then I wanted to go to the Italian across the street and he said no." I shift against my pillows. "He said that the Italians were awful, that the food would get people killed."

"What?" Despite Sarah's nodding, she seems to be completely missing what I'm trying to warn her about, and frustration gets the better of me.

"Oh, my God," I mutter. "The Irish aren't the ones you need to worry about! If you don't do everything you can to make sure Cormac is safe, then there's going to be war between the Irish and the Italians all over the city, and we both know that the law won't stand for anything once that spark ignites."

Sarah's eyes widen, then she cocks her hip slightly as she reaches for her phone. "He's just a friend, huh?"

"That hardly matters right now, does it?" I hiss. "Look, you have to make sure you have good cops around him. All it takes is one wrong injection."

Sarah's busy on her phone, nodding quickly.

"The driver. Were they Italian?"

Sarah shrugs. "They're still unconscious. No clue."

"Please. Please, Sarah. You have to make sure Cormac is safe. Really safe, not just under cop protection safe."

"Evelyn—"

"Please! Do you really think you and the rest of the cops like you will be able to stop what's about to happen if something happens to Cormac?"

She seems to be debating quickly, then Sarah gets a reply ding on her phone. "Don't go anywhere. You'd better answer all of my questions when I get back."

"Sure," is all I get a chance to say before she hurries from the room.

I slump back into my pillows with a groan. Did I say too much? I have no idea how people from these families are supposed to talk to the cops, but unlike Cormac, I have no way of helping anyone. Outside help from people more powerful than me is all I have.

The door has barely closed behind Sarah when it opens again and in walks Saoirse. She flashes me a tight smile as she approaches.

My heart punches into my throat. "Oh, God," I gasp. "Are you going to kill me?"

Saoirse falters. "What? Why would I do that?"

"Because I was talking to the cops."

To my surprise, Saoirse chuckles. "Honey, you didn't reveal anything the cops don't already know. If Sarah has missed the hints on the streets that war is brewing, then that's on her. But you did a decent thing trying to make sure the right kind of cops are around Cormac. We've been having trouble getting men into the hospital."

The relief is so powerful that my vision dims for a moment. "Thank God, I was so scared you were about to shank me for talking to the police."

"Cormac would have my head, and I'd prefer it to stay where it is," she replies, pulling my blankets back. "Come on, I need to get you out of here."

"What about Cormac?"

"Cian has him. At least until backup arrives. We need to get you somewhere safe."

"Why? What's going on? The man who hit us—"

The door to my room suddenly flies wide open. It bounces off the wall with a crack, causing me to jump back in fright. Saoirse spins around, drawing her gun from her belt as a man charges inside and sprints toward Saoirse like a runaway bull.

I glimpse his face as they collide in the middle of the room, and a cold sweat breaks out under my gown.

Noah.

He attacks with a yell. Saoirse and Noah grapple for a few seconds, then she punches him hard in the gut. When he doubles over, she drives her elbow down into his back. He hits the ground and she's on him, but he manages to roll them over and punches her several times in the face. Panicked, I lunge toward them and tackle Noah from behind, grabbing him by the hair and clothes to try and pull him off her. He falls backward, scrambles up, and punches me hard in the face.

I fall back with a cry, stars flashing before my eyes as pain explodes across my jaw. My back throbs as I hit the ground, and the pain from impact against my ribs shocks my lungs into a motionless state. For a few dark seconds, I can't get my body to listen to me and my breathing fails.

Through the dizziness, I watch Saoirse and Noah fight. Thankfully, Saoirse seems to have the upper hand. She's dodging back and forth, avoiding his blows and throwing jabs at his face and body. Until he turns around to me. Saoirse leaps onto his back like a spider monkey and claws at his face.

"Evelyn! Go!" she yells.

It takes every ounce of energy I have left to pull myself up and run for the door. Just as I place one foot out in the hall, a gunshot echoes behind me and I freeze instantly. The corridor is empty, and I scan each doorway in the hopes of seeing someone who can help me. But there's no one. Then I glance back, hoping to see Saoirse standing over Noah.

Instead, she's on the ground grunting with blood pouring from a bullet wound on her thigh, rapidly turning her light blue jeans to black.

"Fucking bitch," Noah garbles through a face full of blood. He lifts the gun and aims it at Saoirse's head.

"No!" I scream, lurching forward. "Don't!"

My scream makes Noah flinch, and he glances at me, his finger on the trigger. "No?" He wipes at his nose and face with his other hand. "There is no 'No' here. I'm the one with the fucking gun."

"I know, I know!" Saoirse's gun is nearby on the floor, but there's no way either she or I can reach it in time. I can barely breathe, desperately seeking a way to save Saoirse's life. "Take me."

"What?" Noah and Saoirse say in unison.

"You came here for me, right? Don't waste bullets on her. She'll bleed out from that wound, anyway!"

Saoirse clutches at her thigh, glaring between me and the barrel of the gun.

"One hostage gives you more leverage than two bodies, right?" I say breathlessly, hoping that Noah's visible desperation will latch onto leverage more than anything else. "So take me. I can walk. She can't."

Noah wipes at his face again, failing to stem the blood flow.

"Fine."

30

CORMAC

"Cormac—"

"Get off me!"

"Cormac, you'll tear open your stitches—"

"I don't care. Get the fuck off me, Cian!"

"No!" Cian snaps, increasing the strength of his grip on my arm. "Not until you calm the fuck down!"

"I am fucking calm," I snarl, attempting to wrench my arm free. "What part of this doesn't exude fucking calmness!"

"Oh, I don't know. Maybe declaring an all-out war on the Italians? Trying to turn the streets into a bloodbath without talking about it first?"

"What's to talk about?" I finally wrench my arm free from Cian's grasp and haul myself out of the hospital bed. "The order is given."

"Cormac—"

"What would you have me do, Cian?" I spin to face him. Anger dulls the pain from my surgery to repair the internal injuries from the crash, and it's more effective than any of the painkillers. "They killed Brenden! And then rather than handing over that fucking rat, Noah, they tried to act like I am unreasonable. And then that son of a bitch strode in here, shot our sister, and kidnapped the woman I love. So tell me, Cian, what the fuck else would you have me do? What kind of talking would fix this, hmm?"

"I don't know!" Cian yells back, situating himself between me and the door. "I just—" He pants softly, seemingly deflating before my eyes. "I just want you to stop and think before—"

"Before what?"

"Before I lose you too!" His voice breaks. "Brenden is dead, okay? Saoirse nearly bled to death in that room because all the fucking cops here are on the Italian payroll. You nearly died in that crash, and I… I was just me, okay? Watching as my family crumbles around me, and I couldn't do anything to help anyone!" He drags his hands through his hair and then points at me. "So if I have to fight you to keep you in here for at least another day, I will. I don't care. I'll fight you for the full twenty-four hours if I have to."

My anger bubbles down to a simmer as my brother looks at me with tears in his eyes, and then it hits me like a bulldozer. Waking up from surgery to learn that two days ago, Noah had swept into this hospital, shot my sister, and kidnapped Evelyn was rage-inducing. Nothing else mattered and I immediately gave the order declaring that no Italian in this city was safe from my wrath.

It didn't cross my mind that for those two days, Cian was suddenly in charge of everything. I know that fear. I felt it when Brenden died and suddenly, I was thrust to the head of the family with no warning. I hadn't thought of Cian feeling the same thing. The urge to punch him fades and I slowly, very slowly, ease back down onto the bed.

"I'm sorry," I say. "Sitting around doing nothing is killing me."

"Running out there," comes Saoirse's voice from the doorway. "That's what will kill you."

"Fuck's sake!" Cian darts forward to grab his twin. "Why can't you fuckers just stay in your beds!"

"Because there's shit to do," Saoirse says, patting Cian's cheek as she braces heavily on a crutch and limps into the room. "I can't stay down either."

"You're both going to be the death of me," Cian groans as he helps Saoirse to a nearby chair.

"Least we'll all go together," I murmur. I rub at my face, trying to ease the tension in my brow and jaw. "Have we heard anything? Anything at all?"

"No," Cian mutters, slumping back against the wall. "Between keeping you two in your beds, calming Ma, trying to keep business running and the Italians away from here, I haven't heard shit."

"What about the fucker that crashed into me?" I ask.

"Pulled a Houdini," Cian grunts. "Vanished."

"Think he ran?" Saoirse asks.

Cian shrugs. "I had too much shit to do, but he's on my list."

"Oh, speaking of. Ma did call with a warning, though," Saoirse says, pulling my attention to her.

"A warning?" I ask.

"She says the deal we have with the Italians is the foundation of where we stand today and that you should retract the call to arms." Saoirse rubs gingerly at her leg. "She also says you've got to call her, or she'll fly out here."

"No. She stays on that ranch. And send some more men out there," I snap.

"Already done," Cian replies. "I wasn't just wailing by your bedside for those two days."

I send him a thankful glance. "I don't give a shit about the deal. Our foundations are our own but they're destroying this family. I don't care about some fucking weapons deal. There's no bridge I won't destroy to get Evelyn back, you hear me?"

"I hear you," Saoirse says, watching me intently. "You really do love her."

"I—" The thought catches in my mind. I'd blurted it out earlier without thinking, but now that thought sits heavily with me. It's a comforting weight, like the warmth of a cat sitting in your lap or the first warm drink after a day spent in the cold. "I do," I say tightly. "I really do."

"Shit," Cian murmurs. "Brenden always said we'd be screwed when you finally fell in love. I thought he meant we'd have to deal with your becoming a sappy bastard."

"No," Saoirse says, her eyes on me. "He knew the world would burn the second Cormac found love. We just hoped it would burn in our favor."

I roll my eyes, curling my hand into a fist against my leg. Sitting around unable to go looking for Evelyn is killing me. Waking to learn that my kidney ruptured in the crash was one thing, but nothing hurt as much as learning Evelyn handed herself over to save Saoirse. I don't know what prompted such a thing, but I'll never be able to repay her for her selflessness.

But I'll try the moment I get her back.

If I get her back.

Because I love her, and I'll tear down the entire city to find her if I have to.

Saoirse and Cian remain in my room for a few hours, quietly discussing our next course of action. Cian's pretty set on making sure we both stay in hospital, but when Saoirse gets up to leave, we exchange a look. She knows I won't stay here, and she won't stop me. She plays up her injury and gets Cian to escort her back to her room, giving me the window I need.

Slipping into the bathroom, I tear off the paper gown and dig my clothes out of the bag. The bloodstains don't faze me. I'd walk out of here stark naked if I needed to. I have no idea where to start looking, but breaking some Italian skulls feels like a good place to begin. Dressed, I quickly wash my face, scarcely feeling the pain of the minor bruises and scratches from the crash. As I walk back into my room, the entrance door closes softly as if someone just left. I'm about to follow when I spot a folder sitting on the tray table with a Post-It note attached.

This is better in your hands than mine.

Opening the file, I'm met with the medical and personal information of a man I don't recognize. It's not until I read further down at the listed injuries that I realize this is the driver from the car crash, the man who vanished from the hospital. According to the report, his injuries are minimal, and he signed himself out against medical advice concerning his dislocated shoulder.

That fucker.

If he were still here, I'd be inclined to think the crash was an accident, but he ran like a fucking rat.

I've found my first face to break.

* * *

"Please!" the man gasps under the weight of my fist around his throat. "Please!"

He squawks like a gull as I haul him off the wall and lift him in the air, then I throw him down onto the nearby table in his shitty living room. Wood splinters and breaks under the force. I don't release my grip. His squawks turn to agonized yells when I press my other hand down onto his injured shoulder—it was easy to tell which one he was favoring due to the way he defended himself when I kicked down his front door.

"Please isn't what I want to hear," I snarl, bringing my face close to his. Tracking him down from the hospital was easy, and finding a gun in his hand answered my questions about whether the driver who hit me was a regular pedestrian or not.

This fucker has some skill. I know a contract killer when I see one.

"Please, I—" The man gargles and chokes around my fist, drowning in the blood streaming from his smashed-in face. The moment he tried to run, my anger overcame me and I poured all my rage into attacking him until he was ready to talk.

He caved disappointingly quickly.

"I want a name," I snarl. "I want to know who the fuck hired you to hit me!"

"I... don't... have a—name!"

"Why the fuck not?"

"No names," he squeaks out, clawing at my arm. "Part–Part of the deal!"

"What was the deal?"

He tries and fails to talk, and it's not until his face turns purple that I realize I'm strangling him a bit too well. Forcing myself to relax my grip around his throat, I glare down as he gasps desperately for air.

"What. Deal."

"It was anonymous," he chokes out through bloodied teeth. "A simple hit. I met with the guy, he gave me a picture and told me to kill her. I failed the first time. She had protection, so I bolted."

"The girl, did you get her name?" I know the answer but I need to hear him say it.

"Evel—Evelyn Morris!"

"And the crash?"

"She vanished and I told him she had protection, so the cost was going up. He agreed, so I tracked down her mother and camped the place. Fucked with the electrics and shit to try and draw her out. And when she did, I tried to run her off the road. Simple accident!"

I tighten my grip once more, and the man squeaks like air escaping a balloon. "Who hired you?"

"No... names!"

Fuck.

Releasing his shoulder, I fish out my phone and quickly scroll until I find a picture of the Italian Don, Matteo Barati. "This guy?"

The assassin shakes his head.

Figures. It wouldn't be Matteo's style to hire an out-of-family assassin. But if he didn't want to be caught, maybe it's precisely the thing he would do. "This guy?" I flash him a photo of Rocky, Matteo's son.

"No!"

"You'd better not be lying to me!"

"I'm not! I swear!"

The last picture I show him is the sketch of Noah.

"That's him! That's the guy! I don't know his name, though, I swear. I swear—" I render him unconscious with a final punch, then straighten up with a wince. Pulling out my gun, a clean shot to the skull ends the assassin's life.

The world tips slightly and my legs feel weak as I pick my way through the destroyed apartment and head for the door.

Noah.

The fucker is at the root of everything.

He hired an assassin to kill Evelyn but failed each time because of me. And now he has her. Once outside, the setting sun burns my eyes. I dial Cian's number.

There's nowhere Noah can hide. The moment he snatched Evelyn is the moment he signed his slow, painful death warrant.

"Where the fuck are you?" Cian screams in my ear. "Do you have any fucking idea how scared I was to find your room empty?"

"Cian." I calmly walk down the street, ignoring the pull of hot pain across my abdomen. "Call Matteo. Tell him I know Italian money paid for an assassin who nearly killed me."

"You fucking… fine," Cian groans. "Fine. I'll tell him. Then what?"

"Then we find Evie, that's what."

This city is hiding my woman. No one rests until she's back by my side.

31

EVELYN

"**D**rink."

Noah shoves the bottle into my face and glares at me. I'd resist if I weren't so damn thirsty. Reluctantly, I part my lips but as I tip my head up to accept the water flow, he tilts the bottle too far. It spills out too fast and washes over my face, flooding my mouth to the point that I have to gulp desperately to get any of it before it all pours away. The bottle empties in a handful of seconds and then he tosses it aside. The plastic bounces on the metal floor and the sound echoes around me. Then he walks away, but not far.

I'm not sure where I am, but since we arrived here he's kept me bound to a rusty metal chair at the bottom of some kind of tank. In my hours alone here, I tried to work out what this was due to the pipes running along the walls and the holes above me that look rusted beyond belief. Maybe water was held in here, or some chemical, judging by how the air carries no scent but stings each time I breathe in.

"Asshole," I croak as he strides away.

Noah stops in his tracks and turns back to me. He reaches me in a few steps then strikes me across the face. "You're lucky I give you anything at all!"

"Lucky?" I gather saliva and fresh blood with a swipe of my tongue and then spit it toward him as my tired heart hammers beneath my aching ribs. "How is it lucky that you've locked me up here and finally remembered to give me water more than once?"

"You're lucky I haven't killed you yet," Noah growls. He carries a handgun in one hand and his knuckles flex slightly when he tightens his grip. That gun stopped scaring me a while ago, although without a clock and sunlight, I can't really tell how long it's been.

"Why haven't you killed me yet, huh?" I press. "Are you keeping me here for entertainment?"

"Entertainment?" He scoffs, looking me over. "Nah. Nah. I just need time. Time to think. And you give me time. So. Yeah. Time." He stumbles away from me again. "Just time to make a plan, that's all."

"A plan? For what, me?"

He ignores me, keeping his back turned.

"Or a plan for you?"

"I don't need a plan," Noah mutters. "I know what I'm doing. It's been good so far. Really good."

"Has it, though?" It's not the brightest idea to question the man with the gun, but he'd left me alone for hours, denying me the chance to get any answers. If I'm going to die here, I want to know why.

"It has." He glances back at me. "I just need some more time and then everything… everything will be fine."

"Are you too scared?" I taunt. "Can't bring yourself to kill me, is that it? Because if you're planning on just letting me starve here, the water was a stupid move."

Noah is suddenly back next to me with his hand around my throat, glaring down into my eyes. "Shut the fuck up! You're all the same, fucking sluts getting in the way of everything. It would have been so easy, so fucking easy if she'd just—" He cuts himself off and glares in silence.

I can't breathe. My lungs try to inflate, forcing a painful pull from my bruised ribs, but there's no air to be had. Clenching my hands into fists, I pull tight against the cold, wet rope keeping me bound, but my skin is so raw from previous struggles that I don't have the strength to struggle again. Just as dark spots dance in front of my eyes, Noah releases me and I sag forward. Harsh, raspy coughs erupt from my chest and each desperate breath tastes like iron.

"Oh, yeah," I croak when I lift my head. "Blame your actions on a woman. Pretty sure the only one responsible for killing anyone here is you. Or did Brenden just fall onto that knife?"

"Brenden?" Noah slaps me hard across the face, snapping my head to the side so forcefully that a stabbing pain lances through my neck. "The fuck do you know about Brenden? That fucking prick."

"I know you killed him," I gasp, straightening myself. My lower lip swells with heat. "And I know he took your girlfriend."

Noah freezes, and a strange, cold look enters his eyes. "Fucking Holly. Fucking bitch. I loved her, y'know? I knew she was a fucking slut but she was mine, and I was gonna give her such a good life. Then she decided I wasn't good enough. Imagine! A whore saying I'm not good enough. If I'd paid her enough, she'd have begged for me."

He rambles and starts to pace back and forth. Clearly, I've touched on a sore spot, but if it gets more information out of him, then I'm relieved.

"And then!" He spins to face me, brandishing the gun, and I shrink back, fearing the explosive pain of a bullet. Thankfully, he doesn't pull the trigger. "Imagine my fucking surprise when she decides that oh, I'm not good enough for her but fucking Brenden Gifford is!"

"That must have hurt," I say cautiously.

"It did! Thank you!" He speaks loudly. "That fucking cunt. As if he didn't already do enough to destroy my family."

"He harmed your family and took your girl?"

"See? He was a fucking snake. You have no idea, no fucking idea how hard I worked. I scraped and I scraped and I scraped together a deal with the Cartel. You got any idea what they ask for when it comes to their deals? Fucking flesh, man. My sister…" He trails off. "But it was worth it because I had the sweetest fucking deal to take to my boss. And the day before, the day before!" Noah kicks hard at the ground. "Fucking Brenden Gifford and the Irish sign a fucking weapons treaty with the Don and my deal is dead in the water. Suddenly, Cartel weapons mean nothing because the Irish think they're fucking superior."

His pacing grows more furious and he lifts the gun to his own temple, tapping slightly. My heart starts to race and an unexpected cold panic sets in.

Why am I scared he will die?

If he shoots himself, I really will starve to death here.

"Is that why you killed him?" I ask. "He ruined your deal?"

"Nah." Noah snorts. "I was gonna, but then the Don was making things good for me, y'know? Even tried to get my sister back from the Cartel, but they killed her, the stupid bitch. Whatever. I moved on. But then I saw him with Holly and I realized this fucker was coming for me again. It was all personal. I didn't see it before. Do you see?" He advances on me with that strange look back in his eyes. "He was after me from the beginning!"

I don't see. Whatever connection he's made in his mind is lost on me. "I see it," I lie. "I'm so sorry."

"Thank you! That fucker. Maybe he was jealous of me, I don't fucking know. Used his fancy status to ruin my business deal so when I saw him with my girl too, I told him I knew his game. I understood now, y'know? He wanted my life, but I wasn't gonna let him take it. He called me crazy, said I was insane, but I could see what he was doing. He couldn't just take Holly from me. She's mine, y'see? All mine. Stupid slut doesn't even know it."

I shake my head slightly, trying to chase away a wave of dizziness that swept over me. Did he really think Brenden was trying to take over his life? I can't imagine he had any idea about the secret Cartel deal and it was terrible timing, but in Noah's eyes, it's all connected.

"You… Do you still want to be with Holly? After everything?"

"She's mine. Are you fucking deaf?" Noah sucks on his teeth and points his gun at me again. "She's always with me, she just doesn't understand yet. But I'll show her. I'll show her she's mine. I just need to explain. Explain to my boss that I was just protecting my life, y'know?"

He was jealous. And crazy.

All this time, Cormac had been searching for the reason Brenden died. He'd accused the Russians and then the Italians, preparing for a war ignited by Brenden's murder, and this entire time, it was Noah. And he did it because he was jealous. Somehow, that's so much worse.

"I understand," I say, wetting my lips. "You have to take care of what's yours."

"Exactly," he mutters. "Exactly."

A terrible idea comes to me painfully quickly. If Noah is this unstable about Holly, maybe I can send him out to find Cormac. Tapping into that jealousy is my only chance because I need Noah to face Cormac.

Cormac would win. I know this for a fact. And then he'd learn where I am.

It's the only chance I have.

"Weird, though, because now Cormac is with Holly," I say cautiously. "I guess she still hasn't learned."

"The fuck you say?" Noah is back in my space and my pulse races fast like a bunny against a drum. "The fuck did you stay?"

"Holly," I gasp. "She's with… she's with Cormac. Why do you think he hasn't come for me? He's busy elsewhere. And Holly, I spoke to her. She's just confused. Maybe he's taking advantage of that."

"Holly…" His face softens slightly. "She's so… fuck. Cormac." And just like that, the cold anger is back. "I thought you were Cormac's bitch so I thought if I take you, then he'll leave me alone. I can use you to make sure he doesn't tell my boss any shit."

"Sure," I reply, and my voice trembles. "But that doesn't get you Holly, does it? You need Cormac off the board for that. Fully."

Noah nods, his eyes darting rapidly back and forth. "That fucker."

"Although it's been a while, who's to say he's not already with her…"

Noah suddenly turns and hurries toward the heavy metal door that stands between me and freedom. "I'll kill him this time," he mutters to himself. "I'll fucking kill both of them, dumb fucking bitch. I'll kill him."

He repeats it like a chant as he hauls the door open with a chilling screech of metal, and my heart finally begins to calm. I have to pray he finds Cormac soon and that somehow, Cormac doesn't kill him.

"Though…" Noah hesitates at the door, then he glances back at me. "You'd better hope I win, or you'll die in here."

A pulse of confusion spreads through my chest. The door slams shut with a final bang that echoes around me, and I breathe as calmly as possible. What relief solitude brings is immediately erased by the sudden chilling clunk of old pipes groaning and creaking.

"Oh, no." The holes above me that I'd been distantly curious about suddenly show their purpose as a gush of cold water sprays out of them and rains down on me like shards of ice.

"Shit!"

32

CORMAC

The air in the Black Ox has never been so tense. Hazel stands at the bar with her shotgun, loaded, on the bar and a warning look in her eyes. It doesn't faze me. There's only one thing keeping me from diving across this table and strangling Matteo Barati and it's not Hazel's shotgun. It's the fact that I have no idea where Evie is and killing the man I suspect won't get me any closer.

Cian and Saoirse flank me, though Saoirse chooses to sit under Cian's watchful eye. He's silent on his anger about our leaving the hospital too soon, but we've wasted too long already.

Matteo sits across from me puffing slowly on his cigar while his son, Rocco, stands off to the left watching me with his dark brows pulled low.

"You have shown me a great deal of disrespect," Matteo begins slowly. "And still I grant you the chance to apologize to me in person."

"Apologize?" My fist slams down onto the table, making the glasses jump sharply. "I'm not here to fucking apologize. I'm here to give you one chance to tell me the fucking truth."

Cian shifts his weight to his other leg and clears his throat.

Matteo is unfazed. "You dare accuse me of lying?"

"I know for a fact that you're lying," I snap. "You can't fucking fool me. And I ain't scared of you either, so you've got one chance to tell me where Evelyn and Noah are or the streets will run red with Italian blood."

"Your threats are baseless," Matteo says quietly. "You yap at my ankles like a young dog. Your brother had infinitely more respect."

In a rage, I snatch up the nearest glass and throw it at the wall. It shatters into a thousand pieces that rain down like starlight while Hazel snatches up her shotgun with a grunt of warning.

"Don't you dare speak about him," I snarl. Every muscle is wound tight with rage, solid and swollen and ready to snap at the barest hint of release. "He was worth ten of you and you still had him killed."

Matteo finally looks at me. "I have told you before, we had no hand in the death of Brenden. Just as we had no issue with you until now. Now, you attack my men in the streets and raid our drug houses. You think such actions won't go answered?"

"My actions are the answer," I snap angrily. "Your little rat Noah just didn't know when to stop, and now he's taken the one thing I will kill everyone to get back. You understand me?"

"Father..." Rocky suddenly steps forward, but he's silenced by a raise of Matteo's hand.

"Your proof?"

"My proof?" I snarl, lunging upward. Italian guards immediately move forward, hands on weapons ready to defend their Don. My own men do the same. "Evelyn was the proof of my brother's murder, the only one who could identify the Italian fuck he was arguing with because she saw it. And then suddenly, he gets his hands on her, and I can prove that with fucking CCTV, you Italian cunt. You've gone too far, you hear me? You took my brother from me, and God as my witness, I will burn your stinking empire to the ground for that, but I won't let you take her too!"

Rage carries me forward as I storm out of the bar, seething with anger. I'm so furious I can barely breathe so when I climb into my car, I tear away from the sidewalk without waiting for any of my guards. My blood boils, and my hands sting hot with fury, searing into the steering wheel. I have no destination in mind and a city far too big to search by hand, but fuck it. I'll do it.

I need her back.

I swore nothing would happen to her again, that I would protect her, and in that I've failed. I can't even stomach imagining what Noah has done to her in the days he's had her, but I swear I will make him pay tenfold.

I drive and drive until a text pings through on my phone, followed by several more. Forced to a stop at a red light, I glance at my phone to see messages from Cian, Saoirse and more, but one makes my heart stall in my chest.

It's a text from Evelyn.

There are no words, just an address. It's Noah. It's got to be.

I slam on the accelerator, ignoring the red light, and spin the car around.

I'm going to make that fucker beg for a quick death.

* * *

"Noah!" I bellow his name as I descend old, dusty steps inside the abandoned theater he dragged me to. I'm under no illusions. This is definitely a trap, but I walk into it willingly for Evelyn. The stage ahead of me is dull and dusty with a few chairs and stage props scattered and abandoned. Old lights dangle overhead and a few frayed ropes twist and sway from the tension they hold.

No one answers me.

I continue down the path and raise my arms. "Noah! Where the fuck are you, you little rat?"

Reaching the stage, I climb the steps two at a time. Still no answer. Despite the low light, several holes in the roof above give me enough light to scan my surroundings, but just as I turn in search of signs of life, Noah attacks from the shadows.

Something solid and heavy collides with the back of my skull, sending me crashing forward. I land hard on my hands and roll over in time to see Noah above me with a baseball bat in his hands.

With a cry of rage, he brings it down on me hard.

I roll out the way, and it splinters the wooden floor where my head just was. He lifts it again. I kick out one leg and hit him behind the knee. As he stumbles, I climb to my feet and punch him hard across the face.

He stumbles and swings the bat hard, catching me in my abdomen across my fresh stitches. Pain explodes through my gut like a gunshot, and I grunt heavily but push through it with a yell of my own.

My fist collides with his jaw, his bat hits my thigh, and then I tackle him down onto the floor.

We grapple like animals. I'm fueled by my rage, and he's driven by insanity if his eyes are anything to go by. What he lacks in strength, he makes up for in how nimble he is.

Each time I punch him and pin him, he wriggles free and quickly realizes my gut is my weak spot. Blood warms my shirt as he kicks me hard, but I grab his leg and flip him over.

His face smashes into a nearby box and it splinters and breaks under him. Then I'm on him, punching him repeatedly.

"Where is she, you fucker?" I rage. "Where the fuck is she?"

His face grows slippery from blood and split flesh, and I have to force myself to stop. Killing him will lose her to me forever.

The moment I hesitate, Noah elbows me in the balls and wriggles free, then he scrambles for his bat. I dodge the first swing, but a wave of agony across my abdomen causes me to falter.

He swings the bat into my face, and it hits me so forcefully that I see stars.

I crash back onto the stage with a pained grunt. Noah scrambles and yells, pushing at one of the stage props. By the time I regain my senses, the wooden cupboard is toppling down on top of me and I have no time to roll out of the way.

I throw my hands up to catch it, preventing it from crushing me, but it leaves me open to everything else.

"Fuck!" I rage, and Noah laughs maniacally as he dances about my head.

"You fuck," he slurs through his mashed up face. "You thought you had me but I have you, and you're gonna stay away from Holly forever, you hear me?"

"Holly?" I gasp, torn between keeping the cupboard from crushing me and trying to talk. "The fuck do you mean?"

"Goodbye, Cormac," Noah says dramatically as he pulls a knife from his pocket. Pictures of Brenden's murder suddenly flash in my mind and my blood runs cold.

No.

But to my surprise—and relief—Noah has other ideas. Instead of slitting my throat while I'm trapped, he moves to one of the ropes nearby. I quickly follow it up to a broken stage light dangling above my head, and my heart sinks.

"Shit."

"Shit indeed." Noah laughs loudly.

He raises his knife, and I screw up my eyes, ready for impact with a broken apology to Evie in my mind. Suddenly, a loud bang echoes around the theater.

I wait for the impending crash of the light, but it doesn't come.

Opening my eyes, I look over to Noah. His arm is still raised with the knife, and blood pours from a gunshot wound to the throat. He gurgles and tries to swing his knife at the rope, but he lacks any kind of strength. The blade slips from his limp fingers and he crumples down off the stage like a broken mannequin.

"What—"

Footsteps echo on the stairs, and I look over. Rocky Barati climbs the steps with a gun in hand and shakes his head. "You drive like a fucking maniac, Cormac."

33

EVELYN

I'm going to die.

And I'm not scared.

Not anymore.

When the cold water covered my toes and kissed my ankles, I was scared. My life wasn't supposed to be like this. I was supposed to keep my head down and work hard at the motel, pay back my debt from the credit cards, and then go on to have a regular, everyday life where my biggest stress was the end-of-year taxes and walking out of a room while leaving a candle lit.

Not this.

Mafia men and their fights, murder and betrayal and psychopathic Italians who can't take no for an answer.

At the time, tricking Noah into going after Cormac felt like such a good idea. In my mind, I was certain Cormac would be unfazed by someone as weedy as Noah and take him out in two seconds, then somehow find out where I was and come to my rescue.

I played out that fantasy as the water slowly crept up to my calves and numbed my feet.

Despite the slow water trickle, the speed at which the tank filled was alarming. One minute, I was certain it would take hours. The next, water swept over my lap each time I moved, and I'd lost track of how long Noah had been gone. I fought like an animal caught in a trap, but the moment the bonds around my wrists became submerged, I knew they'd be impossible to escape.

Now, the water slowly creeps up my abdomen and a strange sense of peace settles in my heart.

I will die here.

I hadn't factored in Cormac's injuries from the crash, whatever they may be. Maybe he hasn't even woken up yet. If Noah goes to him, surely, Cian will be there to stop him. Maybe he will be my savior.

Unless Saoirse didn't survive.

Maybe Cian isn't alive anymore either. Saoirse did say they had trouble getting men into the hospital.

Anything is possible at this point.

My body grows numb as the minutes tick by. Minutes? Hours? I have no idea.

Noah could be on a wild goose chase at this point, and it's my own fault for tricking him. If he were here, I wouldn't be in this position and it strikes me how insane it is for me to wish my kidnapper returned.

What will my mom think? What if they never find my body? To her, I'll just vanish and she'll think I abandoned her. She won't cry. I can already hear her telling people that she expected this of me. That I'm shirking responsibility and running away. When really, I've drowned in some fucking water tank.

I wish Cormac were here.

I wish I got to see him one last time.

Tears warm the corners of my eyes and I close them, sinking into memories of the ranch and the horse ride. Never had my life been so vibrant and full of warmth and love. Clodagh accepted me like I was one of her own. The food was amazing, the animals were adorable, and even the horses were cute as anything. If I survived, I would've liked to try riding one again.

And Cormac. With his squinty smile and constant frown, his deep laugh, and the strong yet tender way he held me like I was the most precious, desirable thing he'd ever come across.

I love him.

It strikes me deep in the middle of my chest as the water finally reaches under my bust.

I love him. And he'll never know.

I try to trick myself into thinking the water is not cold, but warm instead. That my legs are numb from being wrapped up and swaddled next to Cormac for so long that they've just fallen asleep. My hands aren't bound but merely held in Cormac's hands as he cuddles me tight.

These past few weeks have been a whirlwind. The most exciting of my life by far. Sure, they started horribly, but it catapulted me into Cormac's life. He was an asshole who kept an eye on me, protected me, and even paid my credit card debt. Although I never thought to ask what happened to the money after I was stabbed. I presume my debt is clear. He gave me a chance at life, and I did things I never dreamed I'd have the ability to do.

Sure, I broke the law, but looking back, it was pretty damn exciting. If I wish it hard enough, I can almost feel the warm rays of the sun at the ranch and smell Clodagh's bread baking in the oven. I should have told them how happy they made me, should have told them how thankful I was to meet them.

I should have told Cormac how I was feeling before the crash ripped us apart.

Each inch of the rising water washes away my prayers for rescue, replacing them with the painful acceptance that I will die here.

And no one will ever know.

The water creeps up to my chin and I take a deep, painful breath.

This is my end.

34

CORMAC

Out of all the people to walk down those steps, Rocky is not who I expect at all. With the weight of the cupboard pressing down on me and the dangerous light dangling above, there's too much for me to keep track of. I'm a lamb waiting for slaughter at the hands of the Italian Don's son.

To my surprise, when Rocky reaches me, he holsters his weapon and grapples with the cupboard to get it off me. Its bulkiness makes it awkward but together, we're able to shift the cabinet off my body, and I'm able to breathe freely. Then Rocky stands over me and offers his hand down.

I gasp in a deep breath while pain flares across my abdomen, and a hundred thoughts flood through my mind about what it will mean to accept that hand after what happened in the bar.

Then I take it.

Rocky hauls me to my feet and clasps my shoulder, running a concerned eye down my body to where blood soaks into my shirt. "You're hurt?"

"Stitches," I say, immediately retracting my hand. "They burst."

"Shit. Hospital?"

"No time."

"Your girl."

"Aye. What the hell are you even doing here?"

Rocky digs into one of his pockets and pulls out a fabric handkerchief. Offering it to me, he rolls one shoulder in a loose shrug. "I understand love makes you do crazy things," he says. "And my father… he's a bitter man. I don't know why he refuses to see what Noah has done to cause this rift between our families. I think he's so determined to keep up the act that we're innocent, and Noah has been running rampant these past few weeks. Slippery little fuck."

"So you believe me?" I use his handkerchief to dab under my shirt to where a few of my stitches have torn loose.

"Given what you've said and the lack of contact we've had with Noah's family… yes. I don't want the treaty to go up in flames because my father can't see past his own pride. So I followed you, hoping to talk to you." Rocky glances back at where Noah's body lays crumpled just off the stage. "Lucky I did."

"Thought I was next," I mutter, nodding down to his holstered gun.

"Nah. Like I said, the treaty is worth its weight in gold for both of us. My father is just prideful and refuses to let anyone believe that a smaller family could have so much free rein while he's in charge."

Of course. It always comes down to pride with the Italians. My focus returns briefly to my torn stitches, but my concern doesn't linger. "Listen, I'm grateful you saved my life and when there's time, I'll thank you properly, but right now…" My heart pulls painfully in my chest. "You killed my only lead to Evelyn. I…" My throat closes as I stumble down the steps to his body. "There's got to be something."

Pain jolts sharply through my knees as I hit the ground and begin rummaging through Noah's pockets in search of anything that could lead me to Evelyn. I locate keys first, and Rocky snatches them out of my hand.

"I'll find his car." He takes off up the steps two at a time.

Noah's pockets are empty except for a wallet giving me no new information, a receipt for a gas station on the other side of the city, and a few loose coins.

"Fuck!" I yell, grabbing his body by the shirt collar. "Where the fuck is she?"

"Cormac!" Rocky bellows in the distance.

I abandon the corpse and sprint up the steps like the hounds of hell are at my ankles. Outside, the parking lot is filled with cars from people parking here to work nearby. The cool night air clogs my lungs and I wince, briefly feeling every one of my injuries full force when I come to a stop and scan my surroundings for Rocky. Spotting him, I rush over to him. When I'm close enough, he tosses me a small black box.

"GPS. Fucker clearly didn't think about it, or he didn't care. Probably thought he was leaving her victorious."

"Oh, shit," I gasp, my hands trembling. "Thank fuck he was a cocky little shit." I don't need to press anything. Rocky already has the GPS showing his last known location. An old fabric factory on the outskirts of the city. "I have to go."

"I'll drive," Rocky says, snatching the GPS back from me. "You need to fix those stitches and call for backup."

He is helping. Rocky Barati is really standing in front of me, helping me. It could be because he was serious about preserving the treaty, or it's guilt. I can't be certain of his motives, but he makes a decent point so I toss him my car keys.

"Fine, but we're taking my car."

* * *

"Evie!" I bellow her name at the top of my lungs as I run through the fabric factory, stumbling over rusted scraps of metal, clumps of broken glass, and more. This place is huge and on the drive over, I called everyone I knew to get their ass here to find her. Cian's own calls for Evelyn echo somewhere to my right, while Saoirse covers the upstairs offices. Rocky was with me until we located a fork in the corridor and he took the left one, yelling for Evelyn while also explaining that I was here since she wouldn't recognize my voice.

It's been too long.

That single thought taunts me with every step I take. According to his GPS, he left here an hour before we had our fight and in the time it took us to get here, God knows what could have happened in the meantime. Fear grips me with its long, cold fingers, taunting me with the loss of the woman I love, and each step feels weighed down by the intensity of my failure to protect her.

I need her.

I brought her into this.

I turned her life into this.

And if he's harmed her, I will never be able to forgive myself.

"Evie!" I yell, skidding to a stop in a room filled with gigantic empty vats. "Evie, where are you?"

If she's not here, I'll pick apart that fucker's GPS until I find her. I won't stop.

Each room is emptier and more ramshackle than the last. Every so often, I hear the cries of the people here to help me, and each one sends my heart further into my gut that it's not Evelyn's gorgeous voice yelling back at me.

A set of rickety metal stairs takes me down deeper into the factory where a sudden icy chill wraps around me like freezing fog. It's dark, so I pull my phone out to use as a flashlight, and the screen immediately fogs from my fingertips. Under the bright beam of light, I find hope in a few steps.

A chair set up at a table containing fast food wrappers that still shine with grease. Too recent to have been left here before the factory closed.

"Evie?"

I send a message to everyone demanding they get down here immediately, and my pace picks back up into a run as I follow subtle signs of life. Scuffs on the ground, a few empty plastic water bottles, and flickering lights come into view as I round a corner.

And then something odd.

I hear water. Running water inside the walls. "What the...?" This place is long abandoned, so why is there running water? It could be a burst pipe, considering I'm certain I've ventured into the basement, but something pulls me into following it just as footsteps thunder up behind me.

"Got something?" Rocky pants, his face flushed from the sprint. "It's fucking bitter down here."

"Aye, you hear that?"

Rocky tilts his head, then nods. "Water."

"Aye."

"This place shouldn't have anything accessing it," Rocky says. "You think it was Noah?"

"Who else?"

Together we jog down the corridor, hugging close to the wall to ensure we take the right turns with the direction of the water. It grows louder and louder until it's almost deafening, then we stumble to a stop in front of a heavy metal door.

"The fuck is this?"

"Entrance to one of the upstairs vats," Rocky explains. "This place is old. Vats like these were used to house gallons of water or dye for fabrics, but you needed drainage and maintenance. Water-tight door so nothing floods but access for when it's empty and you have drainage issues."

I'd comment on his fabric knowledge if I weren't so overwhelmed by a sudden, sick realization. "Evie!" My fists pound on the door, and I grab the handle, fighting to turn the wheel with all my strength.

"Fuck. It'll be sealed if it detects water!"

"Then find a way to fucking turn it off!" I yell at Rocky. "Evie! Evie, I'm here! Fuck!"

Rocky sprints away in search of exactly that while I pull at the locking mechanism with every ounce of strength I have, and then some. I pull until my muscles burn hot with pain, and still I keep going, straining with everything I have.

It doesn't budge.

"Evie!" I scream her name and pound as hard as I can at the door.

She's in there. I know she is.

I can't lose her.

Not after all this.

Rage and fear consume me, restricting my breathing as I pound with all my might against the old metal door standing between me and the love of my life. Pain is a distant thought, drowned under the white-hot anger that fuels my fury and flailing fists. I punch and punch, throwing shoulder after shoulder at the door. I wrestle with the handle until my fingers are ready to pop right out of their sockets, and still, I fight.

Finally, the metal bends.

35

EVELYN

The water rises torturously slowly when it reaches my face, although that's probably because I'm much more aware of it now. As it crept over my body, I allowed my mind to drift, but now it's right in my face and there's no avoiding my impending death.

Noah didn't return.

Did Cormac kill him? Maybe he forgot about me.

Maybe he's still looking.

This is all my fault.

My body grows numb from the chill of the water, but not enough that I don't feel the pain each time I try to breathe deeply. My bruised ribs complain with every full breath I attempt to take as the water creeps up my cheeks. Soon, even tilting my head back to look straight up fails to save me from the water line. It caresses me like the icy, dead hands of a lover and with one final breath, the water closes over my head.

I blink weakly through the hazy liquid, holding my breath as tightly as I dare. There's a small voice in my head telling me to give in. To just breathe and die quickly so that this will all be over.

I couldn't even if I wanted to.

Something stops me—survival instinct, I suppose. My chest remains tight, and it begins to burn. My abdomen pulls inward as my body battles with itself, fighting the instinctual need for air with the instinctual response to not breathe underwater. My lungs burn, and my throat grows incredibly tickly, giving me an overwhelming urge to cough.

But I can't.

Heat stings behind my eyes, and a final, aching pulse of defeat comes with it. I'd cry, but my tears are lost to the water.

I thought Cormac would find me.

As I cling to my last few seconds, the roaring of my struggling pulse fills my ears and my head throbs painfully. My cheeks bulge and my body screams in strain. Then I give in as the last of my air escapes in tiny bubbles past my lips.

I try to.

The moment I part my lips, warm hands clutch at my face and a familiar set of lips presses against mine. They close over my mouth, creating a seal, and suddenly, air is being forced past my lips and into my lungs. I blink furiously through the murky water, trying to get a glimpse of who is here, but it's so dark that I can't make out any details.

Maybe this is death and I'm dreaming because the mouth and hands vanish after granting me a few precious seconds of air. I cling to it because my body craves life even if my soul accepts defeat. Then the mouth is back, and I know that mouth. I know that mouth so well.

Another kiss of life, another forceful rush of air, and I gain another few seconds. Then more.

It's the most painful thing I've ever experienced. Clinging to the minute oxygen gifted to me from someone else's lungs while every muscle in my body is locked rigid on the brink of death. These precious few seconds stretch on for an eternity. My head swells as if it's about to explode like an overblown balloon, and the pain in my ribs grows sharp and prominent.

I can't do this.

I close my eyes.

"Evie? Come on, Evie, wake up, baby. Please, open your eyes. Wake up. Wake up!"

I do.

My eyes snap open as water bubbles from my lips. I cough weakly, and my body convulses in the firm, chilled arms of the man I love. It feels like a dream. It must be a dream because how can Cormac be here?

"Evie," he gasps, water dripping from his hair like a faucet. "Oh, my God, you're alive. You're alive!" He pulls me close, tucking me to his chest and pressing his lips to my forehead. "I'm so sorry, I'm so fucking sorry!"

I cough again, flaring hot pain in my raw throat. I feel like I've just run a marathon at top speed and everything inside me is raw and inflamed. But Cormac is here, and suddenly, it doesn't matter.

"Cormac," I croak, and he relaxes his grip so I can look up at him. "You came for me."

"I did," he says hurriedly. "I did. I'm here. You're safe, baby. You're safe. The water's draining. You're safe. I'm right here."

The edges of my vision are fuzzy, making Cormac look like he's on the other side of warped glass, and my heart aches with each beat in my chest. Lifting one cold hand, now free from its bonds, I cup his wet cheek.

"I love you," I say, and then darkness descends like a warm blanket.

* * *

"He's really dead?"

Several hours later, I perch on the edge of a hospital bed with a mug of cocoa clasped in my hands. Despite the layers of dry clothing, blankets, and heaters, there's still a chill in my bones that I can't shake. Cormac sits on the chair in front of me, his hands slowly rubbing my legs as he nods.

"He's dead." He glances at the stranger in the corner with olive skin and dark, black hair. "Rocky killed him."

"Thank you," I say to Rocky.

He tips his head as if removing an invisible hat and places one hand over his heart. "The least I could do."

"Did you get a chance to talk to him?" My attention slides back to Cormac. "About anything?"

"No." Cormac abruptly shakes his head. "Fucker had only one intention."

"I'm so sorry," I gasp, reaching for one of Cormac's hands. "That's my fault. I was taunting him because he was talking about Holly and I thought if I tricked him to go and find you, you'd be able to find me."

"Why are you apologizing?" Cormac's brows knit together. "You did the right thing, sweetheart. You were amazing."

I don't feel amazing because the weight of the truth suddenly rests on my shoulders. I don't want to hurt Cormac, but I know what I'm about to share will only cause him pain.

"He... Noah, he told me about Brenden."

Cormac's hands pause on my legs and he looks up at me with dark eyes. "Did he tell you why?"

I nod, hiding my trembling lower lip behind a sip of the hot drink. Rocky shifts off the wall, crossing his arms tight across his chest so his biceps bulge. He looks like he's preparing himself for Cormac lashing out. They both likely still suspect this was some big ploy for power.

Somehow, it's so much sadder knowing it's not.

"He did kill Brenden," I say as softly as I can, stroking Cormac's knuckles. "But not for any kind of power play or anything like that. He said that years ago, he'd worked on a deal to bring Cartel weapons into the family and he was going to make his boss really proud. But before he could, the Irish swept in with their deal and created that treaty."

Rocky frowns deeply. "The Mexican Cartel? We would never make such a deal."

I can only shrug. "That's what he said. He said he had some plan but that the Cartel took his sister. Or he sold her. He wasn't exactly clear."

A flash of recognition washes over Rocky's face. "Oh, my God. I remember that. At least, I remember his sister. He came to us begging for help, claiming that someone had kidnapped his sister. He pointed fingers at the Irish and the Russians, but we later found out she'd died overseas and he went quiet. If he sold her to the Cartel..." Rocky grimaces and his face pales a few shades. "Fucker."

"He was mad about that and blamed the Irish. And then he fell in love with Holly, but she dumped him, and when he saw her with Brenden, he became convinced that Brenden was out to screw him over. That the deal was to ruin him and then stealing his girl was another move against him."

"Fucker was delusional," Rocky mutters. "Absolutely psychotic."

"They argued about it. He said Brenden kept brushing him off as unimportant, so he got him to meet him for one final showdown and then..." I don't need to fill in the gaps. We all know what happened next. Given Cormac's description of the fight with Noah, it's not difficult to envision how that weasel of a man was able to tackle Brenden and slit his throat.

The thought makes my blood run cold, and a shiver moves through my body, eased by Cormac's grip tightening on my leg. He hasn't spoken, merely staring past me into the distance as he listens.

Silence falls and I study his face, catching the pain in his eyes and the subtle downturn of his lips.

"So," Cormac says eventually, his voice gravelly from unshed emotion. "He murdered Brenden, not because he wanted more power for his family, not because he was under orders from the Don, and not because he was planning some insane move. He killed him because—" Cormac cuts himself off.

His hand trembles beneath mine, so I tighten my grasp to try and soothe him.

"Somehow, this is worse," Cormac mutters brokenly. "He didn't die for a reason. Not a real reason. He was just..." His head falls forward, dipping between his shoulders.

"I'm sorry," Rocky says, and he sounds like he genuinely means it.

"I nearly started a war, nearly burned that treaty to the ground," Cormac croaks. "And it wasn't even—"

"Don't." Rocky approaches and places a hand briefly on Cormac's shoulder. "Your grievances are forgotten. Water under the bridge.

Given the circumstances, I don't hold anything against you. And I'll make sure my father won't either."

Cormac lifts his head and his gaze meets Rocky's. There's a moment where they appear to share a silent conversation that ends in a nod of understanding. Then Rocky takes his leave.

As soon as the door closes, Cormac's head falls into my lap. I abandon my drink and thread my fingers into his hair, stroking soothingly. Despite his silence, Cormac begins to shake and he cries silently. I comfort him the best I can.

I imagine it would be easier to know Brenden died for a reason. A real reason. Instead, it was just cruelty, the act of a delusional madman driven by possessive jealousy.

I comfort Cormac the best I can, and my heart breaks each time I hear the smallest sniffle or wounded noise of pain. He will have to break this news to his siblings and his mother. Closing my eyes, I tighten my grip in his hair. It's not going to be easy.

"I'm sorry," Cormac says after a long while. "I pulled you into this world and you have gone through hell because of me." He looks up at me with red-rimmed eyes. "I hope you can forgive me."

"Oh, Cormac." I cup his face and stroke his cheeks with my thumbs. "You saved me. And I don't mean with just the tank. If you hadn't come into my life, I'd be dead by now. I found that body on my own, and the moment the cops questioned me, I was on Noah's radar. If you hadn't taken me that day, then I surely would have died at the hands of his assassin. You saved me, okay? You did."

He surges upward, and our mouths clash in a hot, messy kiss while I slide my hands around his shoulders.

"I promised you that you wouldn't get hurt again and I failed."

"Well," I say against his lips, "you still came for me. You found me and you rescued me, so maybe I can overlook that just this once. Just y'know..." I pull back and gaze deep into his eyes. "Don't let it happen again, yeah?"

He laughs softly, kisses me again, and then moves up onto the bed next to me. As he draws me into his arms, I pull the blankets with me and tuck us in as best I can.

"No one will hurt you ever again," he murmurs with his lips against my hairline. "I swear it."

"Just uhm... keep me away from water for a little while." Never again do I want to be anywhere near water of that level.

Fuck swimming.

Cormac wraps around me and grasps my chin lightly, then tips my head up so our eyes meet. "Never again," he swears. "Did you mean it, what you said?"

"What did I say?" I ask softly, lightly stroking his arm. I ache to comfort him more than this, but if holding me and talking to me is working for him, then I'm here for it. Just being in his arms is chasing away the bone-creaking cold in my soul. I never want to leave.

"When you woke up, you said you loved me."

"Oh." Heat flushes across my cheeks, and I can't stop the small smile that creeps across my lips. "Yeah. I meant it. I love you in this kind of obsessive, really overwhelming way, and I was scared I'd never get to tell you. Convinced, actually. And part of me thought you were a dream so I just... yeah. I said it. And I mean it. I love you."

My pulse quickens suddenly as I'm faced with the prospect that he doesn't feel the same, and a sharp shiver lances down my spine. I shudder in his arms, and Cormac leans so close that the tips of our noses touch.

"Good," Cormac murmurs. "Because I love you too."

36

CORMAC

Breaking the news of why Brenden died was the hardest conversation I've ever had to have with my family. Saoirse and Ma were understandably heartbroken, but Cian's reaction cut the deepest. He was quiet, asking me why over and over as I hugged him until his bones creaked. Senseless killing hurts a thousand times worse than when there's a reason to cling to. The cops finally released his body, and we chose to cremate him since Ma still desired to have him rest in Ireland.

At least with a reason, there's something to focus on and hate. Other than Noah himself, who died far too quickly for my liking, there's nothing to shift that blame onto and so the grief sits like a rock inside me with nowhere to go.

Unless I'm with Evie. Other than the meeting with my family, I refuse to leave her side. The image of her pale and lifeless in my arms after dragging her from that flooded tank will haunt me until the end of my days, and it lingers in my thoughts even now as she flashes me a bright smile and answers her phone, resting her head down in my lap.

"Hello? Oh, Detective Cogs!" Her eyes widen and she gazes up at me while I twirl some of her hair around my fingers.

Since returning to my penthouse, Evelyn has been recovering well these past few weeks and her warmth is the only thing helping me find light at the end of a dark tunnel. A call from the cops, however, is never a good sign.

She subtly puts the call on speaker and Sarah's voice crackles though. "I was concerned when you vanished from the hospital. Is everything alright in that regard?"

"Yes," Evie replies. "I was desperate to get home and back to something normal. I'm sick of hospitals now."

"Understandable," Sarah replies. "I'm incredibly relieved that you were found safe and alive. It was a scary few days."

Evie looks up at me. "Yes," she says. "It really was."

"I trust my assistance was well received?"

Evie frowns. "Your assistance?"

"When we last spoke, you made a good point about the level of effectiveness I held in the situation between Families. Oddly, there was a file on a suspect that went missing and I can only assume it ended up in the right hands."

As Evie and I stare at each other, it suddenly clicks in my mind and I mute the microphone on the call. "It was her. She left the file on the driver, which eventually led me to you. It was a small crumb, but still a crumb."

Evie nods and unmutes. "It was received well," she replies. "Thank you. That can't have been an easy decision for you to make."

"It wasn't, but I believe there's a time and a place for the law, and sometimes, there's a need for other things. We also pulled the body of a man from the river this morning. He was bloated, but fingerprints helped us identify him. It turns out he was a match for the man we were looking for regarding the body you found."

My heart squeezes faintly in my chest, and Evie lifts her hand to cup my cheek. "Oh?"

"I'll be clear with you, Evelyn. Does that body mean I don't have to worry about my city turning into a warzone?"

"Yes," Evie replies. "You're safe in that regard. There won't be any further issues."

Sarah sighs deeply, like the years are being stripped away from her. "Alright. Well, I say this with as much respect as I can muster, but I hope I never see you again—either of you."

The call ends and Evie laughs loudly. "Did she know she was on speaker?"

"Probably." I lean down and kiss her sweetly. "She's pretty sharp for a detective."

"Aren't they all sharp? Isn't that why they're detectives?"

"You and I have different definitions of sharp." I kiss her nose. "But now I'm in debt to a detective and I don't like it, so I'd better find a way I can help her with something, and quickly."

"Her help puts you in debt?"

"I don't like owing anyone anything."

"Even me?" Evie flutters her lashes, and I claim her lips in a deep kiss.

"I owe you everything."

Our mouths weave poetry together until Evie suddenly jerks away and sits up. "Oh, no. I'm late to see my mother!"

* * *

Evie's visit with her mother went smoother than expected. She walked inside with confidence and was honest with her, to a point. She confessed about her credit card debt but puts focus on how she got her act together and found a way to pay it off. She tells her straight how happy she is forging her own path in life and that she wants her mother to be by her side but refuses to tolerate the bullying and disrespect anymore. She spoke with such confidence that I fell in love with her all over again. She's so different from the scared, quiet girl I snatched up all those weeks ago.

Trauma shapes people, but it makes me giddy to see Evie grow into this strong woman who wears survival like a badge.

Evie then introduces me formally as her boyfriend, and I remain as pleasant as I can be as her mother breaks down in tears. There's a moment where the tears feel manipulative as her mother expresses how deeply lonely she is and all she wants is a daughter who will care for her. The tears turn genuine when Evie assures her that she will always be there for her and always a phone call away. Evie promises that even though they will never see eye to eye, she loves her and all her mother needs to do is call.

I've never been prouder. That pride remains blooming in my chest when we make our next stop of the day. Holly.

She greets us warmly but breaks down as Evelyn gently tells her the truth surrounding Brenden's death.

"Is it my fault?" She sobs, struggling to light her cigarette. "Is it my fault he's dead?"

Evie sits by her side on the couch and takes the cigarette from her trembling fingers. Then she lights it herself and hands it back. "Of course it's not your fault. Noah was insane. While his jealousy was a contributing factor, he was disillusioned about an old deal long before you were in the picture."

"My God," Holly whimpers, drawing desperately on her cigarette.

"You should know, Holly," I say quietly. "Brenden kept you a secret. I knew my brother inside and out, and the only reason he would do that was because you were incredibly dear to him. He really loved you."

Holly weeps harder, and I immediately understand that she feels the same way. Their love was real, and she carries as much pain as the rest of us.

"Is there anything I can do for you?" Evie takes her hand and squeezes, while Holly shakes her head.

"You can't bring him back, can you?"

"No," I say, and warmth burns behind my eyes. "But from this day forward, you are under our protection. Brenden cared for you deeply, and we will continue to do so in his absence. Anything you need, no matter how small or dire, and we will be there. Saoirse, my sister, will visit soon to sort out a few things with you."

"Why?" Holly looks up at me through her sparkling lashes. "Why do you even care?"

"Because Brenden was my brother and I know he would protect Evie if our roles were switched."

Evie looks at me with wide eyes. Then she flashes me a soft smile.

"Okay." Holly nods. "Thank you."

We stay with her for a few hours, and she shares stories of the times she spent with Brenden. By the time we leave, I feel a little lighter knowing Brenden had someone truly good in his life. It seems she's from the same vein as Evie—a ball of warmth and light to reach dangerous men and soften their edges.

"Did you mean what you said?" Evie asks me later as we drive toward the day's last destination.

"Which part?"

"That Brenden truly loved her? Or did you just say that because you knew it would make her feel better?"

"I meant it." I reach across for her hand. "The life I lead, or led until you, is the same as my brother's. We shared the same loneliness and for me, I didn't even realize it was there until you came into my life and showed me that there was a gigantic cold hole in my soul. Brenden was like me. He kept Holly a secret for the same reason I couldn't let you go even after you walked away. I was in love with you before I even knew it. And I wanted to keep it secret and protect it so I wouldn't lose it."

"Wow," Evie murmurs, and she brings my knuckles to her lips. "You're so romantic when you want to be."

"Oh, I can be romantic," I say, smirking at her. "I just hope that I can be to you what you are to me. Even just a fraction."

"You're everything," she replies immediately. "You opened my eyes to this whole new world and have given me more excitement than I've had in my entire life. In a few short weeks, you showed me more affection than I've ever felt. In fact, you made me feel like I had worth. That I was worth protecting and saving and caring for."

"Evie, darling. Of course you have worth."

"I know. And I knew it. But now I feel it, and that's so much different."

I pull the car to a stop and smile. "I'll make sure you never stop feeling that way."

Evie looks out the window and grimaces. "Why are we here?"

I've stopped us outside the Sunrise Motel. Reaching into the glove compartment, I pull out some paperwork and hand it to her.

"What are these?"

"Construction plans. We've bought the place. It's going to be bulldozed and a new motel will be built in its place. A motel, under our leadership and yours, that will serve as a safe haven for people like Holly or yourself. Anyone in trouble who needs a place to stay."

"Oh, wow!" Her eyes widen as she flicks through the plans. "I can't believe you did this."

"I wanted to do something for you. How you are with Holly, the way you were kind with her and got her to open up… I realized you have a knack for helping people, and I want to give you space to do that. And I want the place where Brenden died to mean something more than this fucking place."

"What about the employees?"

It's impossible to miss the excitement in her eyes. "You can go and fire that shit stain of a boss."

She looks at me, grinning. "Really?"

"Really."

"Oh, this is going to be so fucking good."

"Do you want me to come with you?"

She contemplates for a second, then shakes her head. "Nah, I don't want him to be intimidated by you. I want to do that all by myself."

"Okay. I'll be here."

She kisses my cheek and darts from the car, jogging lightly to the motel entrance. I keep one eye on her as a call comes through from Saoirse.

"All set?" I ask.

"All set," she replies. "Is it weird that I'm kinda nervous?"

"Not at all. We haven't seen him in a few years."

"He won't even recognize us."

"I know. But Brenden deserves to see him one last time."

"True." She sighs deeply. "I hate flying."

"It'll be over before you know it."

"True. Okay, see you in a few hours."

I remain in the car, mulling over my plans and waiting on Evie. Before long, she comes dancing out of the building with the biggest smile on her face that I've ever seen. When she reaches the car, she flops inside and wiggles in her seat.

"That is the most satisfying thing I have ever done," she declares.

"Did he take it well?"

"Oh, not at all. I thought he was going to burst something in his fat face." She laughs. "It was amazing. I hope he rots."

"I can organize that—"

"No!" She lightly smacks my arm. "Don't you dare."

"Okay, well, we have one more stop. We can't get there until later tonight."

"Another?" Evie whines slightly. "I'm tired. Where are we going?"

"Ireland."

37

EVELYN

"**Y**ou look beautiful."

Cormac lounges back in bed with the sheets pooled around his naked hips. His bare chest rises slowly as he breathes, and one arm rests tucked behind his head. Dark eyes follow me about the room as I apply some cream to my hands, and his words make me pause near the window.

"Really?" I tilt my hips to the side and look down at the silken nightgown. "In this?"

"It's not the clothing that makes you beautiful," Cormac says. "It's you. Your presence. Your smile. Your warmth."

"Are you trying to lure me into bed with sweet talk, Mister?"

"Maybe." Cormac smirks softly. "It's always good to rest before a long flight. It keeps the body relaxed."

"What time do we fly out tomorrow?"

"Six a.m."

"Gross."

"Agreed."

"Won't we get into trouble?"

Cormac's brows pull softly together. "For?"

"I don't have a passport, remember? Isn't it illegal for me to leave here and fly to Ireland?"

Cormac laughs deeply, tilting his head back and looking more relaxed than I've ever seen him. "You know who I am. The life I lead. Everything you've seen, and flying without a passport is where you worry about the law?"

"Don't make fun! I don't know how serious these things are!"

"I'm sorry." He chuckles. "Trust me. It will not be an issue."

"You'll protect me?"

"Always. Now come to bed."

I linger near the glass doors leading to the small balcony attached to Cormac's bedroom. The city twinkles below us like a thousand scattered stars, but something about it all feels different.

"What's wrong?" Cormac asks when I don't move.

"Don't you think the city looks different?"

"Different how?"

"I don't know. Just… different. Maybe it's me. I feel different."

"You've been through a lot. More than anyone should go through."

"Isn't it common in your world, though?" I glance back up at him. "Danger?"

"Yes. But what you've witnessed and experienced in just a month is intense for anyone."

Casting one last look at the city, I turn toward the bed and finally slide on it and into Cormac's waiting open arms. "Can you teach me to be like you?"

"Like me?" Cormac winds both thick arms around me, cuddling me close and nuzzling into my hairline.

"Yeah. I want to know how to shoot a gun. And how to fight."

Cormac pulls back slightly and angles himself so we're face to face. "Why?"

"I... when I was with Noah, all I felt was powerless. There was nothing I could do against him."

"You weren't the only one," Cormac assures me softly.

"I know, but I couldn't try. I don't want to feel like that again. I want to be able to defend myself for me. I want to feel stronger than I was in that moment." His body radiates heat, and there's slight concern hidden in his eyes, but to my relief, Cormac nods.

"Of course," he says. "I understand. Although I am the only protection you need."

"Oh, really?" My lips pull into a warm smile and I reach up to caress his cheek. "And just how do you plan to do that?"

"Easily." His voice drops to a low whisper and he tilts his head down.

The moment his lips press against mine, a deep pull of relaxation moves through my body. I melt back into his hold and kiss him back just as deeply while stroking his cheekbone and the coarser hairs of his well-kept beard. One of Cormac's hands skims down my body, following the seam of my nightdress to where the lace hem sits loose against my thigh. In the same movement, his hand slips underneath the material and presses firmly between my legs. He cups my heat and uses that grip to pull my hips back against him as I gasp softly into his mouth.

"And who will protect me from you?" I whisper, staring deep into his eyes when the kiss breaks.

The tips of our noses brush together as Cormac tilts his head, and he holds my gaze as two thick fingers press between my folds, lightly caressing my vulva as he replies, "The other me."

"The other you?" I ask, tilting my head up while a soft moan bubbles at the base of my throat. Warm curls of pleasure sweep through my belly and settle south in my core as my pelvic muscles pull up at Cormac's next teasing stroke of his fingers.

"Exactly," he whispers huskily. "You get every version of me." He kisses me softly. "You get the soft me who's so in love with you that I want to be inside you all the time so you never stop feeling me." He kisses me again, increasing the pressure of his fingers over my clit. "You get the desperate me who constantly calculates how to give you the best life you deserve." Another kiss as each backward stroke of his fingers teases one digit around my entrance. "You get the tough me who will fight and do everything he can to protect you and your future." Another kiss, and as his finger enters me, his thumb grazes over my clit at just the right angle. Stars explode across my eyes, but I'm hooked under his gaze and can't look away.

"And you get the scared me who just wants to make everyone proud and make sure no one gets let down." He kisses me again, and this one lingers as he slides knuckle deep into my pussy. "You get all of me, Evie."

It might—no, it is. This is the most romantic thing anyone has ever said to me. My heart swells in my chest like I've taken in too much air, and warmth prickles behind my eyes. It's not upset that rises in me but an overwhelming surge of love at how this man has changed my life. I've done things I never thought I was capable of, and he was the ignition.

Even if our meeting was highly unconventional.

"Wow," I gasp, panting softly as one finger inside me becomes two. My hips rock back and forth in time to the thrusting of his fingers while his thumb keeps up an insistent pattern across my clit. "You really know how to get a girl going."

"That I do." He kisses me harder this time, and as my lips part to moan louder, his tongue snakes into my mouth and he devours my sounds. My pulse races and heat bursts across my skin like fireworks, making contact with Cormac's bare chest all the more exhilarating. He thrusts his fingers deep and my body opens up to him. I'm soaked before long, and my dampness coats Cormac's palm and fingers as he works. Distantly, I feel the tell-tale rise of arousal at my ass, but Cormac is so focused on me that I don't think about it yet.

Soon, my need to pant and moan overwhelms my desire for a kiss and my head falls back against his shoulder. A string of moans dances past my lips and I writhe in his arms, closing my thighs around his wrist as he draws me closer and closer to orgasm. His other arm, curled underneath me, fondles my breasts until my nipples are stiff and aching. Each rock of pleasure is amplified by his lips and tongue kissing and weaving silent words of love against my throat and jaw.

Every muscle of my core pulls tight and I arch into his hold, my breath catching in my throat. For a few hot seconds, I'm merely pressed against him on the cusp of orgasm while he continues to pleasure me. Then I come, and it hits like a punch through my body. I'd curl in on myself if not for his arms around me. Every wave causes me to shiver and twitch. My toes curl and my eyes screw up so hard, I see sparkling colors.

I can feel Cormac smiling against my throat, and it makes it all the sweeter. When the pulses of pleasure begin to fade, I slump down in his arms and pant. "Wow." Cupping his cheek, I guide him in for a kiss and he leads it by sliding his tongue briefly into my mouth and pulling me even closer.

"Wow indeed," he murmurs, staying so close that his lips write those words against my cheek.

"We should plan long flights more often."

"Easily," Cormac replies. "Although I don't need an excuse to play with you."

"Mmmhmm." I kiss him again and then remember the arch of his arousal pressing into the crease of my ass. "My turn."

"Hmm?"

Sliding from his grasp, I miss the warmth of his chest immediately, but I want to feel his cock inside me, and knowing how hard he is just arouses me further. I push at his shoulder, and Cormac slowly rolls onto his back as I climb on top of him, mindful of the lingering injuries we both share from the car crash and more. Externally, we're looking good, but I'm hyperaware of Cormac's surgery scar. Just as he was of mine.

"Evie, you don't—"

"Do you want me to beg?" I ask, situating myself on his thighs. "Should I detail how horny I am or how much I want to feel your cock inside me reaching deeper than your fingers ever can?"

The rise in his pants gives a very visible twitch at my words, and I smirk up at Cormac, who merely rolls his eyes. "Nothing gets past you."

"It's true." Crawling over him, I kiss him on the mouth and then pepper an array of gentle kisses over his broad torso. By the time I reach his abdomen, my pussy already aches at the thought of his being inside me and I can't wait any longer. The blankets fall away, and I pull down the hem of his silken pants to expose his long, thick cock to my hungry gaze.

Cormac moves only once to grab some lube from the bedside table and pass it to me. The sound he makes when I wrap my slicked hand around his cock is a sweet sound that I never want to forget. His abdominal muscles shift and contract as I stroke him from base to tip, slicking up his cock as needed.

"Ready?"

"I'd wait forever for you, but holy fuck, I'm ready."

Bliss comes in the form of Cormac's cock stretching me wide and filling me in just the right way. Using gravity and my body weight, I slowly sink down onto his cock with a long, slow moan, and my mind goes blank. His hands lightly rest on my hips with his thumbs caressing in slow circles. Each inch drives me to new heights as he reaches every hidden bundle of nerves inside me, and a warm shiver of delight curls down my spine.

I'm lost to him. Setting up a slow rhythm, I rise and fall over his cock with liquid movements. There's no rush. There's just him and me, soaking up the moment. Each rise leaves me hungry for him to be fully inside me once more, and each rock down leaves me eager to feel the pull of his cock. I brace my hands lightly on his lower abdomen as I move, but soon, they're on my own body as I caress my abdomen, fondle my breasts, and then pull the nightdress over my head. The fabric was suddenly too smothering for my skin.

I hear Cormac's moans of approval and he caresses my waist and back. His hips occasionally rise to meet mine, trusting that bit deeper, but it remains with me in control, and I'm in heaven. The slow curl of pleasure warms inside me just below my navel, and a sheen of sweat breaks out across my oversensitive skin. Each touch from Cormac is like a flash of electricity skimming over my limbs. Needy moans spill unhindered past my parted lips until suddenly, Cormac sits up and winds his arms around me.

It's harder to rise in his lap now as our lips gently collide so instead, we're rocking together, allowing me to get delicious pressure against my clit. My arms circle his shoulders with one hand sliding into his thick hair. He holds me close, tight enough to make me feel utterly protected, and my heart soars.

We orgasm together, rocking slowly and reaching heights I never knew were possible. Every single part of me feels alive with light and sensation, and my orgasm lasts so long. My core ripples, clenching around his cock and milking him for everything he's worth. We kiss so deeply that I can't remember the last time I took a breath, and my body burns so hot that I can't tell where I end and he begins.

It's pure ecstasy.

"I love you," Cormac whispers against me, and the power of those words makes me melt.

"I love you too."

38

CORMAC

It's been years since I last set foot on Irish soil. The last time I was here, it was for a similar reason to why I'm here now.

To say goodbye.

With Evie's hand in mine, I climb the steps up to a white front door and press the buzzer. The noise jolts through me, setting my heart off-rhythm, and Evie clasps our joined hands in her other hand in silent comfort.

The home where my father stays is quite nice at a glance. A beautiful garden for the residents to spend their time, cozy bedrooms that they can decorate themselves, a games room with everything from cards to board games, and even a safe kitchen for those still eager to try a little cooking. Everything looks exactly as I remember as we're led through the home to one of the sitting rooms near the back of the building.

"How has he been?" I ask the man escorting us.

"Conor is an absolute pleasure to be around," he replies. "Keeps his head down, never causes a fuss. He's very partial to a raspberry trifle." He chuckles as he holds open the door. "Take all the time you need."

I walk in first with Evie by my side. Cian and Saoirse walk silently at my back, less inclined to see our father in such a position. It's hard for them—it's hard for all of us. Ma stayed back at the farm because she couldn't handle looking into the eyes of the man she loved and not seeing that love returned. I don't blame her.

My father sits near the window, engrossed in an old book with thick spectacles hanging from his crooked nose. He wears the same cardigan I saw him in last, and he taps one foot along to the radio playing nearby. He looks every bit my father and my chest aches painfully. My grip tightens further on Evie's hand until I realize it's probably too tight and break the contact.

"Dad?" I approach him slowly. He doesn't react. "Conor? Conor Gifford?"

Only then does he lift his head. He peers over the top of his glasses, looking at me as if I'm a stranger. There isn't a hint of recognition in those eyes but he does lower his book.

"Dad? It's me, Cormac. Your son. Do you... do you remember me?"

Dad looks me over, then his lips press into a firm, frail line. "You have the wrong person." He returns to his book.

"I'm sorry," Saoirse says behind me. As I turn, she takes her leave and Cian follows a moment later. I half want to follow them, but I came here for a reason. Moving closer to my dad, I sit on the small stool nearby and rest my elbows atop my knees.

"Dad, I have to tell you something important and it's not going to be easy."

He lowers his book again and looks at me as if I'm bothering him. It's a look I grew up with as a child and it's painfully familiar. Cotton forms in my throat and I swallow hard.

"Boy," he says sharply, and the nerves down my back jump. But for some reason, he doesn't continue. He just watches me, so I take my chance.

"Dad, do you remember Brenden? Your son? He was older than me by just a couple of years. You used to always yell at him for climbing in the orchard, said it would affect the harvest and then each spring, he would get the first bite of the sourest apples."

Dad doesn't respond.

"Well, he…" Suddenly, words become impossible. Then Evie's hand lands on my shoulder. "Dad, I'm really sorry to tell you this but Brenden… he passed away. He's gone. But he was a good man, Dad. You would have been so proud of him. I know you would."

The words don't sound like they're coming from me. It's like another voice has taken over in an attempt to reach my father, and my heart thumps painfully.

Then my father reaches out. He places a frail hand on my arm and squeezes suddenly. Tears instantly spring into my eyes.

"You look sad, Son," he says. "Go and speak to Mabel. She'll cheer you right up!"

His touch is painfully familiar, even if his words speak of unfamiliarity. Suddenly, when our eyes meet, I feel at peace. It's as if some part of him understands what I'm trying to tell him, and that is the part that reached out. He leans back, returning to his book, and I give him my strongest smile.

"I'll do that." I sniffle, gathering myself. "Thanks, Dad. Also, this is Evie. She's my girlfriend."

Dad glances up at her and smiles. "What a bonnie lass."

"Aye. She is." I stand and loop my arm around Evie. "Love you, Da."

He doesn't respond, but I don't need him to. I came here and did what I needed to do, and I'm certain he understood. Somehow.

With a final glance, I head back out of the building to find Saoirse and Cian hugging in the parking lot.

"Did you tell him?" Saoirse asks as they break apart.

"Yeah."

"What did he say?"

"Told me I looked sad and to go and speak to someone called Mabel." I scoff softly. "But the strangest thing… I felt like he understood."

"You're just convincing yourself of that," Cian says.

"No. He reached out, and for a moment, it was like…" I shake my head. "I don't know. Maybe it was nothing, but I'm convinced he understood. He heard me. He knows."

"I think so too," Evie says.

"You have to have his back." Saoirse chuckles, wiping her eyes. "You're his girlfriend."

"Maybe, but he did seem tender. Just from an outside perspective," she adds hurriedly.

"Dad would have loved you," Cian says with a smile. "He had a soft spot for soft people."

"I'm not soft!" Evie protests, to which we all laugh.

"Sure, sweetie." She elbows me in the ribs as I pull her in for a kiss.

"Right." Saoirse claps her hands together. "Ready to say goodbye?"

* * *

"Is there anything you need?" Evie stands in front of me, adjusting my tie with her delicate fingers. "Anything I can get you?"

"Just you," I say softly.

"You have me." She cups my cheek with one hand and guides me down to a soft, tender kiss.

"And I am forever grateful." As the kiss breaks, I stand back to admire us in the mirror. Evie wears a black dress on loan from Saoirse and I wear a black suit with a white shirt and black tie. We might be at the old family farm, which hasn't seen this much activity in years, but it's the perfect place to lay Brenden to rest. And as per Ma's sharp instructions, we all have to dress respectfully.

"Did you grow up here?" Evie asks as we duck through the low hallway and move down through the farmhouse.

"Not as much as I would have liked. I was born in the States, but about half, maybe three-quarters of my childhood was spent here."

"Is this where you'd also want to be laid to rest?" She looks up at me. "Here?"

"As long as it's next to you, I won't care," I reply easily. "But here would be good."

"Noted."

"Why, planning on bumping me off?"

"It's crossed my mind. A lot of money in ranch inheritance, right?"

"Millions," I tease, kissing her temple.

We head outside and follow an old cobblestone path through the overgrown garden to a large pond out the back of the house. Ma is there holding a back marble urn, with Cian and Saoirse around her.

"Why the pond?" Evie asks, her voice low.

"Brenden loved the pond. He spent a lot of time there raising a family of goslings he rescued. It was adorable looking back then, but at the time I was so jealous. He told me he was raising an army of swans that would eat me in my sleep."

Evie stifles a laugh. "Must have been some shit swans."

"To this day whenever I hear a honk, I fear it's his promise coming true." I grin. As we reach the pond, Ma immediately pulls me in and presses a powdery kiss to my cheek.

"Thank you for talking to Da'."

"Aye." I nod. "I'm glad I did."

"How was he?"

"Just the same," I assure her. "Healthy."

She nods curtly, then turns to Evie and kisses her cheek. "Welcome, dear."

"Thank you for having me," Evie replies.

"Fuck," Cian mutters, suddenly wiping his eyes. "Shitty fucking—"

"Come here, little brother." I loop my arm around his shoulders and pull him in for a tight hug. Saoirse joins us and together, the three of us squeeze onto one another until a demand for air and space breaks us apart.

"Y'alright?" I clutch Cian's shoulder, and he nods, wiping at his eyes.

"Aye. Just… why'd he have t'die, y'know? Fucker was supposed to be old and gray."

"No one in this life makes it old and gray," Saoirse says.

"Oi, cheeky. I did," Ma remarks. "Brenden… what happened was horrible, but I choose to think he's looking down on us happy that we dealt with the fucker who took him from us. And we'll make him proud. All of us."

We all nod. I reach for Evie's hand, and she flashes me a comforting smile. Ma removes the lid of the urn and then takes out a handful of ashes. Whatever she says to them is so quiet that I don't catch it, then she scatters them into the pond where they drift down onto the water.

"I love you, Son," she says tearfully.

Cian is next. He takes a handful, and whatever he says as goodbye is only for his ears as he doesn't speak a word of it aloud. Then he scatters his handful and clears his throat. "Man, I'm kinda pissed you died so early. All these pranks I never got a chance to play, and I wanted to wreck one of your fancy fast cars just once."

A rumble of amusement moves through us.

Saoirse steps up next. "You were the best brother I ever had and you've left me with these two fucks," she mumbles. "But I'm so happy that you found someone to love and I'm totally stealing your diamond watch. Love you." She scatters the ashes and dusts her hands off.

My turn.

The ash is heavy in my hands and a thousand thoughts burst through my mind, but nothing feels right. Slowly, I spread my fingers and watch the ash trickle down into the water.

"I'll make you proud, Brother," is all I say.

I stare down until the last of the ash melts into the water that rocks softly back and forth from the movement of fish, frogs, and other animals that live here now. Then Ma offers the urn to Evie and her eyes widen.

"Are you sure?" she asks.

Ma nods. "You're family, dear."

She takes a handful, looking uncertain, then approaches the water's edge. "I didn't know you, but if you were even half the man your brother is then I know you were great. I'm sorry I didn't get to meet you." She scatters the ashes, then steps back into my arms.

Ma moves forward and turns the urn upside down, pouring the rest of the ash out into the pond. Just as she does, a gust of wind kicks up and blows the ash back at all of us, invading eyes, noses, and throats.

A flurry of coughing rises up in all of us as we turn to avoid Brenden's ashes getting carried in the wind and caught on us. Coughs that then turn to laughter.

"That fucker." Cian laughs, brushing ash out of his suit. "I knew he'd pull something like this."

"Always had to make his presence known," Saoirse groans.

"That's my boy." Ma laughs along with them.

"Oh, God." Evie coughs and coughs until I take her hand and help her brush the ash from her hair. When she looks up at me, her eyes are bright and a swell of love overtakes the grief in my chest.

"I love you," I say, cupping the side of her neck. "So much. Thank you for being here."

"Of course," she says. "I love you too. And I'll always be here."

"My strongest pillar," I say. She leans up onto her tiptoes and kisses me tearily.

"Right!" Cian declares, slapping his hands together. "Enough crying. Time for the pub!"

39

EVELYN

Cormac swings his leg outward and I side-step, drawing my hands up to my chest and quickly returning a few light jabs to his shoulder. He spins, his fist lightly colliding with my ribs. I grab it and turn, twisting in the way he taught me and drawing a grunt of pain from him as I spin us both and force his arm up his back.

"Do you concede?" I ask breathlessly, having spent the past four hours sparring with Cormac in the gym.

In a flash, Cormac slips out of my grip and faces me, then he hooks one ankle around my leg and sends us both tumbling down onto the mat with a grunt. He rests above me, grinning as he pins me there firmly.

"Do you concede?"

I jerk upward and crash our lips together, pressing my knee into his crotch and using that leverage to roll us over until I'm on top and it's my turn to smirk down at him.

"Do you?"

"You play dirty," Cormac says accusingly.

"And I win."

"In a real fight, this won't work."

"I know. But here, I win."

"You do." Cormac cups my face and teases his thumb along the bottom swell of my lower lip. "You're getting faster."

A final kiss and we climb to our feet. I push sweaty strands of my hair out of my face and groan softly. "Not fast enough."

"What counts as fast enough?"

"I don't know." Walking over the mat, I snatch up a bottle of water from the bench. "I want to beat you properly."

"You won't be able to."

"Why not?"

"Because I'm much bigger than you and I've been fighting since I was a kid. You've been training for six months." Cormac stands next to me and gently nudges my shoulder. "But that's not a big thing."

"Isn't it?" I gaze up at him as I gulp mouthfuls of cool, refreshing water. "I mean, most people are bigger than me. If I can't take you down, what hope do I have?"

Cormac affectionately nudges at the bottom of my bottle, then he steals it to drink his fill. "Saoirse is smaller too, remember."

"And she can kick your ass."

"Again, there's a huge time difference there. My point is that you are learning for survival and your goal to take me down will take a lot longer than six months. We have to play to your strengths. Your speed. Using your opponent's strength against them."

He speaks sense, and in the past six months, it has felt amazing to learn how to defend myself at different levels. The first time I shot a rifle was scary, but now it's as easy as curling my hair.

"Do you want to go again?" Cormac asks, passing my water back.

"No, we'll be late for lunch."

"Race you to the shower?" He smirks at me, and I laugh.

"Fine. But no cheating this time—Cormac!" The words are barely out of my mouth when Cormac scoops me up onto his shoulder and sprints with me to the showers.

After an intimate shower to wash away the sweat, Cormac decides against the car and instead we walk arm in arm through the streets toward the restaurant with the warm sun beating down from above. Our guards do an excellent job of blending with the crowd so it almost feels like we're a normal couple heading to lunch.

"Rocky called earlier, when you were drying off," Cormac says. "He wanted to know how many spaces you have at the shelter near the docks. He's got some people he wants you to take care of."

"The docks?"

The past six months have been a whirlwind. Cormac wasn't kidding when he said he wanted me in charge of the motels he was building, and Sunrise was demolished and rebuilt with impressive speed. That was only the beginning. Within two months, I found myself in charge of multiple shelters around the city and several motels that I turned into safe havens. They became beacons for people like Holly, who settled easily into the manager role at Sunrise, or for people like me, growing up in a cold home and needing love that didn't come from credit cards. With Rocky becoming a firm friend after he saved Cormac's life and helped rescue me, helping him is a guarantee.

"I can check the rosters, but I'm pretty sure we have some rooms free down there. If not, I can put them up at Sunrise because I know we have three rooms there."

"I'll let him know." Cormac tightens his grip briefly around my shoulders. "He was concerned you would say no."

"In what life would I say no?" I gaze up at him, squinting slightly in the sun. "Is this because I had dinner with Anastasia?"

Thankfully, the Russians were finding internal peace, which meant Anastasia finally had time to focus on issues outside of her internal dealings. She'd voiced an interest in the shelters I offered around the city. So far, all she wanted was to provide a monetary contribution, but I still hadn't settled on whether to accept her offer.

"Perhaps. The Italians and Russians have a lot of bad blood. Old bad blood thanks to her father, but it's the kind of pain that isn't forgotten," Cormac explains. "Maybe he thought you were favoring them more."

"I think we can be amicable with both," I say, glancing into the windows of shops we stroll past. "There's nothing I wouldn't accept from Rocky after what he did. His father, on the other hand…" I trail off. That man had been salty ever since Rocky had stepped in to smooth things over with Cormac. There are rumors that he still holds some resentment to the accusations and refuses to accept Noah's guilt. It's an odd hill to die on.

"His father is a whole other deal," Cormac agrees. "But don't think about him. Think about the good you are doing. Rocky will be pleased that you can help."

"Of course. Oh, is Cian back from Ireland yet?"

"Next week," Cormac replies. "He's really intent on renovating that farm."

"I think it's sweet." His passion for all things heritage really exploded after he experienced two days fearing his family was about to crumble underneath him. He's putting us to shame with the amount of time he spends back at the ranch.

"It's certainly a choice." Cormac chuckles. "But he's happy and that's all I can ask for."

"Speaking of happy." I glance back up at Cormac. "Don't you think we're due a holiday?"

"A holiday?"

"Yeah. Somewhere nice and hot where we can just be me and you and not worry about anything else."

Cormac tilts his head and hums softly. "Sometimes, I feel like you read my mind."

"Really? Why?"

As we reach the restaurant, Cormac winks at me but he doesn't reply. Instead, he holds the door open and ushers me inside with a sweep of his arm. I'm hit with the scents of spices and cream, along with a few floral notes that put my soul at ease while reminding me how hungry I am.

However, instead of being faced with a bustling restaurant, the place is empty.

A thousand twinkling droplet lights dangle from the ceiling, sparkling away like the night sky has made an appearance just for me. The floor is covered in deep red rose petals, and every single table has a single candle burning away, creating a warm, cozy aura under the sparkling lights. If I squint, I'd swear there was glitter shimmering in the air, but I can't pinpoint the source. Soft flute music fills the air, and my stomach twists into knots as confusion warms in my mind.

"Cormac, I think we've walked in on—" I turn to him, and my heart stops dead in my chest.

Cormac is down on one knee, smiling softly while holding a sparkling ring. The emerald cut stone at the center gleams at me, surrounded by an array of colorful smaller gemstones that all wink in the light.

I can't breathe. Heat pours over my skin as if I've just walked into a sauna and the maxi dress I'm wearing suddenly doesn't feel good enough.

"Evelyn."

Oh, my God.

"Cormac, what are you—"

"I love you. I know you know this, but I don't think you realize just how much I love you. I spend every waking moment eager for a glimpse of your smile or the sparkle in your eyes. My heart lurches every time you send me a text or call me to fill me in on your day. My soul ties into knots each time you're delayed at work and I have to wait to see you, which is why most of the time, I'll just drive to see you. The best part of my day is when you come home and flop into my lap with stories of everything you've been up to, and I drink it all up because I want to see the world through your eyes for the rest of my days. At night, I dream of you and can't wait to wake up and see you again. Your laughter gives me life. I adore the way your nose crinkles when you're confused, how you constantly twirl the same strand of hair around your finger when you're cooking. I ache to be inside you as often as I can, and each time we part, I hunger for the next time I'll get to kiss you again. I love you, Evelyn Morris, every single part of you, and I have since I met you."

Cormac takes a breath and for the first time in my life, he sounds nervous.

"So I'm here, kneeling before you and asking you to marry me because I can't imagine living without you. You're already a part of my family, but I want you to be a part in every possible way. So, Evie... will you marry me?"

I have no words.

Everything he says sounds like a dream, and I almost pinch myself to make sure I'm awake. There are times I worry that rambling about my day is boring to a man like Cormac since he is involved in deals that are much more exciting, but every word from him feels powerfully genuine. My heart pounds like a drum beneath my chest and every breath I take trembles like a loose leaf in the wind.

He watches me intently as my lips part and no words come. My stomach knots tighter, and pressure swells in my chest as I stare at the ring and then Cormac's eyes.

There's only one answer.

There's only one thing I want in this life and it's Cormac. The love I feel for him is limitless, and what he gives me in return feels like everything I deserve and everything I'm owed from our time apart.

I step forward as tears burst into my eyes and blur the ring until it looks like Cormac is offering me a palmful of pure light. I touch his cheek, and he turns his face into my hand, briefly closing his eyes.

"Yes," I say hoarsely, shaking from the rush of excitement and adrenaline that follows. "Oh, my fucking God, yes. Yes, yes, yes!"

Cormac surges up to kiss me, gathering me in his arms and spinning me around so fast that the world blurs. I cling to him tightly, swearing to never let go.

"I will marry you," I repeat over and over. "I will. I will!"

"I love you," Cormac gasps. His lips meet mine in a warm, powerful kiss as the cool metal of the ring glides over my finger.

My life is complete.

"I love you too."

Printed in Dunstable, United Kingdom